D0835129

TRADE OFF

TRADE OFF

Nader Hossain Salehi

Heliotrope Books

New York City

Copyright © 2017, Nader Hossain Salehi

All rights reserved. No part of this book may be reproduced or transmitted in any form or by any means, electronic or mechanical, including photocopying, recording or by an information storage or retrieval system now known or heretoafter invented — except by a reviewer who may quote brief passages in a review to be printed in a magazine or newspaper — without permission in writing from the publisher.
Heliotrope Books LLC
heliotropebooks@gmail.com

This is a work of fiction. Names, characters, places, and incidents either are products of the author's imagination, or are used fictitiously. Any resemblance to actual events or persons, living or dead, is coincidental.

Cover Design by Katya Mezhibovskaya

For K, P, and R

The world is waiting to hear your stories.

PROLOGUE

It was the beginning of the end for Colonel Shirvani when the bearded man came out from Qom. No one knew, of course, way back then in 1964, that the Shah one day would fall, and that the Colonel and so many others would perish. How could they? The Shah had fantastic wealth, the Imperial Iranian Armed Forces, the United States, and the awe of the Pahlavi dynasty behind him.

Neither the Shah nor the military would tolerate the provocations and insults of this unsophisticated cleric from Qom – his pious and mystical insistence on the destiny of his cause notwithstanding. In those days, he was already an old man, with a long, gray beard and an inconsequential following, so they arrested him and then banished him first to Turkey, then to Iraq, and eventually to France. Their actions were quick and decisive. It should have taken care of the problem.

Yet for fourteen more years the exile lingered, steadfast in his resolve, declaiming the Shah and biding his time. Ultimately it was the death of the old man's son in Iraq – in a car accident, of all things – that sparked a few hundred militants to protest. At first, in 1977, it was considered by Colonel Shirvani and his friends to be a small and insignificant event. But despite the material wealth delivered to them by the Shah, the Iranian people were restless, and they demanded greater freedom and civil rights. Maybe the youth had little else to command their attention. Revolutions can start like that sometimes.

As the months went by the unrest didn't stop, and the popular protests intensified. By the new year of 1978, they had grown into revolt and insurrection. The Shah's tanks crushed hundreds of Islamic students in Qom – the place from which the old man had sprung, suddenly, like a pernicious weed – killing several. That led to retaliation and more death. The bearded cleric issued edicts from France, directing work stoppages and urging Iranians not to compromise. The people responded with strikes and sabotage, purposefully crashing the economy. Liquor stores were looted and destroyed. By late summer, martial law was imposed. And then, on a black Friday, in September, the Army, ill-equipped to deal with civil unrest, shot and killed dozens in the street. Millions swore they saw the old man's face in the full moon.

By the end of 1978, the Shah, the head of all Imperial Armed Forces, brooded like a paralyzed Persian Hamlet in his palace. While the fate of his country hung in the balance, the King of Kings simply begged for leave to live quietly in the country. In December, two million people marched in Tehran, and up to ten million throughout the country. Shirvani and his soldiers stood down. By what means can millions of people be suppressed? Even the Colonel had had enough.

Eventually, like thousands of his colleagues, Colonel Shirvani stopped reporting to his post and, with his family, lay low in the home and gardens of his father-in-law, a retired government minister, in a northern district of Tehran. In the early mornings of January, Shirvani, in his mid-40s now, balding but still fit, would run up and down the empty winter streets, in the shadows of the Alborz mountains, the trickles of melted snows flowing south down wide, deep gutters. His five-kilometer route was the same each day, though it had no particular destination. Upon his return, and after he'd shower, his wife, Laleh, set for him a meal of flat breads, butter, and feta cheese, and thick yogurt with jams and honey. When there was no school, Reza, his nine-year-old son, and Maryam, his five-year-old daughter, would join him for the meal, but no one would talk. At least not until the Colonel said something first.

But on this morning, the seventeenth of January, Laleh spoke up. "The Shah has left for Egypt."

Shirvani bit into a dry, hard cracker. "He'll be back soon enough."

"He's not coming back. Khomeini is."

He glared at her and then gestured toward the children. "This is a conversation for another time."

"Maybe we should go for a short holiday, until things settle down? We've been talking for so long about taking the kids to London."

"We're going to London?" Reza asked.

The Colonel stood. "No. We're not going anywhere. Eat your breakfast."

He left the dining area and, through a sliding door, entered into a backyard garden, past trellises of barren grape vines still months away from bearing fruit. Laleh followed.

"I'm not suggesting that we abandon our home and run away, like the others. Just a short holiday, until we see how things resolve themselves," she said, wiping her hands on a blue apron.

He grunted. "Nonsense. What have we done for which we can't answer?"

She walked to the end of a trellis, to face him. "People are getting killed. Do you think the *Mujaheddin* and the *Pasdaran* are interested in dialogue? Do you think they want to engage in question-and-answer sessions?"

He brushed a lock of brown hair from her eyes. "Don't worry. Everything will calm down once Bakhtiar installs a new government. And Khomeini will have his seat in Qom."

Laleh stared at him. The Colonel was usually right, but what if this time were different?

"Like a Vatican," he added.

Khomeini, now the Grand Ayatollah and soon to be Supreme Leader of the Islamic Republic of Iran, returned to his country in February 1979, promising a popularly elected government without interference from the clergy. But instead, Islamic law, *sharia*, was introduced. Women were forced to cover their hair. Alcohol was banned. Only martial or religious music was broadcast. Armed gangs, the *komitehs*, started to patrol Tehran, arresting those suspected of aristocratic leanings, loyalty to the Shah or to the communist agitators still vying for power in the wake of the Shah's flight.

In April they rang the bell of Laleh's father's house.

It was just after two a.m. The Colonel ordered his children into the basement and opened the door. He was not entirely unprepared. Eight bearded men burst in, armed, and with guns to Shirvani's head and neck, they forced him back, to the lushly carpeted living room area. Laleh screamed for them to stop. Her father, an elderly man, the former minister of justice for Iran, came down the stairs to intercede. He was knocked to the floor. Reza, in the cellar, hid Maryam under a pile of blankets and tattered bedding, warning her to be still. The boy, clutching a broom, escaped up into the hall and tiptoed toward the commotion near the front of the house. He saw his grandfather on the soft, green rug that Reza, when he was little, would imagine to be a field of grass. There was blood on his old man's lips.

His mother shouted: "Reza!"

The son lunged toward his father, but one of the men extended a long arm and kept him at bay. "*Aroom*, little man," he said, "we just want to talk with your father."

Then two of them frog-marched the Colonel toward the door.

"I'll be home soon," Shirvani said, calmly.

They warned Laleh not to follow. She glowered at them, murmuring prayers, willing herself not to cry.

The Colonel was blindfolded and led to a bus with a dozen other suspected collaborators. Hours later, the vehicle pulled up to what had been a local police station. The makeshift officers in ill-matched uniforms didn't know him, but they yelled at each other and argued the charges against him: murder, treason, conspiracy, fraud and blasphemy. It would all be so farcical, he thought, were it not so serious. At long last, he exploded: "Who the hell are you sons-of-bitches to handle me like this? Let me speak with whoever is in charge of this circus!"

He was led to a locked room, the entrance guarded by a young man, a scruffy teenager in fact, armed with what Shirvani recognized to be a Heckler & Koch MPT-9 submachine gun. Not a bad weapon: lightweight, air-cooled, with a roller-delayed bolt. He sat alone on the floor, now more composed, awaiting their next move. There was no judge or jury, no proceeding or tribunal.

Two hours later the Colonel was bound and taken outside to a yard beside the police station. He was made to stand against a wall. No explanations were offered. In the black of the moonless night he heard the clicks of cocking guns. And then he was shot dead in the chest.

When is it time to flee one's country? To leave all your possessions, your family, your friends, and everything you know behind? How do you decide to turn away from the only place you ever knew, taking with you only your breath and the certain knowledge that you'll never return? Laleh had known it was time. She had known it as soon as the Shah had equivocated, but she hadn't pressed the point. Now this, for long years and forever after, would be her eternal regret.

Still, Laleh was young, she was determined, and she had her faith. And she now also had her parents and her two little children to care for. Little Maryam, in particular, had been hardest hit by the Colonel's sudden absence, and she required almost constant reassurance that Laleh too would not disappear. Clearly, leaving Iran was no longer an option. But for months after the Colonel's death, their situation had only grown worse: her father had been repeatedly questioned. And, more frightening, the country had slipped into a bloody war with its hostile neighbor Iraq. Although Iran was larger and stronger, Saddam Hussein had calculated that he would catch his enemy at a weak moment. With their military and defense forces in shambles, the Iranians threw human waves at the better-equipped and organized Iraqi forces. Soon, even boys as young as Reza were sent to the front lines to defend Iran's honor. It was true what they said – once a fire is lit, both the dry and the damp all burn.

Laleh would not lose Reza too.

They left Tehran a year later, before dawn on a windswept day in March, after Laleh managed to pull together the 800,000 rials the

Kurdish smugglers demanded to take Reza out of Iran. The boy didn't know yet that at the border he would travel alone – otherwise he would never have gone. They stayed one night in Zanjan, the city of knives, and then were hustled by Kurdish drivers to the shores of Lake Urmia.

Reza stared out of a truck window at the green, salty sea, its glittering minerals sparkling in the dusk. Strange lumps of white rock, like mounds of hard chalk, rose from the still surface. Pink and purple rays of gentle sunlight skittered on the skin of the water, and Reza, tired from the drive and scared to be far from home, lost himself in the alien landscape: desiccated, barren and unknown.

From just outside of Urmia they travelled by horseback, north into the cool mountains and the no-man's land of Turkey and Iran. Reza could ride a little; his father had taught him well. Their trail rose into the Taurus Mountains, steep and haunted by the calls of unseen animals. But where was the border? And who, besides some long-dead English cartographer, would even know where it might have been drawn?

Their guides were thin, with long, bony noses and weathered, pockmarked faces. The leader was Barzani; his assistant was called Rami. They rarely spoke, even to each other, communicating instead with quick but deliberate gestures. Often, they gazed far into the distance, as if the mountains were their only friends. Their red, gold and white turbans, their *jamadanis*, seemed to swirl peacock-like against their dark horses and long black coats. They had Reza dressed all in black from head to toe, a color that blended into the slate hillsides and suited his coal-colored eyes. Laleh, since they had left Tehran, still wore a simple, black chador. The trail was rocky, and Reza's horse would sometimes slip. He forced himself to only look ahead, not down into the valleys of wolves and leopards. At night, when they camped, Reza peeked from below his blankets into the bruised canopy above him. A beautiful falcon had accompanied them on the trek, from the very first day, as if it were an advance scout, leading him and his mother, and their guides, over and through the desolate terrain. Reza imagined that it was the

Colonel, keeping a vigilant watch. The trip took three days. At the end of the third afternoon, Barzani pulled up their horses in a small, shaded field and announced that they were on the threshold of Turkish land.

Reza gazed down a hill from the meadow, and to him the trees all looked the same. He turned to Barzani. "How do you know where Iran ends and Turkey begins?"

Barzani smiled, and his face folded into a hundred creases. "This way, you find Turks. That way, you find Persians. But in my heart, and across all these valleys, *insha'allah*, you find Kurdistan." His arms opened as if to encompass all they could see.

The younger of the two guides took the reins of Laleh's horse. Laleh, like stone, turned stiffly to her son.

"Mother, what is it?" he asked.

"You're going on now. And I'm returning to Maryam and our home in Tehran."

"What? No! Where will I go?"

She wiped some dust from her eyes. "Into Turkey. Barzani will get you to Ankara. From there, you'll fly to Hamburg, to Germany. Your aunt is expecting you. Take this."

She pressed a large roll of Turkish lira into his palm.

"Mother – "

She was firm and unrelenting. "Call me from Ankara, and again from Hamburg, so I know that you're well."

"When are you and Maryam coming? When will you meet me?"

She pressed another paper containing a German address and phone number, this time into his left hand. "'We will come as soon as we can."

"When?" Reza pleaded.

Laleh took the money from his trembling right hand and placed it in a secure pouch on his pack. She then kissed him on the forehead and removed another paper from the folds of her now limp and dirty chador. She pressed that into his palm. "Read this after you cross the border."

Barzani took the reins of Reza's horse. They sloped down the hill to the west, toward Turkey, while Laleh, with her guide Rami, disappeared in the other direction, below the bluff, returning into the newly created Islamic Republic of Iran. Reza, wanting to cry, hating his now upside-down world, turned to watch his mother's back slowly diminish towards the horizon, like a sun setting incongruously to the east.

"I'll be back to get you," he screamed as loudly as he could at the silent, observant sky. "Do you hear me? I'll be back to get you if you and Maryam are not in Germany by the new year."

After twenty minutes of smooth, downhill cantering, Barzani directed their horses to a stream, where they drank. "We're in Turkey now," he said.

A soft wind chilled Reza and made him shiver. He remembered the folded paper his mother gave him and opened it up to read. He recognized it: a verse of the Persian poet Hafez:

Don't surrender your loneliness
So quickly.
Let it cut more deep.
Let it ferment and season you
As few human
Or even divine ingredients can.
Something missing in my heart tonight
Has made my eyes so soft,
My voice
So tender,
My need of God
Absolutely
Clear.

CHAPTER ONE

George Gibran smiled and nodded as the boyish waiter handed him the Trinidad cigar that the hotel's manager had saved for him. Of course the waiter, who had been with London's prestigious Dorchester Hotel for more than three years, since late 2000, knew that smoking was strictly forbidden. Yet his manager was not only going to permit this guest to smoke in the stately lobby, he was also going to give him the cigar to light. The white-gloved waiter had known enough not to ask any questions when he was handed the Trinidad, the gold cutter and malachite ashtray, but surely he wondered to himself – who was this man who so comfortably flouted the rules at the landmark hotel?

Gibran sat straight in a green upholstered, high-backed chair in the shade of an indoor palm plant. Heavy, amber colored curtains covered the windows looking out toward Hyde Park's barren, December trees. Gibran was in his early fifties, fit, fashionably dressed in a dark, classically tailored suit, olive-complexioned but of unclear ethnic origin, and regal in his manner. "Thank you, young man," he said.

The waiter, caught off guard, snapped to attention. Delivered with an accent that bore a slight French trace, Gibran's tone implied more of a dismissal than a gesture of gratitude. The waiter had continued to stand above him for several moments too many. "Right, sir, please do not hesitate to let me know if I can be of further service," and then he hurried away.

"You don't mind?" Gibran politely asked Sheik Ahmed, his companion, as he snipped off one end of his cigar and methodically lit the other, not really waiting for an objection and knowing well that none would be forthcoming.

"Of course not, of course not, *sadiqi*. Smoke, smoke away," the sheik replied, the words rapid and thick with an Arabic accent. "I've become well accustomed to this filthy habit of yours," he added, waving toward the smoke emanating from Gibran's cigar.

The sheik was heavy-set and dark, well into his sixties, with a white goatee that hadn't sprouted black for years. He wore a beige, wool *thobe*, the traditional, ankle-length garment reserved by Saudis for the winter months. His head was covered by a green and white checkered *Ghutra* scarf, held in place by a thick, black cord. Despite the cold London weather, he sported only canvas sandals over his fatty, scaly feet. He appeared uncomfortable, and shifted in his large chair.

"How was your flight?" Gibran asked mischievously, knowing well how much Ahmed feared to fly, even in the plush first-class compartments of Saudi Airlines.

"Awful. Very turbulent. But I arrived safely, *al-hamdul-Allah*," Ahmed said, raising his gaze and hand toward the ceiling.

"Well, that is what matters, isn't it?"

He harrumphed. "The driver from Heathrow was chatty. From where did you hire him? He asked too many questions."

Gibran exhaled smoke. "Don't worry, sheik, he is very reliable. I'll have a word with him."

Ahmed spied, across the lobby, his large and muscular bodyguard, stuffed uncomfortably into a too-small seat. Otherwise, they were well enough alone.

"Is the staff here treating you well?" Gibran asked.

Ahmed remembered the large basket he had found in his suite upon arrival the day before. "Yes, yes. And thank you, *shukran*. The fruits are delicious. It was a very nice treat."

Gibran also knew that Ahmed disliked being in London. In fact, he hated being anywhere other than in Saudi Arabia. He was afraid of being followed or watched and uncomfortable with the way people interacted in the West, with the way they lived their lives, and, of course, with the foods they ate. Ahmed often complained about the British taste for highly processed meats and, always, of the lack of fresh fruit in London. So Gibran arranged for crisp pears, oranges, pineapple, bananas and berries to be delivered to Ahmed's room every day – a table overflowing with freshness, prepared for his companion before dawn.

Gibran smoked and stared across the table, through the bluish haze of the Trinidad, comfortable and calculating, while offering pleasantries in an earnest manner. "You're most welcome, Ahmed. And your children and grandchildren, they are well?"

"Yes, *al-hamdul-Allah*, they are fine."

"Shame it's not an ideal time to visit. Too cold for a Bedouin, I would imagine. And, of course, by now, after the holidays, Harrod's has been picked clean."

The sheik grew restless. "We need to talk."

Gibran remained unfazed. "I thought that this is what we were doing."

"Stop the silliness, please. I enjoy your company, but I did not risk my life or liberty flying here from Jeddah to discuss the weather." Ahmed slammed his glass of orange juice on the marble-top table.

Gibran chuckled, slapped his knee, and stood up. "Let's go for a walk. It's a tad bit chilly, but I think you'll enjoy a stroll through the park, no?"

"Yes. Good."

It was a typically misty, December day, and the two men left the hotel and crossed the street into Hyde Park. The sheik's sullen bodyguard wandered behind them. They found a bench at the edge of the lake, under a leafless tree, and sat. A lone two-seated pedalo eased its way over the murky water, toward the Serpentine Bridge in the distance. The bodyguard stood against the tree.

Gibran, smiling, nodded toward the water. "Perhaps we'd enjoy more privacy out there on a boat?"

Ahmed released his hand. "You know I can't swim."

"It's a useful skill to pick up, my dear friend."

"Not in the desert."

Gibran looked at the choppy waves. "Once, long ago, there was a girl. One of those perky, blue-eyed, freckled English types I'd met at a bar near the business school, soon after I started. I must have been twenty-two at the time. At five a.m. this one morning she decides to sneak us into the park. I remember the streets leading us in, all freshly washed and dead empty and sparkling from the electric lights. And so I follow her into this darkness. I'll tell you, it was eerie rattling around here in the middle of the night. Well, we get to the edge of this lake, the Serpentine, and she unbuttons my shirt and my pants. You might imagine how I, a poor and impressionable boy from Beirut, trembled as I held her." He paused to relight his cigar.

"You're a devil," the sheik said. *"La ilaha ill-Allah.* If it weren't for me and my prayers, you would surely end in Hell."

"I didn't sleep with the girl, my dear friend, I merely swam with her!" Gibran gazed into the distance, somewhere past the bridge. "But to be, once again, young and care-free in London."

Ahmed stared at Gibran and opened wide his puffy eyes. "So these were your glorious days of study?"

"Quite." Gibran puffed hard, and the fire on the tobacco burned bright.

The sheik leaned in so close to the well-tailored man that he could smell his Clive Christian cologne. "And how well have you studied since then?"

As it turned out, exceedingly well. Gibran had established his Geneva-based asset management fund at the beginning of 1979, investing money for a few wealthy Lebanese and French families. By 2004, Gibran Asset Management, or GAM as it was more commonly known, man-

aged well more than thirty billion dollars in European and Middle East-
ern money. Part of GAM's capital growth, of course, was tied to the oil
revenues that flooded the world markets over the years since GAM first
opened its doors for business.   And part was due to the relative lack
of oversight that fund managers enjoy in Europe. Over the past four
years, in particular, Gibran's returns had averaged close to 30 percent
– an astounding rate of success, especially in the wake of the busted
technology bubble two years before.

Gibran's investors ranged from high net worth individuals to corporations and even some sovereign funds. And because he cared so much
for his impeccable image, he didn't open his fund to any known mob-
sters, arms dealers or other rogues. But he also did not make a habit
of asking his investors unnecessary questions. If clients needed funds
wired across borders in a discrete or invisible manner, or he'd be happy
to assist them if they needed their holdings disguised.

Gibran moved with ease through the opaque and quirky worlds of international finance, as comfortable in a Swiss vault as he was in a Manx
bank. But Gibran also understood that money itself meant nothing. The
game was only about amassing it, and then using it to get the things
that really mattered. Money itself never made anyone happy – you can't
eat it, you can't live in it, and it doesn't heal a wound. Money's a neutral.
It's just a current like electricity. All the billions and trillions of coins and
cash and gold and silver zipping across the planet, around and around
like schools of fish: all one has to know is how and when to cast the net.
That and how to acquire an edge over the competitors standing beside
you.

That edge is what Sheik Ahmed delivered.

Gibran and the sheik were old friends, dating back to GAM's early
funding by the Saudi royal family. Ahmed was always more of a mar-
ginal figure, a cousin of the Sauds but several generations removed. His
job, as long as Gibran knew him, was to maintain various Saudi charities
and to distribute the largesse of those pious contributions to the needy

in Arab lands. Throughout the years, of course, and not the least of which due to his regular visits to mosques worldwide, the sheik came to know many of these poor Muslims personally, scattered as they were throughout the West. They trusted him. And so back in the late 1990s, when he approached Gibran with his idea – the brilliant epiphany which struck him during prayer, a true and literal gift from Allah, Blessed Be His Name – he already had the network in place to support its execution.

Sheik Ahmed's people came from North Africa and Pakistan and from the less fortunate of the Sunni Gulf States – the ones, like Yemen, with no oil. They fled the lack of jobs in their homes and migrated to Europe's free cities and capitals. For years many hoped for work but their situations, over a generation, failed to improve. Their children lost their mother tongues. They were despised and feared now in the so-called enlightened West. And in return, they hated everyone right back. The diaspora was widespread: they sunk roots in Amsterdam, in Brussels, in Cologne and in London's East End. Marseilles now could hardly be called French. And when they did find work, these poor, non-European Europeans, it was more often than not as janitors or as maids. And this made them quite useful for Ahmed and, eventually, Gibran.

The operation started in 1999. The Muslim janitors cleaning the hallways of the rich and powerful, the ones gathering the papers and trash of the law firms and investment banks of the elite, were trained by Ahmed and his associates to not dump all of them and every night to bring some documents home. Once a week, they would be collected and boxed and shipped to an East End warehouse controlled by GAM. There, Gibran's more junior employees, trained in finance and driven to find every possible trading edge, would review each document and highlight those that could contain some material information – information that could be worth a fortune in the hands of an expert trader. Sometimes the documents reflected non-public earnings forecasts. Other times they discussed planned transactions that were known only to those most intimately involved in the proposed deal. This information was then forwarded to and digested by a more experienced and more senior group of GAM analysts. These more senior analysts then prepared detailed research reports for Gibran's consideration, reports which were derived from — but never, ever made any mention of – the documents brought home by the janitors only weeks earlier.

As far as Gibran was concerned, you probe the market until you find some advantage, and then you exploit it with the maximum amount of leverage possible. Simple. Stay a step ahead and make yourself a bit smarter than the competition. And if the regulators ever asked any questions about the basis for Gibran's trading and success, he could point to and rely on the detailed research reports that were prepared by his senior analyst team.

Gibran eventually brought Ahmed in as a GAM director, and he received a piece of all profits derived from their operations. The sheik's earnings, in turn, were dispersed to the janitors, and the rest Ahmed directed to Islamic organizations, which he called charities but others called terrorists, in Palestine, Iraq, Pakistan and Afghanistan. The proceeds were funneled through networks of shell corporations in various countries. The money might be routed through Switzerland to Cyprus to the Isle of Man, and then through India, before it ever hit an account of an Afghan charity or warlord, operating under a fictitious name, and controlled by a single director. But that was Ahmed's business. Gibran's well-manicured hands were clean.

"Some of what was turned up last week I found to be of exceptional interest," Gibran said. "And yes, Ahmed, I have studied it well."

The sheik was pleased. "I put a new man in place, an uneducated man, but a man of deep faith and struggle, a man of determination."

Gibran glanced toward him. "Yes, well, we haven't many educated janitors to call on, do we?"

"His name is Tareek Abdul-Majeed."

"May his garbage collection skills live up to his glorious surname."

"He is very simple, but that's his strength. He lives quietly and devoutly, and he does not ask unnecessary questions. When he speaks, he speaks sensibly and politely. His wife and each of his seven children are, *al-hamdul-Allah*, good Muslims. He is, as far as anyone can determine, beyond reproach."

"He appears to grasp the nature of the market implicitly."

The sheik raised his open right hand. "He prays five times a day."

"I mean to say that he has a keen eye for information that, while not obviously meaningful, can provide a substantial trading advantage in the right hands."

"He has performed *umrah* and *hajj*."

Gibran puffed his cigar. "As if he were trained in finance."

"He follows the straight path of Allah."

"His information about Northern Control Systems was extremely helpful."

"Who are they?"

"Exterminators. Listed on the LSE. His documents revealed a drop in fortunes, loss of material contracts, higher costs. We're shorting them."

"How much will it generate?"

"It depends how far the stock falls. Within six weeks, I'd venture this short alone may generate twenty to twenty-five million pounds."

The two men rose and began to walk again, toward the bridge, to warm themselves. The lumbering bodyguard followed. Gibran was aware that they had had a very good five-year run, but he sensed that it was time for a correction in course. He turned again to the sheik, crunching on the dry, brown leaves in their path. "I should say, Ahmed, it's never in our interest to be subject to scrutiny."

"Yes, yes," the sheik agreed, panting to keep up with the younger and more fit Gibran. "No attention, of course, *naam naam*. But why mention this? Is someone watching?"

"No, but our strategies are working too well and the trading patterns are too profitable. Eventually, even the Financial Services Authority will be hard to assuage."

Ahmed took his hand again. "So what shall we do?"

Gibran tossed his half-smoked cigar in the trash. "We change direction."

The sheik seemed puzzled. "Which way?"

"This way." He pointed ahead.

"Toward the bridge?"

"Toward the West."

Ahmed immediately understood the implication. "*La, la*. No. Not the United States."

"Imagine the possibilities!"

"No."

They approached the entrance to the Lido Café, on the bank of the Serpentine. Gibran dashed up two brick steps between the simple white columns and held open the door for the sheik to walk through. "Come, come Ahmed. How beautiful it can be! You use their own money to defeat them."

Ahmed directed the bodyguard to linger outside. "I can't travel there even if I want to. I'm on a list."

"What list?"

"Somewhere there's a list."

That was no obstacle to Gibran. If anything, he preferred to have the sheik's influence attenuated. Let him deal with gathering information. Gibran would focus on raising new funds from a whole new set of investors, and establishing brand new entities through which to carry out the trades. It would be like starting a race again, with a fresh group of competitors whom he could crush. After all, he would still have the same edge when it came to research. "We'll create a different network of investment funds and trading accounts. Of course, we'll be just as discrete and discriminating as we always are in terms of the people whose funds we accept and the professionals with whom we work."

Ahmed selected a corner booth, near the bar. "It won't be easy to find good Muslims there to work with."

"We'll do exactly what we do here, except we'll do it with new money that we raise there," Gibran said, ignoring Ahmed's admonition. "If anything, our trades will be even more difficult for any authorities to trace. The connection between the janitors here in Europe and the trades in America will be harder to discern. And, from the perspective of regulatory scrutiny, we get a brand new start. All new trades and all new patterns. Plus, we'll find a reliable new beard, a front for our work who is not connected in any way to what we do here in in Europe."

"Another Ahmed?" the sheik grumbled.

Gibran placed his hand over the sheik's. "If I had ten thousand lives on a thousand planets I would never find another Ahmed."

Ahmed pulled his hand away. "And if I had a single pound in my pocket you would take it."

"And turn it into ten."

"Of which eight becomes yours."

"Indeed." Gibran stood, walked to a counter and ordered a white wine for himself, and for Ahmed a dish of vanilla ice cream. He returned to their booth and served him.

"It is *halal*?"

Gibran shrugged. "It's organic."

"Maybe I should not."

"Come now, you're not in Jeddah, you're on vacation. Eat."

Ahmed dipped the very tip of a teaspoon into the scoop and licked a sweet drop. "I don't like any part of this, George. Even your idea for a reliable new beard, as you put it, makes no sense. How can you find someone who is totally reliable, is fully acceptable to the Americans, and in no way connected to us?"

Gibran sipped his wine. "Ah, but we already have such a person. You remember Clara?"

"No, I don't think so."

Gibran was aware that the sheik knew her full well. "Of course you do! She's in Geneva, my General Counsel, she sits just two doors down from my office. So very smart and capable too."

"The blonde?"

"Yes, the exquisite blonde, tall and with perfect breasts like small, firm peaches."

Ahmed had another lick of ice cream. "I've seen her."

Gibran slapped his knee and laughed out loud, with a tone that bore a hint of condescension. He quickly gathered himself. "She's going to connect us with a very successful attorney in the States, an old friend whom she trusts completely. He's at a tip-top, law firm. A white-shoe firm, as they call it. And based on my research, I believe he fits our needs perfectly."

"What makes you think so? Is he Muslim?"

"Indeed, he is. And, more importantly, he has some particular sensitivities that we can leverage, if that ever becomes necessary, to ensure that he makes the right decisions."

The sheik looked out of the cafe's window, out into the *haram* world of England, at the people walking without thinking, passing through life with no purpose, no sense of service to either the truth or to the divine. "It's too dangerous. We should stick to working with people we know, people who are already tested."

"And whom might that be?" Gibran asked rhetorically. "Which devout, American lawyer have you placed in a top U.S. firm?" He lowered his voice. "Which cell of your extensive network do you plan to activate?"

Ahmed had never been to America, let alone placed any brother there on a long-term mission or path. "Look, the whole thing is too risky. You're in arbitrage, so by your nature, you take too many risks."

Gibran took that as a compliment. "It's true, I am by nature a risk taker. But have I not proven adept at choosing which risks to take and when? Have our causes not benefitted from my willingness to take risks that others would not? Plus, my dear brother, if you just keep doing the same thing over and over again while the whole world continues to change around you, isn't that itself the most risky path?"

The sheik brought a full teaspoon of ice cream to his mouth and swallowed. The sweetness spread through his chest, and he closed his eyes and smiled. "Tell me more about this attorney who will be your beard. What is his family background?"

"Iranian."

A Shi'a. Ahmed rolled his eyes, as if that were already a problem. "His name?"

Gibran turned his head toward an Asian family seated close by, preoccupied with the cries of a small child. He then locked back onto the sheik's eyes and replied in a very soft voice: "Shirvani. His first name is Reza."

CHAPTER TWO

The Federal-style row house where Reza lived, like most everything else in Washington, D.C., was garish. The H Street dwelling, a simple, boxy place, flaunted bricks painted in a color that fell somewhere in the range between blood and fire-engine red. Its stoop was crumbling, and the rusted front yard fence had started to come apart and curl, but his home had history and character and, more importantly, was close to his office: the place where Reza, for the most part, could be found.

He grabbed a bottle of Poland Spring as he rushed out of the house this December morning, in 2003, following the headline news that most of Washington's water supply was for years contaminated with lead. A bitter wind slapped his face and froze his just-washed, thick black hair. It was only a brisk, twenty-minute walk past the FBI Building, the Doric columns of the Smithsonian's art museum, and down Pennsylvania Avenue to the twelve-story offices of the Henderson & Humphries corporate law firm.

Reza glanced at his watch as he rode the elevator from the spacious marble lobby to the eighth floor where his office at "Double H" was located. He calculated that he would be sitting at his desk by nine a.m., and while that was not particularly early, it was not so late as to be embarrassing. It was, in fact, an impressive start given that Reza had not reached his bed the night before until about 2:30 a.m. A glaring, winter sun flooded the elevator car as the doors opened, and Reza squinted.

He still felt the effects of the previous night's drinking.

Reza unlocked and opened the door to his office about two minutes later, juggling his briefcase, coffee, and keys. Once inside, he turned on his computer, and opened the daily diary with which he tracked his tasks and activities. He knew from the flashing orange light on his telephone that he had voicemails awaiting him, and that is where he turned his attention while his computer booted-up. To his mild surprise, the computerized voice on the other end of the telephone informed him that he already had three new messages.

The first was from Jane Erlich, secretary to John Burlington, the senior partner with whom Reza worked most closely. "Good morning, Reza. Mr. Burlington would like to know if you wouldn't mind pushing back his annual review meeting with you to three p.m. Please call or drop me a line and let me know." Her Southern accent, combined with a charming and reassuring tone, caused her to extend the word "you" so that it sounded more like "yew." Reza jotted Jane's name in the column in his diary where he kept track of the calls he needed to return.

The second message was from Gil Vargas of the office services department. "You know that thing I talked to you about last week? It worked just like you said it would. Thanks, man, I owe you, big time. I'll catch-up with you later today." Reza made a mental note to find and speak to Vargas. Because Gil's primary job at Double H was to deliver mail to the attorneys' offices, he was rarely in the same place for more than a few minutes and could be difficult to locate.

The third and final message was from the General Counsel of Microtrade Brokerage Services. "Good morning, Reza. It's Jessica Blount. I'm calling to see if you've had a chance to think further about that e-mail exchange, and how we want to present it to the S.E.C. staff. I'm in and out of meetings, but generally around all day." Reza added her name to the list.

By the time he had finished listening to these voicemails, Reza's computer had fully booted, and he turned back to his terminal and the thirty-four new e-mail messages that awaited him. He skipped through them quickly, responding only to the most urgent ones. He then called Jane Erlich, and confirmed his review meeting with Burlington later that afternoon. And then his phone rang from an international line.

"Reza, it's Maryam."

His sister. *"Salam,* Maryam jan. How are you? How is mother?" he asked.

"We are the same Reza. She says she is fine, but you know she would never say otherwise. I think her eyesight is deteriorating, but she pretends that it's my imagination."

He gazed out of his window toward the Washington Mall. "My mother was born in exhaustion. Didn't see dawn or dusk. The chariot of time, wheeled her by the hair, in the thorny desert of life."

"What are you talking about?"

New e-mails continued to pop on his screen. "It's a poem by Reza Farmand."

"I've never heard of him."

"He's banned in Iran."

"Reza, listen, that doesn't help us right now. We're stuck in Afghanistan, and we are no closer to finding a way to get to America. It's been six months already and I found out this morning that our visa applications were denied again."

His morning coffee left a bitter taste in his mouth. Or maybe it was the lead in the water. "Damn it. They told me it would go through this time. I've spent months talking to them at State. I had assurances from very senior people."

"Please find out what happened!"

"You're an Iranian in Afghanistan two years after 9/11, that's what happened." He would have to call the State Department again. "I'm sorry. I'll ask around."

She paused. "It's been going on for too long. I wish we had just stayed in Iran. At least we had our home and our normal lives there. It wasn't supposed to take this long. Is there anything else you can do?"

He unknotted his tie, having noticed a coffee stain, and squeezed the receiver. "I'm working on it, Maryam, I swear I'm doing my best."

"Look, Reza, there is another way out of this mess. I know it's not the way you like to do things, but if we can pull together some money, mother and I can buy our way to America. I've been talking with people here, and there is a powerful tribal leader, Rashid Agha Khan, he is very close with the Americans, with the military, and he can arrange for a green card for us – not just visas, green cards. He is very reliable and has done this for many others. It costs a lot, five hundred thousand dollars for the two of us, but our troubles would be over if we had green cards."

Reza opened the bottom drawer of his desk to search for a new tie. He thought of his annual review meeting later that afternoon and the fact that he had picked an awful day to spill coffee on himself. "Wow, Maryam, even if this was a reliable option, that's an awful lot of money. You do know that, right?"

"I know it's a lot of money, but it can get us to America once and for all. If you can find a way to get us the money, I can work the rest out with Rashid. And of course, when I come to America, I'll get a job and I'll earn the money to pay you back —"

He found a lilac Brioni. Not quite the bright blue Zegna he'd stained, but it would work. "I would happily send the money if I had it. And you know that I don't want you to pay me back. That's not the point." He didn't mean to be, but he was yelling.

"Calm down. This isn't about you and your feelings. For six months we have been living as refugees in a run-down house outside of Farah, and you have no idea what it's like — "

"Maryam — "

"It's a God-forsaken place. It's dry, it's crumbling, and there is violence and death everywhere. If I knew that I could get us back to Iran safely, I would. But because we left illegally, you know we can't. I know you told us not to try to come out through Afghanistan, but that's what we did, and mother and I don't have a lot of options at this point. Please, see what you can do about the money. I'm begging you!"

Why should she beg? Was there some question in her mind about his devotion to his family? "Enough, I understand. I'll see about the money. In the meantime, see if you can find out more about this guy, Rashid, and how reliable he really is. I'm sure there are a lot of bad guys out there who wouldn't think twice about taking advantage of you, and for a lot less money."

"I know, I'm the one living here, remember? Anyway, I know you are doing your best. Thank you."

He searched for a note he made in his diary, a message for his mother: "A man is insensible to the relish of prosperity 'til he has tasted adversity."

"Reza, this is serious."

"It's Saadi. Tell it to Mother, and tell her it's from me."

He repeated the verse and hung up the phone. He knew he'd have to find a way to get hold of the cash. He already had about fifty thousand in the bank, and that was a reasonable start. The only other money he had was the ten thousand in cash that he always kept in his closet for emergencies — he wasn't going to touch that, it was saved for life and death situations. But he was going to make partner soon — he expected to hear about it from Burlington later in the day – and that would certainly make it easier to get the rest of the money together.

Reza spent the rest of the morning working on the presentation that he would soon have to make to the Securities and Exchange Commission staff concerning its investigation of his client, Microtrade. The S.E.C. had been investigating Microtrade's sales practices for more than two years and, to Reza's delight, they had not discovered any wrongdoing, at least not on the part of any senior officers. Only a batch of unsuitable trades carried out by a handful of low-level brokers. That could be dealt with. Their most recent subpoena to Microtrade, however, required the production of a number of e-mail messages, including a highly problematic one between Microtrade's C.E.O. and one of its retail brokers. Reza knew that the S.E.C. staff would, absent the necessary context, view the e-mail exchange as a smoking gun, one that implicated the C.E.O. in the unsuitable sale of complex products to a number of elderly and unsophisticated investors. His job was to make sure that the S.E.C. staff had the necessary context, so they would not interpret the email to mean what it plainly seemed to say – that the C.E.O. was not only aware of the unsuitable sales, but that he actively encouraged the brokers who carried them out. It was going to be a tough job, and Microtrade's C.E.O. was rightfully nervous. But if Reza was good at anything, it was spin.

Shortly before three p.m., and after a typically late lunch at his desk, he left his office and made his way toward the Lincoln Conference Room. Even more so than usual, he was conscious of his pace. It was brisk enough to inform any observer that he was a man whose time was valued. But his open posture, combined with the confident smile that broke almost imperceptibly across his handsome face, also informed anyone he passed that he was not too busy to be approached. Reza had worked hard over the course of his eight years at Double H to perfect that appearance. And it had, over time, become a very comfortable uniform for him. So much so that he adopted it now, only semi-consciously, to calm his nerves.

He contemplated that point as he reached the end of the wide hallway. Inside the glass-walled conference room, senior partners John Burlington and Bob Abramowitz waited to deliver Reza his final review as an associate at the prestigious law firm. The final review, Reza knew very well, always included a message about the associate's partnership prospects within the next year. And 2004, he was certain, would be his year. The metal handle felt unusually cold as Reza pulled open the heavy door. Burlington, who appeared to Reza to be in the midst of a heated exchange with Abramowitz, stopped mid-sentence, smiled, and waved Reza into the room. "Come on in, have a seat," he said.

Abramowitz continued to stare out of the window, toward the Washington Monument, apparently engrossed in thought. His jacket was off
and his sleeves rolled up to his elbows – unusually casual, Reza thought.

Reza made his way to one of the many soft, empty, leather chairs
across the long conference room table, and they then exchanged the
obligatory pleasantries. Burlington, attired impeccably, as always, in a
dark gray, pinstriped Gieves & Hawkes suit, asked Reza in sincere tones
how things were going. Reza, as he always would, replied that things
were going well. He then added, casually and cheerfully, that he was
a bit busy but that that was certainly better than the alternative. That
statement, or variations of it, was standard code at every major corporate law firm. It meant that you were, in fact, very busy, but that you
were not the type of person who was going to complain about it.

"Reza, as you know, Bob and I are here to provide you with your for-
mal, annual evaluation. Do you have any questions for us before we
start?"

Yes, he thought to himself. Can you help get my mother and sister
out of Afghanistan? How do you think I can most reliably buy them a
green card from a warlord in Farah province called Rashid Agha Khan?
Do warlords have bank accounts that you can wire money to? "No,
thanks, though I may have some after you begin."

"Fair enough. Bob, do you have anything before we jump in?"

An awkward moment of silence ensued before Abramowitz, who had
continued to stare out the window, suddenly realized that Burlington
had been speaking to him. "No, go right ahead," he stammered. "I'll
jump in if necessary."

John Burlington was a legend not only at Double H, but throughout
the legal profession more broadly. The rotund, sixty-two year old had
been one of the founders of the firm, and the tales of his heroic bat-
tles with government regulators and private plaintiffs initially seemed
at odds with his jolly demeanor. But Reza had worked with Burlington
long enough that he had come to see the full range of his prodigious

talents. They had worked closely together over the past five years, and Reza had come to consider Burlington to be his primary, professional mentor. Burlington, for his part, relied on Reza for his most difficult and thorny client needs. And Reza had never let him down.

Burlington picked up several loose sheets of paper from the table before him. "Let's begin with a summary of your accomplishments over the last year." Yes, Reza thought sarcastically, my accomplishments. He was reminded again of his mother and sister and his failure to secure them a visa to the United States. But this was no time to lose focus, and he quickly brought his mind back to the room before him. "Of course," he replied, continuing the polite pretense that his interviewer, the man who held sway over the younger man's professional future, had actually asked him permission to begin the review in that way.

"You're an incredibly valuable member of the firm, Reza, and our colleagues and clients have turned to you with some of our most important and difficult investigations. You've shown that you possess all of the analytical skills required to perform this job at a high level, and you inspire confidence in those with whom you work."

Even though Burlington glanced at the several sheets of papers balanced in his plump hands, Reza knew that he wasn't actually reading from them.

"Your writing skills are superb, and the brief that you drafted in the Intrepid Funds case last summer was outstanding Reza," Burlington said, pronouncing his name perfectly. "It's rare that the S.E.C. is persuaded to drop insider trading charges completely, and the credit for that belongs to you."

Reza's face remained expressionless, but inside he was thrilled – the Intrepid case had been a remarkable success. Burlington's commentary, he knew, had to be leading to the very message that he yearned to hear. He recalled their first private dinner together in 1997 when he had taught Burlington, over several Martinis, precisely how his name should be pronounced — *Reh-Zah*. It had taken some time for the old man to get it, but he had never mispronounced his name again. "Thank you, John."

"Because of your efforts — "

Abramowitz cut in: "Oh, and don't forget Rockefeller Bank."

Brilliant, Reza thought. Even Abramowitz was supportive! The meeting couldn't be going any better.

"Yes, yes, I'm getting to that," Burlington assured his colleague. "Indeed, Reza, we've expanded several important client relationships because of you, including the one with Rockefeller Bank, which had looked for some time as though it might diminish. On a personal level, you've been a delight to work with, and your collegial nature is an asset to the entire firm." Reza quickly classified Burlington's last set of statements as positive but somewhat formulaic.

Burlington, whose ability to read others never ceased to amaze Reza, continued: "I know you're dismissing this praise, but rest assured that this is not puffery."

"Thank you for saying that, John, but I promise that I wasn't dismissing any of it. It's just that it's been a long time since anyone has said more than two nice things to me in a row." Reza was simultaneously pleased by the fact that he had deflected John's volley, and upset that he had allowed John to so easily read his mind.

"Really, there are no weaknesses whatsoever in your performance, and that is no light statement given the complexity of the matters that you've handled," John continued. "And, if you're able to continue performing at this level, your partnership prospects are very strong."

Very strong.

Reza had just received his final associate review message. It had come rather quickly, and he had not been fully ready for it. It also was not at all the message that he had hoped to hear.

Reza worked hard to maintain his smile as he leaned back and replayed John's words in his mind. There were four possible messages at Double H. You could be told that you were "unlikely" to be made a partnership offer; that your partnership prospects were "open;" that your partnership prospects were "very strong;" or that your partnership prospects were "excellent." An "excellent" message meant that unless you screwed something up on a colossal scale, you would be offered partnership within the year. And partnership, of course, brought with it both professional recognition and steady financial profit. "Very strong" simply meant that it was more likely than not, but by no means guaranteed that you would be offered partnership with the next year. Maybe it was the pressure from his mother and Maryam in Afghanistan, but he had allowed himself all day to imagine – perhaps even assume – that he would be receiving an excellent message. Yes, it was a rarely shared message, but he also knew that he had done everything necessary to deserve it.

Reza suddenly felt weary, and his mind began to wander again. He didn't hear Burlington ask Abramowitz whether he had anything to add, and he also didn't hear Abramowitz go on to describe in exuberant tones the creative ways in which Reza had helped Hunterland Financial acquire and license its investment advisory business. Instead, he returned to his office and clocked a few more Microtrade hours. It always helped him, in times of stress, to do something productive, even if the task with which he occupied himself had nothing to do with the source of the stress.   Then he left work early, by six p.m., and made his way home through a freezing rain. His housemate and best friend, Travis Meadows, was already there, working at a laptop in their living room, the music from an obscure D.C. rap band shaking the floors and walls:

I'ma sleep in yo lobby,
I won't pay no rent,
Yeah, that is my hobby,
Now you know what I meant.
When I said that yo mine, girl,
It don't matter what you think,

My word is word,
I need your sink cuz I stink.

Reza dropped his bag near the front door and shouted toward Travis: "Can you please turn that shit off?"

Travis didn't look up from his laptop. "Huh?"

"That crap you're listening to. It's terrible. Seriously, it's like being stabbed in the ears!"

Travis pressed a button on a remote beside him, and the amplified rant stopped. His movements were quick, and he spoke fast. "That was poetry, dude!" he said.

That could be many things, Reza thought, but poetry was not one of them. "You're the only black guy I know who can't tell good rap from bad."

Travis was brilliant, he was unflinchingly loyal, and he had what was possibly the coolest job on the planet, black-hatting Al-Qaeda websites for an unknown government employer – but Travis also had worse taste in music than anyone else Reza had ever met. Still, each young man was the closest thing to family that the other had around.

Travis thought for a moment about Reza's charge but didn't reply. "Why're you back so early?"

"My review meeting didn't go well. I'm not sure if I'm going to make partner this year, so I didn't feel like working all night."

Travis set aside the laptop and stood up off of their battered, rose-flowered couch. He grabbed a small bag of cheese puffs, threw one in the air, and snatched it proudly with his mouth. He was tall and bone-thin, with large, alert eyes and a short, flat-top hairstyle that he trimmed meticulously every day. He had grown up as a half-black kid who looked totally black in a northern California town called Ukiah, which, as he liked to point out, is haiku spelled backwards. His family stopped supporting him after he was ejected from Stanford for breaking into the school's intranet and financial management systems. Yes, he had done it, he'd insisted, not for any nefarious purpose but only to prove that he could. He never quite understood why that had not been an adequate explanation for the authorities or his parents. They eventually disowned him, or, in Travis' telling, he disowned them.

"Dude, to hell with those guys. You bust your hump for them day and night, and you do it knowing that they don't really care about you. Aren't you tired of them riding you the way they do, just to protect a bunch of fat cats on Wall Street? I'm telling you, it's time you redirect your efforts, it's not too late to do something more meaningful with your life. Perhaps something that might actually make you happy." He slapped Reza on the back with a powdered-cheese covered hand.

"So should I just quit and sit around all day playing Nintendo and tossing cheese puffs in the air?"

Travis shrugged, as if it wasn't such a bad idea.

"Let's go get a drink," Reza said.

"Fine, but you're buying."

Travis grabbed his leather, California highway patrolman's jacket, and they fought their way through the rain to Granville Moore's, a tiny H Street bar that Reza liked because it looked like a miniature castle. They were early and sat on stools at the rough-cut butcher-block bar. The beer menu listed La Trappe Quad, Poperings Hommel, Saison Dupont, Staffe Quad and Orval. Reza ordered the La Trappe; Travis, a Red Stripe Jamaican draught lager.

"Listen, I've found this beautiful little hotel in St. Martin, on Orient beach, that we can buy for about $2 million," Travis said. "It's called *Le Coloniale*. It has ten guest rooms and a direct view of St. Barth's that you can wake up to. All you have to do is get us a loan and help manage the financial side of things. After that, you can just sit in a hammock nursing boat drinks."

Reza sipped his beer. "Boat drinks, huh? If I could find a way to get my hands on $2 million, then I'd have my sister and mother here in the States, instead of them being stuck in some hell-hole in Afghanistan.

I think you overestimate my ability to manage the financial side of things."

Travis was undeterred. "Seriously, you need to consider this plan. Heck, if it's important to you, bring your sister and mother down there to St. Martin. We'll find something for them to do at the hotel. Somebody has to put the little umbrellas in the pina coladas."

Reza stared into his designer microbrew. "I'm not even going to dignify that with a response."

"You're right, it won't work. They even have boat drinks in Afghanistan? Do they even have boats?"

"You're an ass," Reza replied.

Travis erupted with the contagious laughter that came so naturally to him, and he motioned for Bobby, the boyish but heavily tattooed bartender, to double-up their beers.

"You know, maybe I'm over-thinking the meeting today," Reza continued. "Maybe it wasn't so bad. This is one of the best law firms in the world. I've busted my ass for seven years for a shot at partnership there, and my odds are still pretty good. Better than fifty-fifty, in fact. I just have to buckle down for one more year and see this thing through. Then I'm set."

"Set with what, man? You want to be one of those walking corpses, shuffling around, out of shape, wearing a frumpy Brooks Brothers suit and proud that you finally leased a Lexus sedan? Congratulations. You're almost there."

"That's not what it's about. I've got responsibilities. Maryam needs me to raise half a million dollars to help her and my mother buy their way into the States. They're out of options, and I'm the only hope they have left. If I can make partner soon, then I can probably find a way to earn or borrow the kind of money I need to bring them over."

Travis stared over Reza's shoulder.

Reza took a long swig. "How am I going to get my hands on that kind of cash if I'm nursing boat drinks with you in a hammock?"

But Travis was looking past Reza, wearing that expression of confusion and amusement that always overcame him, Reza knew, when he set his sights on female prey. "Are you listening? I'm pouring my heart out here." He waved his open hand directly in front of Travis's face.

"Definitely, I'm listening. I heard you clearly. Words, words, words. And something about a hammock."

Travis walked past Reza, toward an attractive, olive-complexioned, young woman who was sitting alone at a table near the corner of the room. In a matter of moments, he sat comfortably across from her, with his hands resting lightly on hers. It never ceased to amaze Reza, the ease and confidence with which Travis approached women he didn't know.

Travis returned to the bar area ten minutes later, and he flashed Reza, and then Bobby, the napkin on which she appeared to have written her telephone number in brown lipstick. "I hope you enjoyed today's lesson, boys!"

"Thanks Travis, it was really valuable," Reza said. "But if I have any questions, can I call that number? And by the way, what kind of area code is 555?"

Travis worked hard to keep his composure, but he only was able to do so for several seconds. Visibly panicked, he turned the napkin toward himself and confirmed that the area code she had provided him was in fact 202 and not 555. By the time he looked back up, Reza and Bobby were doubled over with laughter. He couldn't help but join them.

They remained at the bar for several hours, laughing and drinking. And, like countless other nights, Reza ultimately found himself with Travis at Vincent's Deli, at 1:30 a.m., hoping against all hope that a steak and cheese sandwich might somehow help him to sober up more quickly. He washed his face in the deli's bathroom, splashing cold, fresh water on his cheeks and neck. Lead-laced water. It was then that he realized he could have spent that evening In a more productive way: one in which he might have figured out how to raise the very necessary cash. And fast.

CHAPTER THREE

The green, walled gardens of the Kabul compound occupied by Rashid Agha Khan were designed to flourish at the peak of the highest, otherwise desolate mountain that rose on the immediate outskirts of the city. From there, Rashid's men, sipping tea to stay warm after the previous night's crunching snow, could guard the approaches from all directions, although these days most visitors – beggars, merchants and American military representatives – made their way up from the east, from the city, on a rutted, one-lane road choked with too many cars and trucks. Rashid controlled a critical area in the western part of the country, about the size of Maryland, that stretched from Farah to Shindand and across to the Iranian border. This month, however, he was based in Kabul as part of the *loya jurga* for the newly proposed Afghan constitution and government.

Since the Taliban were routed, Kabul had become overwhelmed with millions of rural refugees, their stinking trash and sewage flowing in open channels down the city's dilapidated streets. But apart from the overcrowding and the fetid roads, the affairs of Kabul were stable in January 2004. A rocket might land in the capital, a compound raided, or a car bomb occasionally explode, but the U.S. Army's operations in Nuristan, Helmand and Kandahar left the capitol, in the context of Afghanistan, a relatively secure and functioning commercial city.

It was early in the morning, not long after the *fajr* prayer, but already a long line of visitors waited for Rashid in the adjacent residence. Screams and laughter floated from his gardens, where his youngest wife, Jala, played with several children. He rose from his cushion, fixed his *pakol* on his head, slipped into his boots and a heavy beige *chapan* and walked outside. Rashid was old by Afghan standards, having just turned fifty, his beard half-gray and his own parents long since dead. He smiled when his beautiful Jala turned to him. Like a child herself, Jala sat on a small, purple sled, her blue burkha cinched at her waist, shivering but snug in red boots and polka dotted blankets. The boys ran to Rashid, and he patted the coarse black hair on the tops of their heads. They searched his pockets for stray candies or other unanticipated treats. Rashid said nothing to each but rather tromped through the crystal snow to the rear of the garden where he raised his pigeons and rabbits.

He opened the pigeon coop first and found two eggs, a warm and perfect little clutch, which he seized and placed into a black felt bag. He then sprinkled handfuls of seeds and crushed granite throughout the fenced coop, and the pigeons, with their swallowing coos, stamped and fluttered to position themselves for breakfast. The rabbit runs were built into the other side of a plywood wall, separating them from the birds. These hutches were more elaborate than the pigeon coops, and Rashid shuffled to their side with a large bag of hay. He grabbed a hose and filled each of the almost twenty water bottles scattered throughout the system of hutches and wire fences and then dumped the hay, along with treats of carrots and fruit, into each of the various caged rooms. The rabbits, unlike the pigeons, at first scattered, but then scampered toward the carrots as soon as the commotion died down. Rashid lifted a fat rabbit, a one-eyed one he privately called Omar, and brushed his gray, matted fur. Then he seized the animal by the scruff of its neck and turned it toward him, so the rabbit, powerless, was vulnerable, its white underbelly exposed and a look of panic, or perhaps terror, in its one good eye. Rashid laughed and stroked his rough beard across the rabbit's face. Then, in quick motions, he sprung open a door to the hutch, tossed the rabbit back inside, clapped his hands, gazed into the clear, winter sky and murmured a prayer for the day. He returned to his home, stamped the snow off of his boots, removed the *chapan* and took his seat in an adjoining tent, in an honored place on the Persian carpets, among his group of black-robed, turbaned men, their submachine guns and various other weapons across their laps or propped up on the walls. "The Americans can wait. Bring me first the women and children," he said.

Rashid's supplicants were still streaming with purpose up the winding, steep and unpaved road to the top of his hill. The women, like Jala, wore full yet colorful burkas; the bearded men in loose, pajama-like tunics called *shalwar kameez*. Peddlers sold herbs, roots and vegetables from three-wheeled carts and flimsy tables on the approach to the main gate. Their goods were pulled by scrawny donkeys, if they were lucky, or by hand for the rest. A tea-seller with a rich, white beard squatted in a pool of melted snow with his steaming samovar and dirty cups. Young boys hawked phone credit cards, scraps of brick, rubber or wood, and DVDs of either Islamic sermons or Russian pornography, and sometimes even doses of crystal meth. Children in torn clothing, bored waiting, played with stones just inside of the compound, beyond the matrix of thick concrete walls topped with barbed wire. Rashid's men patrolled inside and outside of the gates and searched with dogs and metal detectors every car that dared to approach before allowing them to pass through the large hescoes, or sand-bagged outer walls, pilfered from NATO bases. Many of the surrounding homes were bombed out and abandoned, their gaping wounds a testament to the crumbling remains of a war of total destruction. The land was cratered. Outside of Rashid's gardens, there were no longer any standing trees.

A young woman looking old entered Rashid's tent on crutches and fell to her one knee. She was missing a leg and a hand. Her three children, none older than eight, hid behind the folds of her tattered, stained brown burka. She muttered devotions to the Prophet, as well as to Rashid, and he motioned for her to be brought closer to his feet. Two of his men rose and herded the family toward him. He held a paper in his shaky hand.

"You are from Farah?"

She looked down and not into his eyes. "Yes."

"Your husband?"

"Killed three years ago," she looked up, "defending our tribe."

Rashid pulled on his beard, "Hmm. And this?" he asked, motioning toward her missing limbs. "Land mine?"

"I must beg everyday just to feed my children. We live near the river with no roof above to stop the snow."

"Some have no walls." A few of his men smiled. "Is that all what you do? Beg?"

She hesitated. "It's very cold now. When it's warmer sometimes I wash clothes in the river."

"Yes. In the stinking river. Why not return now to Farah?"

She held up toward him the stump of her hand. "Like this?"

"You have family there. They will care for you."

"I can't. I am a source of shame and embarrassment." The woman began to cry.

"Hmm. Bring me the eldest one." A soldier tore the eight-year-old boy from the clutches of his mother and presented him to the warlord. Rashid looked him up and down, and then held his bony chin in the clench of his calloused hand. "Take your family to Farah, I will give you a home with four walls and a roof."

The woman muttered her thanks and blessings, prostrated before him at his feet. His men nodded their heads in approval.

"This eldest boy will stay with me. He will work for me, and I will be as I were his father."

The destiny of the child was determined. "Yes. Thank you, thank you Rashid Khan, may God smile upon you and your children," she blubbered with joy.

Rashid glanced at the stunned boy, gently touching his cheek with the back of his fingers. "We will teach you to work. Something more than how to pick up garbage or clean shit from shoes. You will learn to fight. And perhaps, someday, you'll learn to read and write."

The older men next to him smiled.

"God willing, you might even read poetry to your mother, and think of my generosity this day."

The men smiled again.

Then the mother and her children were escorted out. The boy was taken away to the garden.

The morning, like most mornings for Rashid, went like this, his bowls of dates and almonds occasionally replaced, his mint tea kept warm and fresh. His visitors, invariably, were Hamid Karzai's men, representatives of other *loya gurja* leaders, Afghan businessmen in shiny suits and with cheap black briefcases, or others from Farah or Herat paying their respects. Rashid looked at his watch; the midday *zhur* prayers were approaching. He motioned for the two armed guards at the entrance to his tent to finally bring him the Americans and their party. The guards disappeared into the adjoining residence and after a minute returned with three men.

Rashid recognized one as Major Jeffrey from the American base at Camp Eggers. He was tall, like so many Americans, with a shaved head and thick black eyebrows that almost connected above the bridge of an imperial nose. He was dressed, as Rashid expected, in desert camouflage and spotless, shiny black boots. The other two were unfamiliar but Rashid was certain one was a military contractor of sorts: the thick mustache, cargo pants and nylon Under Armour shirt gave him away. The third man, much smaller, was dressed in jeans, sandals with rubber soles and carried his own water bottle. Rashid motioned to have it taken away and replaced with a glass of hot tea. The three men sat cross-legged on the red carpet before him with boxes of gifts at their feet.

"Welcome to my make-shift home Major Jeffrey, it is always a pleasure when we meet. Don't you agree?"

Jeffrey responded with a slow drawl, like a character, Rashid thought, from the American Westerns that sometimes played on TV. "Indeed it is Rashid Khan. You have been more generous with your time and support than we would have any right to expect. I will try to keep our imposition to a minimum. I'm present today with two of my brothers. Tony Nicholas here is with our forces, or in support of them to be precise, and Joseph Burroughs, right next to him, is with an organization called the IFMA."

An interpreter whispered into Rashid's ear. During the pause, Burroughs softly spoke up. "If I may, sir, and I am really honored to finally meet you, I'd like to tell you about IFMA, the International Friendship and Management Association. We've been around since 1914, since the start of the First World War, and we help people to build sustainable communities. We've trained and brought professional development expertise all over the world since that time from small villages to big metropolitan areas. It's basically grant and contract funded work to develop professional practices and ethical, transparent governmental bodies."

Rashid sat and peered at him without expression. The interpreter had been silent since just after Burroughs started to speak. As soon as the IFMA man stopped talking, Jeffrey, who was staring holes through Burroughs the whole time, spoke up. "Rashid Khan, it is so darn inconsiderate of me to have forgotten this, but we've brought you some presents, unworthy ones I am sure, but ones that I hope you'll find useful." He bowed slightly and pointed to six unmarked, wooden boxes that lay before them.

Several of Rashid's young soldiers made their way to the front of the three Americans, and they lifted and carried the boxes to another room.

Rashid bowed deeply in response. "Thank you, Major. You are kind as always."

"Actually, Rashid Khan, I am Lieutenant Colonel Jeffrey now."

"A promotion?"

"Yes sir."

"Ah, your talent has been recognized and appreciated."

"I wish that were so. The truth is that I've learned not to get shot and not make waves."

Rashid fingered his prayer beads. "What brings you here today, with your brothers, Lieutenant Colonel?"

Although Burroughs and the other man had started to recline, Jeffrey sat at attention, his back as straight as a rod of steel. "My colleague here from the IFMA has a proposal for your consideration Rashid Khan, and I think it's one that advances both of our strategic interests. I hope you agree."

"The idea," Burroughs said, again interrupting Jeffrey's lead, "is to work together to clean up the river and the city, to start organizing garbage pick ups and to get the sewage out of the Kabul River. It's not, of course, sir, that the Afghans themselves are doing a bad job but there's a lot of other stuff on everyone's mind. Everyone's busy. Something like three million new people have moved to Kabul since 2001."

Rashid smiled benevolently.

Burroughs was slight and thin, with stringy blonde hair, pale blue eyes and an earnest appearance, as if he hadn't recognized yet the practical weakness of idealism. "You've got a growing population with deteriorated roads, congested streets, garbage flowing in the streets, there's no trash removal, and everything is falling apart."

"And so what do you suggest?" Rashid asked.

"We tackle this together. We'll form work crews, each of which will have representatives from IFMA, from the Ministry of Urban Development and Housing, and from the general civilian population. Once the crews are up and running, we will monitor and track their performance every day. We'll develop performance criteria – you know, qualitative and quantitative ones – and create a system of awards for good performance. Once we get these systems in place here in Kabul, we can replicate them all over the country."

"In Farah?"

Burroughs crossed and uncrossed his legs. "Absolutely Mr. Rashid. We can turn to Farah next."

"The Kabul River is indeed a sewer," Rashid added. "We were talking about it just this morning." The men around him solemnly shook their heads in agreement.

"It smells horrible," Burroughs added.

"So what do you need from me?"

"Men to help staff the work crews, sir. We need people to plant trees, pick up trash on a regular basis, drive dump trucks, even people with wheelbarrows, shovels or picks can contribute."

Rashid sipped his tea. The several men on either side of him did the same. "So you are looking for me lend you my men for free?"

Burroughs laughed, which to Rashid sounded more like a woman's giggle. "No, sir. Not at all. I should have mentioned that earlier. We fully intend to pay you and your people a satisfactory fee. We just need you to lend us your support."

In Rashid's experience, things like this were never so straightforward. And so, he probed further. "Who pays for everything? Where does the money come from?"

"Membership dues – "

Jeffrey interrupted: "If I may, sir, IFMA receives certain support from the United States Government and its military services branches on a project by project basis. We in the U.S. Army have determined that it is in our strategic interest to have Kabul cleaned up. IFMA seems to be good at that kind of thing, so we are funding them. We hope you share that interest."

"Perhaps," Rashid chuckled in a manner that appeared to unnerve Burroughs. "Still, that is not why you are all here, today, is it? There is something more that you want from me, no?"

The third American, Nicholas, stirred and sat up straight. "Yes, sir, we do. We want the ammunition flow from Iran to the Taliban to stop."

Rashid stroked his beard and eyed the military contractor. He was fat and out of shape, as if he did too much of his business over too many rich meals. And while Rashid appreciated the directness of his approach, he did not intend to reciprocate so quickly. "I have no influence over Iran or the Talib. What can a simple Afghan like me do?"

"Your men maintain the border with Iran, sir," Nicholas said.

"Borders? What borders? These lines exist in your maps and GPS systems only. There are no lines in mountains." Rashid's men laughed at the remark.

"We believe that the majority of arms are coming over by road. Convoys of trucks, sir."

"So if you know all of that, why do you need me? You can shoot them with your planes and drones."

"Rashid Khan, you're right," Jeffrey said. "We could blow them to pieces any time we want. But right now, we're not in the business of blowing up Iranians. It would create an unnecessary distraction from our main mission. We believe that our strategic interest would be advanced significantly if we could rely on you and your men to help us in this regard. We know that you control the roads in the west. You have the means to inspect all the trucks coming in from Iran. That, sir, is what we're asking of you."

He drained his tea. It was almost time now to pray. "As I think you know, I am happy to help the United States whenever I can. But this is risky business, both for me and my men."

"Yes, sir, we do appreciate that. And we are fully prepared to compensate you and your men for the risks that they may face." Jeffrey drew a large envelope out from a case at his side. "I believe it contains two hundred and fifty thousand United States dollars. We stand ready to revisit this amount in a month's time if you are able to help us."

Rashid rose, and each of the men, including the Americans, stood with him. "That will help, of course. I can assure my men that their families will be taken care of if they die. But what sometimes will go even further in helping me provide for the welfare of my people, those whose husbands or fathers perish, is travel documents. Passports, green cards, and the promise of safe passage to America." He paused deliberately.

"Yes, naturally, Rashid Khan. You can rest assured that, should that come to pass, you can count on us to deliver those necessary travel documents as well. Provided of course that the recipients aren't on the Terrorist Watchlist."

"Of course." The tribal leader rose. "Very well then, Lieutenant Colonel. It has been a pleasure, as always, to see you."

Jeffrey smiled and handed the large envelope to one of Rashid's lieutenants. «Likewise, Rashid Khan. May peace be with you. Oh, and we'll be in touch on the sanitation project we discussed."

"Right. I will lend you ten men in Kabul on the promise that you turn to Farah next."

Rashid left the tent and fought through crowds of other Afghan men, shouting at him for assistance with land disputes and other matters, and he pushed his way toward a small mosque on the grounds of the compound. There, he washed his hands and his feet and entered the mosque with his hands up toward the sky. "Allahu Akbar!"

His men joined him: "Allahu Akbar!!"

Rashid folded his hands over his chest and recited the first chapter of the Qu'ran.

Jeffrey and the other Americans walked out of the grounds, to their truck, past the mosque, where the lieutenant colonel managed to catch a snippet of the prayer. "Sam'l Allahu liman hamidah."

He turned to Burroughs: "God hears those who call upon Him."

"Yeah, and so many do," Nicholas added.

Jeffrey unlocked the car doors.

"So let me ask you guys," Nicholas said as he entered the vehicle, "does the U.S. military really provide passports and green cards to

Afghan warlords?"

"Of course not," Jeffrey replied with a chuckle. "But we do to Afghan freedom fighters who help us kill the bad guys."

CHAPTER FOUR

As the days went by, Reza worked hard to stay as focused on his assignments at Double H as he had been for the prior seven years. It wasn't easy, given the new doubts that now filled his head following his most recent associate evaluation and the accompanying partnership message. Had all his efforts at the firm, all the sleepless nights and personal sacrifices been for nothing? He certainly hoped not, but he found himself asking the questions all the same. Reza also spent more and more time thinking of ways to raise the money that his sister and mother needed to get to the United States. That too had proven difficult. It was not easy for an associate at a law firm – even a very good one, with very strong partnership prospects – to get his hands on $500,000. Reza's highest annual compensation, including his bonus, had been less than half that amount. And on top of all that, Reza could not help but feel frustrated that for all his supposed legal skills and Washington contacts, he had been unable to get his mother and sister to the United States through an above-board channel and that he had been reduced to bribing – no, trying to find the money to bribe – an Afghan warlord.

That last thought had made it very hard for him to sleep the night before, and that in turn led him to arrive at work a bit later than usual this cold February morning. Without much deliberation, Reza decided that his first call would be to a legal recruiter, an ex-lawyer he once practiced with at Double H named Edith O'Leary. She had been telling him for months that several other law firms were interested in recruiting him and that some may be willing to bring him over as a partner. Moreover, she had hinted in the past, some may be willing to pay him a signing bonus. That could prove useful, Reza thought, given his present circumstances. He closed his door when she picked up the line.

"It's me, Reza," he whispered – unnecessary, given the purposefully thick walls at Double H.

"Who?"

"Reza!"

"Oh, hi, I couldn't hear you."

Reza cupped his hand around the phone. "I need to keep this very quiet."

"Of course, dear. You know I couldn't do what I do for a living – at least not very well, anyway – if I wasn't able to be discrete. And you know that I do my job very well," she snorted. "So, to what do I owe the pleasure?"

Reza bent low, down to his lap and almost under his desk, and continued to cup his hand on the receiver. "I'm not at all sure that I'm interested in moving, but I think I'd like to hear a bit more about that opportunity you mentioned the last time we spoke."

"Oh, you mean Greenberg Platt? They've had their eye on you for a long time."

Even though he knew it was part of her job to blow sunshine all day long, Reza couldn't help but feel flattered. "Tell me a bit more about them. What're they up to these days?"

"They are a terrific firm. Maybe not up to Double H's level yet, but moving up the ranks quickly. And they're very aggressive when it comes to investing in talent they believe in. In fact, Reza, I'm working on a big deal now, bringing several very high profile litigators over there. Perhaps we could look into attaching you to that team."

"Really, why would that make sense? Wouldn't it just make the discussions more complicated?"

"Normally it would, but, in this case – and this is between us, Reza, I'm getting a bit over my skis here – the team I'm recruiting is from your firm. And it's a really impressive group."

That surprised him. People did not leave Double H very often for other firms, especially not in groups. "Seriously?"

"Yes. But again, don't whisper a word to anybody. I'll tell you more as it pans out."

"Sounds good. And maybe you can explore what they might be willing to do in terms of compensation if I were to consider a move."

"Of course! They'd be delighted to explore that, I'm sure. Do you have some dollar range in mind?"

"Not really," Reza replied, trying his best to maintain the casual tone. "But it would be important to me that they include a significant signing bonus, a lump sum up front."

There was a knock on Reza's door, and he sat up suddenly. "I've got to go, but let's keep in touch."

It was Vargas, from office services, who seemed not to care in the slightest that Reza was on the telephone. He squeezed into the small office with his cart of mail and closed the door behind him. "Lemme talk to you, man."

"Come on in."

He stared at Reza. "I'm already in."

Doesn't anyone get sarcasm anymore? "What's up?"

"I bought that co-op you told me about."

"Wow. Which one?"

"On Virginia Avenue. Near Georgetown. Got them down to a hundred fifty thou. Made my brother the purchaser, you know, the one who runs that bagel place in Alexandria, he got through the co-op board. We gonna close next week."

Reza picked some lint off of his knee. "Schmears?"

"That's the one."

"Nice."

"Yeah. We goin' to rent it out to like Europeans, they come over, can't afford the hotels, stay with us for like $200 a night. Mortgage and maintenance for me is like $1500 a month, we make that back in a week, and then it's gravy."

"Seems like you got it all figured out."

He patted his chest with a clenched fist. "I appreciate you turnin' me on to it."

Reza took an envelope of inter-office mail from him. "Let me ask you, though, didn't I warn you that co-ops don't usually allow short-term rentals?"

Vargas waved his hand. "They not gonna find out. We just say they're relatives."

"From Sweden?"

"Yeah. Why not?"

Reza looked at Gil's chinstrap beard. "I don't know. Forget it. I've got to get back to work."

Vargas pushed his mail cart back out of the office and shut Reza's heavy door behind him. Everyone was hustling, Reza thought. Why should he judge Gil for doing the same, for fighting for his share of the pie? At least Gil was showing some ingenuity. Reza then turned to his voicemails. The first was from Burlington, wanting to meet with him at ten a.m. Reza looked at his watch. Ten minutes to go. The next message was unexpected:

"Ah, *bonjour*, Reza. In case you don't remember who this is, it's me, Clara. It's been a long time since we've spoken, no? Anyway, I wanted to say hello, but I am also calling on business. I'm still working with Gibran Asset Management, here in Geneva, and we are looking for some legal assistance in the U.S. Naturally, I thought of you. I was hoping you might be free to meet with me and my boss, George Gibran? We are planning to be in Washington for meetings the week of the fourteenth. Oh, Valentine's Day! Ha ha! Anyway, let me know if you are free that week and if we could block some time to meet. *Ciao*, Reza."

She left her number.

Reza listened to the message again. The soft laugh, the French accent. Ha ha, Valentine's Day indeed! Clara Fournier — the beautiful French woman from Chamonix, the small town at the foot of Mont Blanc, the highest mountain in the Alps — was someone whom Reza had dated for about a year while they were both at New York University Law School. He had spent the first two years of law school pursuing her, but she'd spent those summers in Morocco, and it was not until the beginning of their final year that she agreed to see him. He had fallen in love with her during that last year, and she had, it seemed to him at the time anyway, reciprocated. But then school ended, and she left just as abruptly for a rare job opportunity in Geneva. Reza, for his part, moved on to Double H but thought of her often. He had tried on several occasions during the early years after law school to connect with her, but she had declined his every overture; she always had a good excuse handy. Eventually, he gave up altogether.

The phone rang, and Reza looked at his watch – damn, he was going to be late. He ignored the phone, grabbed his suit jacket off the back of his chair and raced down the hall to Burlington's office. He winked at Jane, Burlington's assistant, and slipped in through the half-opened door. She smiled and shook her head. Jane was pretty, he thought. In her mid-forties, reddish hair and slim: in another time, and definitely another place, he might have found her attractive.

John Burlington's office was a unique blend of old and new. The heavy furniture, the antique grandfather clock, and the leather-bound law books that filled the built-in shelves around the room could very well have been found in a barrister's office many, many decades earlier. They stood in stark contrast, however, to the sleek flat-screen monitor, the thin laptop computer, and wireless, telephone headset that Burlington used to carry out his work.

He pointed Reza toward a classic, brown leather couch, with ruffling, tufting and buttons, and indicated with his index finger and thumb that the call he was on would be ending shortly. Reza had spent many hours over the course of seven years in John's office, waiting for John to finish other, similar "short" calls. He smiled, nodded, and made his way to his familiar place across from Burlington's desk. He spied a copy of the *Wall Street Journal* on Burlington's desk and grabbed it, collapsing into the leather couch. But Reza found it particularly difficult that day to tune out the animated conversation that Burlington was having with an obstinate client. It did not help Reza's cause that Burlington paced the office as he spoke, like a caged and unhappy animal.

"You can take a horse to water, but you can't make him drink," Burlington said several minutes later, removing his telephone headset and tossing it onto his large and overcrowded, French Empire style desk.

"I'm sure that if anyone can make him drink, it's you," Reza replied with a grin.

"In this case, it may be that no one can."

Reza put the newspaper down on the table, and waited for Burlington to join him on the well-worn couch.

"How are things going?" Burlington asked.

"Fine, thanks. I've been working on the outline for the Microtrade S.E.C. meeting."

"Good. I know Jessica's pretty anxious about that meeting. Sounds like their C.E.O. has some real exposure if thing break badly."

"She's right to be worried, but we'll see what we can do to get that investigation shut down soon."

"Okay," Burlington said, pausing long enough to let Reza know that he would be changing the subject. "I want to talk with you about the review that you received a few weeks back. I know you weren't pleased, but I want to let you know exactly what it all means. There are a lot of things going on here that have nothing to do with you, but they are going to impact you nonetheless. And I think it's important and fair, really, for you to know about them."

Reza wasn't surprised that Burlington wanted to discuss his review.

In fact, he had expected to receive a pep talk from him earlier. This conversation appeared, however, to be going down a different path.

"What I'm about to tell you is highly confidential. You cannot share it with anyone. In fact, there are many partners here who are not privy to it. Do you understand that?"

"Sure." Reza knew that Burlington did not make such requests casually.

"You've probably had no reason to track the firm's financial performance in *American Lawyer*, but, over the last five years, our profit per partner numbers have fallen dramatically. Actually, it's not that they've fallen, it's that others have passed us, some by a mile. This year, for the first time, we're not going to be in the top twenty in profits per partner."

Reza knew the *American Lawyer* financial rankings were closely tracked by law firms throughout the country and, whether they liked it or not, these rankings impacted their ability to attract and retain talent. If a firm's financial performance and rankings weakened significantly compared to the competition, they started to lose their top rainmakers to more profitable, better-paying competitors. Less rainmakers meant worse financial performance, and that was often the start of a vicious cycle that was very difficult to break, one that had more than once led to the demise of otherwise successful firms. Made sense now that O'Leary had senior partners from Double H looking to leave.

"The fact of the matter is that we have not done as good a job as we should have diversifying our practice," Burlington continued. "We've become too reliant on our core litigation and regulatory practices, and we never developed a strong corporate practice like some of our competitors. Those practices aren't often glamorous, but they sure do generate billings. So what does this have to do with the review you received?"

Reza had been trying hard to digest where Burlington was going and had almost forgotten that the conversation was intended to relate to his review. "I wasn't asking myself that just yet, but I suppose it would be nice to know the connection."

"We're officially worried. That's the connection. We have to raise our profits per partner. And when you and others in your position are considered for partnership, well, that dilutes the profits for the rest of us. So next year the firm will examine, in a way it really has never done before, what revenue we think each partnership candidate can generate. What impact will that person's promotion have on the profit per partner calculations? It sounds crass, but that's the reality we're in."

Burlington stood. He walked slowly across the thick, blue and red Persian rug that covered his office floor, and he turned his gaze west, out of his window, past the treetops, the office buildings, the Washington Monument, and beyond. His voice grew softer, and more wistful. "It's not the profession that it was when I started my practice, Reza, but change is the only constant, I suppose."

Reza had the distinct impression that Burlington had forgotten that he was still in the room. For several moments, neither man broke the uncomfortable silence that followed. "Remember," Burlington finally snapped, "this conversation never happened."

When Reza left the office several minutes later, he found himself more than a bit disoriented. It was going to take some time to understand all of the things that he had heard. First, he had to get his head around the idea that Double H was worried about its financial performance and its ability to stay competitive. This was the same blue-chip firm that had mastered the most difficult and high profile legal cases in the country for the last fifty years. It was the can't-miss firm that deep-pocket clients turned to when the stakes were the highest possible, when careers, fortunes and liberties were on the line. This firm was now worried about the diversity of its business mix?

Even when he was able to consider all of that, Reza would have to confront the second, more important message that he'd received: that his partnership prospects were going to turn, more so than on anything else, on his ability to generate revenue. It was not going to be the case, as he had been assured for seven years, that all he needed to demonstrate was top-notch lawyering. In fact, the quality of his lawyering, what he had spent seven long years proving, may be substantially less relevant than a demonstrated ability to bring in money.

He returned to his office and listened again to Clara's message. Her beautiful, lilting voice had once been like heroin to him. In the evenings, when she would stay through the night, her head on his chest and her soft lips so near to his cheek, she would murmur words to him, words that slowly lost their meaning as they melted into each other, and then into a soft melodic hum. Her golden brown hair, straight and so long it reached her waist, would cascade across his belly. She was thin, with narrow hips and skinny thighs, but her skin, especially on the outer sides of her small breasts, near her arms, was for him the softest place on earth. His fingertips would linger there, or he would nuzzle, his whiskers scratching her.

Reza snapped out of his memories. She surely had called him on business, nothing more. And, of course, that's what it was always all about for her. He had found out the hard way: the cold and calculating decision she'd secretly made to move to Geneva had been sprung on him with no warning during a rainy night's dinner. The plane ticket had already been purchased, and the flight was to leave the next day. It had been so much fun, she'd said, but now it was over. It was time for the next chapter in their respective lives. The opportunity she was presented at the Swiss hedge fund could not be refused. She enthused over a string of bitter nothings about asset allocation, leverage, and internal rates of return: suddenly her voice had sounded a lot less sweet to him.

Reza should have known from the start that she was not a sentimentalist. She came from a very modest background, and her father was an abusive alcoholic who had left Clara and her mother when she was thirteen. Everything Clara had achieved in life, she had achieved through sheer, dogged determination. She once told Reza a chilling story of an old and dented pot that her mother kept stowed in her bedroom closet. It was the pot that her father would beat her and her mother with – the dents were from blows to their heads.

It was a little after 10:30 a.m. in Washington, and just past 4:30 p.m. in Geneva.

He placed the call.

The voice on the other end was breathless. *"Oui, hallo."*

"Clara," he cooed, in a rumbling, low voice. "It was so nice to hear from you. It's been far too long."

"Ah. Ms. Fournier? Just a moment, please."

Reza winced.

After a few seconds, Clara picked up the phone.

"Clara," Reza cooed again, in a rumbling, but even lower voice. "It's been so long, I was so happy to hear from you again."

She giggled. "Reza? You sound different."

He coughed. "Ah, yes, I'm getting over a cold."

They exchanged customary pleasantries.

"As I said in my message, I'll be in Washington for a few days, around the fourteenth. I'm traveling with my boss, George Gibran. Do you know him?"

Reza typed the name into a Google search. "Of course, but not personally."

"He's a very big player here in Europe. In fact, we're now managing north of thirty billion dollars in assets."

Reza balanced the receiver between his shoulder and ear and began typing furiously. "Wow, that's real money."

"Yes, it is," she replied. "And we're interested now in establishing a presence in the U.S. We want to set up a series of new, U.S. based funds, and we want to market to large institutional investors in America. We need a top-notch, well-connected law firm to help us do all of that, and to do it quickly. And so, of course, I thought of you."

"That's very flattering, Clara, and I'd love to be of help, but you know there are lots of lawyers, including here at Double H, with more experience than me in this particular area. I'd be happy to connect you with them."

She paused. "I know that Reza. We can call any lawyer in the country and they would jump on the opportunity. I'm sure you understand that this has the potential to be a very substantial and lucrative assignment. But we believe in personal relationships at GAM. That's how we've become as successful as we have. And I want to work with someone that I can trust. That is much harder to find than someone who just knows the law in this area. Plus, you're a damn good lawyer, Reza. Give yourself more credit."

How would she know that? Had she been interested enough to watch him from afar? He recalled his recent conversation with Burlington. "Right. Of course I would be happy to discuss this further. When would you like to meet?"

"Dinner on February 14th?"

"Sure, why not?" He paused. "I have no plans that night."

"Mr. Gibran will join me."

"Great. I'll ask one of senior partners with an investment management background to come along as well."

"No, Reza," she said quickly. "Only you. Let's just meet, the three of us, and explore if this is a good fit. We know Double H is a great firm with lots of prominent lawyers. We are really interested in exploring the personal connection."

"Sure, that's fine too."

After hanging up, Reza pulled up several articles about Gibran Asset Management and shot an optimistic email to Burlington about his new prospect.

At the same time, Clara slipped out of her office to see Gibran.

She paused before his door, knocked and entered before he said to come in. His office was sumptuous, too fancy for Clara's taste, but Gibran intentionally went for the more ostentatious, Versailles look. From the outside, the GAM building was simple: sand-colored with green shutters on a hilly street in the old city district. But the fixtures inside Gibran's office were made of gold, marble and crystal. He sat behind an ornate, wooden, gilt-inlaid desk in front of a marble fireplace with brass candelabras and an antique Swiss clock on its mantel. She stood before him under a massive chandelier with hundreds of teardrops, her reflection in the mirror above the fireplace. Sunlight streamed in through the floor to ceiling windows, the office's yellow and red curtains, tapestries and straight-back chairs sparkling in its shafts. Clara's hair, too, appeared to shimmer golden in its rays.

Gibran motioned for her to come around his desk and when she did he slipped a hand below her skirt.

She backed away. "I think this is not such a good idea."

He smirked. "It's chilly this afternoon."

"You've ignored me for days, stewing in your own head about I don't know what, and when I've approached you, you act like I'm not there. So fine, I have my own life to live. But don't just squeeze my ass and expect me to act like nothing's going on. You want to talk to me about work, then fine, we'll talk. But please stop trying to treat me like I'm your whore. I won't allow it."

He knew he should say no, of course you're not my whore, but he didn't. "I received a call from the Financial Services Authority. I've been preoccupied with that, I'm sorry."

Clara walked back around to the other side of his desk, sat in a chair and crossed her legs. "That's fine. I just talked to Reza Shirvani."

Gibran raised an eyebrow. "And?"

"We're meeting with him, of course, on the fourteenth."

"In Washington?"

"Yes. I'll make the arrangements when I get back to the office."

"Only the three of us?"

"Yes, I made that clear." She paused. "You know, I'll say it again, I'm not sure why you're so insistent on meeting him alone. This is a big project. Don't you want to meet some of the senior partners at Double H?"

"Yes, in due time, we can meet all of them. But for now, I want to meet this young Mr. Shirvani. You said he's smart and loyal, and that I can trust him, no? That is what matters most in this business."

She picked up a letter opener from a tray on his desk. It was shaped like a sword. "I don't think you really trust anyone, George."

He smiled. She'd learned well. "But I do. I trust people to always act in an economically rational way, to always seek the advancement of their personal interest above all else. I've not been let down yet."

A subtle smile creased her pretty face. "You remind me that I need a raise. It's been a while."

Gibran walked around his side of the desk to the rear of her chair. He placed his hands on her slight shoulders and sniffed her neck. "Chantal Thomass?"

"*Osez-Moi!*"

"Dare me? I believe I will."

She slipped from his grasp and stood, facing him. The subtle smile, again.

He held her by her chin.

She draped her right arm around his neck and playfully drew the letter opener across his throat. "Careful, *monsieur*, I'm armed."

He seized her narrow wrist, shook it, and the opener dropped to the floor. "Everyone close to me is. Life would be pretty boring otherwise."

CHAPTER FIVE

Reza and Travis sat on a couch in their living room with their feet up on a battered and stained coffee table. Travis had a bottle of Red Stripe in his left hand and the TV remote in his right. Reza, having just returned from a run, held a bottle of Fiji spring water in his still sweaty hands. It was late on Saturday afternoon, hours before he was to meet Clara and Gibran. A re-run of The Cosby Show flashed on the screen.

"I hate Valentine's Day." Reza muttered.

"It's a bullshit, Hallmark holiday," Travis replied as he nursed his beer.

"Ironic that I have a work dinner with my ex-girlfriend and her boss tonight, huh?"

"I wouldn't call it irony, really. More like an uncomfortable coincidence."

"True. It's going to be a little weird, seeing her again tonight."

Travis ignored him and squinted toward the television. "Lisa Bonet was hot," he said.

"I never really liked her. I couldn't get past those crazy parachute pants."

"Ain't nothing wrong with her pants, man. What were you wearing in 1980 when you stepped off the boat?"

"*Touchez.*"

Reza's brain was filled, all day, with thoughts of Clara, as if he were in law school again. Like an unconscious muscle memory, she stimulated his thoughts. He had hoped that a brisk run would clear his head. It did not. "Can I borrow the Benz tonight?"

Travis lifted his feet off of the table and sat up straight. "That's asking a lot."

"I know, but I'd like to arrive in respectable fashion."

The Benz – Travis's 1972 Mercedes-Benz 280SE 4.5 – was among his most prized possessions. Despite its boxy, upright, stuffy look and an original swimming pool, blue-green color, the Benz was a beautiful beast. Its V-8 engine was packed with torque and easily cruised at 100 mph with only two fingers on the wheel. Its heavy doors slammed shut like a bank vault. The switches on its dash were as solid as those on tractors, making perceptible clicks and chunks when turned or positioned. Its brown leather seats were well worn, as was the thin carpet on its floor. Travis kept it in their driveway, Clubbed and rarely used. Although it wasn't actually worth all that much – Reza had seen the model sell for as low as fifteen thousand dollars – Travis treated it as he would a museum piece.

"Why is that? You still into her?"

"What? No, of course not. It's a work dinner. She's here with her boss. They're Europeans, and I'm meeting them at Cafe Milano. I need to look respectable. That's it."

Travis tilted his head slightly to the left and focused his gaze on Reza. "Yep, you're definitely still into her."

"Come on, man, if you won't lend me the car, just say so and I'll call for a car service instead."

Travis turned his head toward him. "You know you're not getting laid just cause you drive the Benz, right?"

Reza hadn't even thought of that possibility. "Look, I'm Persian. The Benz just fits."

"You're not rich, you're not hairy, you don't have long eyelashes, you suck at soccer. I'm more Persian than you. I'm the Black Persian."

"You don't wear cologne."

"That's the only thing Persian about you."

"Just tell me this," Travis asked, "is she hot?"

"I don't know, I haven't seen her in years. I know she was hot, back in the day. But this is a work dinner. It's actually a pretty big opportunity for me. Now can I have the keys?"

"Name?"

"What?"

"I need her name."

"Why?"

"You want the car or not?" Travis pulled and flashed the keys.

"Clara Fournier. Now give me the keys."

Travis threw the keys to Reza, and Reza went upstairs to shower. Halfway through his shower, Travis opened the bathroom door and walked in with an open lap-top computer. "Thought you'd like to know that as of about six months ago, she was indeed still hot!"

Reza poked his head out from behind the shower curtain. A picture of Clara, wearing a stern expression at a recent hedge fund conference, appeared on the screen.

"Congratulations, now can I have some privacy please?"

Travis looked again at her photo. "I'm hoping you can do this, man, but I'm not sure. Look, just try to be cool. Don't do something silly like hanging on too long when you hug her hello."

"I wouldn't do that." Shower water ran down Reza's face.

Travis raised one eyebrow. "You would. And don't try to be funny."

The water started to pool on the floor. "I'm funny."

"No, you're definitely not funny. Your best bet, without a doubt, is to be cool, aloof, almost uninterested. And then, when she least expects it, when she's decided that you're completely callous, hit her with a really great compliment, something totally unconventional."

The soap fell out of Reza's hand. "Thanks, really, I appreciate it, now can you please get out?"

"It can't be trite. It has to be something unpredictable. Something like complimenting her skin tone. And I know this is hard, but whatever you do, don't talk too much."

"I never talk too much!"

Reza shut the shower curtain, and Travis finally left him. He shaved, dressed and prepared for the meeting. An hour later, the Benz roared to life at the turn of the key and then idled to a soothing, rumbling hum. Reza opened the gate, backed out of the driveway onto H Street, closed the gate and then made his way to Cafe Milano, weaving through slower-moving traffic. He tried hard to keep his gaze fixed on the cars that flashed by at unnaturally close distances rather than the picturesque Potomac River views on his right. He looked at the dashboard. He was late.

Cafe Milano is a tony and modern Italian eatery in the heart of Georgetown. Though the food is generally expensive and almost always mediocre, the landmark restaurant has been known for years by Washington insiders as the place to see and be seen by the city's social elite. Getting a table on the evening of Valentine's Day must not have been an easy task, though Reza knew it would not present a problem for Clara.

He arrived at the restaurant after some fifteen minutes – just in time. A team of blue-jacketed valet attendants appeared to be overwhelmed by the many luxury sedans that blared their horns and demanded immediate attention.

"Damn it," Reza muttered and, without pause, he maneuvered the Benz into the left lane of the narrow, two-lane road and pulled to the front of the line of stopped cars. In doing so, he narrowly avoided a head-on collision with a minivan whose lane he had invaded. He avoided eye contact with the startled driver, as well the passengers of the cars whom he had unceremoniously passed. He tossed his car keys to a young valet, spotted him a twenty, and sauntered toward the entrance to the warm, brightly lit restaurant, under trees decorated with strings of white lights.

Clara and Gibran were already seated. She waved to him, and the host escorted Reza to their corner table, candlelit and below a poster of a red heart. Reza pulled sharply at the lapels of his blue blazer and walked straight to Clara. Her beautiful blondish-brown hair was piled high up in a bun, and two curled strands framed her white face. She stood, as did Gibran, and Reza looked her up and down, admiring her shimmering, green blouse, her tight black skirt, her dark stockings and delicate black heels wrapped around her ankles with two gold-studded straps. "*Bon soir*, darling, how nice to see you again," she said, leaning in to kiss him.

Reza, unnerved, momentarily pulled back before bending forward to return the gesture by kissing her on both cheeks. He wondered whether he let his hand linger too long on the small of her petite back, like Travis had warned him not to do. Bad start, he thought.

"Good evening, Clara. Wonderful to see you."

"Reza, this is George Gibran."

"Hello. Uh... Nice to... uh... meet you," Reza stammered, as he unintentionally bumped Clara and stepped forward to shake hands with Gibran.

If Clara was at all uncomfortable, she certainly hid it well. "Reza and I were very close friends in New York many years ago, in our student days. It's been too long, *n'est-ce pas?*"

"Yes, it has been indeed. I'm very glad you reached out."

"Not at all," Gibran said, as they all took their places at the table. "Thank you for joining us, Reza. "You know, I'm always amazed that when I see old friends they seem to have aged so much, yet I, of course, always look the same."

Clara laughed at Gibran's comment, and Reza was simply glad to now be seated. He remembered Travis's admonition — just be cool.

A waiter came, and they ordered salads and entrees, along with more wine. Reza tried hard to focus on Gibran, rather than Clara, and the conversation skipped along above the gentle waves of pleasantries: the quality of their Swiss Air flight, the powder over the holidays at Davos, the dryness of the wine, and the recent cold spell in Washington. Gibran received a call, and he excused himself.

Clara finished less than half of her salad, dabbed the corners of her mouth with her napkin and sat erect, staring at Reza affectionately. "You look very well."

He wanted to return the compliment. He even considered, for a brief moment, telling her that she looked beautiful, that he has missed her terribly, and that he had hoped for years that they would again be sitting across the table from each other, like they were tonight. Instead, he chose to follow Travis's advice. "Thanks." Polite but aloof.

"When George returns, you should ask him about his plans for expanding into the U.S. This could be a very large and profitable project for you and Double H. Don't be coy, for heaven's sake!"

Right, Reza reminded himself, that's why he was here after all. "Yes, of course. So tell me, what exactly is it that you are hoping to do in the U.S.?"

"We've run out of room for growth in Europe. So what we want to do is to set up a series of brand new funds that are registered here in the U.S., and we want to market them to institutional investors throughout America. This will allow us to leverage significantly the brand and experience that we developed in Europe. Once that's done, we'll need to establish prime brokerage and trading accounts at the largest banks in New York, so we can trade on behalf of the funds. Just like we do in Europe. But setting all of that up from scratch here in the U.S. will be no small feat." She stroked a strand of long, golden hair out of her eye.

"That sounds like a pretty large project. I really appreciate you thinking of me."

Gibran returned and came around the table, touching Clara's shoulder before taking his seat. "I was just noticing, Clara, the tone of your skin. I hope you don't think me impertinent. Perhaps it's the light, or the air here in the U.S., but it really has a wonderful glow tonight." Clara giggled and flashed a coy smile toward Gibran. Damn, Reza thought,

Travis *was* right.

Their entrees were served: Costaletta di Vitello da Latte al Marsala for Gibran; Branzino del Mediterraneo al Forno con Rosemarino e Verdure for Clara; and an organic chicken dish for Reza.

"I understand from Clara," Reza said, "that you may require legal assistance here in the U.S. I was hoping that I could tell you a bit about Henderson & Humphries. It is, as you may very well know, one of the best firms in America."

The investment banker cut into his veal. "Yes, I'm well aware of your firm's stellar reputation. But you know, Reza, this is a city full of top-notch lawyers. I have very particular needs, and so I'm looking for just the right representation."

"Well, we serve numerous investment banks, and prominent hedge funds just like yours, including the Regal Funds, Magna — "

Gibran pointed a fork toward Reza, and the younger man abruptly stopped speaking. Over a silent minute, Gibran attacked his veal, cutting it into small pieces and piercing them one at a time, placing each in his mouth until his right cheek was stuffed. He chewed hard and swallowed, wiped his mouth and smiled. "It's quite delicious, don't you think?"

Clara agreed. Reza had yet to touch his plate.

"I'm planning to raise and deploy as much as twenty billion dollars in the United States. As you undoubtedly recognize, this will require the establishment of dozens of new corporate entities, including a series of brand new investment funds. Some will be on-shore, and some will be off-shore. All of them will be marketed here in the U.S., so we will need prospectuses, marketing materials, and the like. Of course, we also will need to establish and register an investment advisor with the S.E.C., to run the funds. Later, we can turn our attention to the establishment of prime brokerage and other trading relationships. But what makes all of this particularly challenging, is that all of this needs to be done very quickly. In other words, I need a team of totally dedicated attorneys willing and able to work around the clock, and I want this work done right the first time."

Reza's goose had just laid its golden egg. To do all of the things that Gibran had described would cost millions of dollars in legal fees alone. And if Reza could guide this project and the associated revenue to Double H, then he surely would have demonstrated his revenue generation skills beyond any doubt whatsoever. That would certainly lead to partnership for him, and – perhaps – even help him raise the money he needed to bring his mother and sister to the U.S. "Clara can assure you, I believe, that there is no one more committed to client service than we are at Double H. Our lawyers simply cannot be out-worked."

"Oui, il est plus American qu'Iranian á cet égard," she added, for only Gibran.

The older man leaned toward him. "Most of all, Reza, I need a point person whom I can rely on. I value personal trust. I value personal loyalty. If I turn this over to Double H, I want to know that you – Reza Shirvani – will be fully involved in every aspect of the project, and that you will be available to me when I need you. Always. And in return I will pay you and your firm very handsomely."

"Of course. I understand. Those are my values as well."

Gibran retreated back to his seat and smiled. He grabbed a roll from the basket, sliced it in half, and put a tab of butter on each side. *"Est comme ça il est plus Iranian."* And in this way more Iranian, he said softly to Clara.

"It would be fun, Reza, to be together again," Clara added, putting her hand on top of Reza's.

"Please, go ahead and eat," Gibran said. "You haven't touched your meal."

Reza stared down at the heat swirling from his hand into Clara's, but he willed his arm to slip away so he could lift his fork. To be together again? "Thank you."

"Clara tells me you're originally from Tehran."

"Yes, that's right."

"And your family is here?"

Reza paused. "No. Still there. Sort of. My mother and sister are actually in Afghanistan now, but we are hoping that that won't be the case for much longer."

"Indeed. Afghanistan these days is, as I'm sure you know, a difficult place. Where exactly are they?"

"Farah province. For the time being," Reza added quickly.

"Actually I know that area well. It's a shame what has happened there over the last twenty years. I myself am Lebanese. A Maronite."

Reza looked up. "A Phoenician."

"You know your history."

"No more than most, I'm sure. But I know your poets."

"Are you familiar with Said Akl?" Gibran asked.

"I would cut off my right hand just not to be an Arab."

Upon hearing the Akl quote, Gibran banged his fist on the table so hard that the wineglasses and candle nearly toppled over. "I like you already! A Persian and a Maronite together in America! What a country!"

Reza pushed his half-eaten dish away; he was done. He would draft a retainer agreement that night and send it to Gibran in the morning. Burlington would be thrilled.

They left the restaurant, each man on either side of Clara, and Reza waited with them as Gibran's driver was summoned to arrive.

"Do you need a ride?" Gibran asked.

"No, my car is parked right here," he said while pointing conspicuously to Travis's Benz.

"Okay, *ciao*, Reza. Great to see you again." Clara kissed him on both cheeks and slipped into the deep back seat of a black Maybach.

"I look forward to hearing from you shortly, young Mr. Shirvani," Gibran said to Reza as he slapped his back and followed Clara into the car.

Five minutes later, Reza was behind the seat of Travis's car. He revved the engine, and before he shifted into drive, Reza noticed what he thought he saw a familiar figure exiting Cafe Milano's. He looked more closely at a female form entering the passenger side of a waiting Cadillac. Yes, he was almost certain it was Jane Erlich, Burlington's assistant. What a small world. It must have been her husband behind the wheel of the Cadillac. Who would have thought she would frequent a venue as flashy as Milano's? On Valentine's Day no less. He would have to tease her about that.

He smiled to himself as he pulled out onto Prospect Street. A black Jaguar with tinted windows came quickly into his rear mirror view. They'd just have to slow down, Reza thought. He turned on the CD player and the haunting voice of Tupac Shakur filled the car. Did Travis did know something about good music after all? Suddenly, the road felt wide open to him. If things played out the right way with Gibran, there would be millions of dollars pouring into the law firm, thanks to him. That had to make his partnership prospects almost certain. And he'd have the funds, soon enough, to get his mother and sister out of Afghanistan. On top of all that he was again in touch with Clara. Whatever her status was with Gibran – that was far from clear, Reza thought – she was now back in his life. What a wonderful night this had turned out to to be after all.

He made a right on Wisconsin. The black Jaguar did as well, right on his tail. Idiot driver, Reza thought. Why couldn't they keep a reasonable breaking distance? Probably a diplomatic vehicle, even though the car didn't seem to have any number plate in the front. The last thing he wanted was to ruin his night with a fender-bender. He picked up his phone and called Travis.

"I'm on my way back," he said. "We're going out for drinks. I'm buying."

"Yeah? The car okay?"

"Car's fine. I think I locked the client down. Could be a huge deal."

"Cool. What about the girl, Clara?"

Right. He had told him her name. "I don't know. I told you, this was a business dinner. Plus, I think she's with her boss."

"You stayed cool, right?"

Reza turned left, onto K Street, past the Potomac and Georgetown Waterfront Park. "I'm always cool."

"Okay, sure, you can tell yourself that if it makes you feel better. Please at least tell me you didn't try to be funny."

"No. But only because it was a work dinner. I could've been very funny if I'd wanted to."

Reza looked back in his mirror to find the black Jaguar, again, trailing him. "Listen, I know this sounds crazy, but I think someone's following me. This Jaguar is on my tail whichever way I turn. Is that possible?"

"Shit."

"What do you mean, shit?"

"They're probably following me," Travis said.

"What? Why?"

"It's the car. They think they're following me. Listen, just turn left on New Hampshire and try to lose them on Dupont Circle."

"Are you serious?"

"Yah. Be cool. This happens sometimes. Not a big deal."

"Really? It is to me!"

Reza made a quick left on New Hampshire and sped through a line of green lights toward Dupont. "Should I blow through red lights?"

"No, no need to get dramatic. Just do what I tell you and let me know if they stay on you."

Tupac's voice growled from the stereo.

"*Now let me welcome everybody to the wild, wild West,*
A state that's untouchable like Elliot Ness,
The track hits ya eardrum like a slug to ya chest..."

"What the fuck do you do for work anyway, Travis?"

"Not important right now, just be calm."

The Jaguar was right on Reza's tail. He thought he could see two men sitting in front, but the heavily tinted windows made it hard to be sure. "I think I should call 911."

"No, no, don't do that. Where are you now?"

"Coming up on Dupont."

"Hard left on N!" Travis shouted.

Reza swerved to the left. The Jaguar, screeching, followed.

"Left on 21st!"

"This isn't a video game!"

"Left on L!"

"Got it!"

"Still behind you?"

Reza looked into the mirror. "Yeah!"

"Catch the green lights and burn it down L."

Reza hit 70, but the Jaguar kept pace. He flew past office buildings and old row houses, the Benz bouncing over asphalt dips and crashing down onto potholes. He accelerated past slower cars, whether to the right or the left, but slowed when he got close to the Metro Station. "Do these guys have guns?"

Travis didn't respond.

"Travis?"

"They're not gonna shoot you, man. They could've done that by now if they wanted. They're just fucking with you."

And doing so very well, Reza thought. Reza made a right on 17th and then another quick turn back onto K Street. The Jaguar, keeping pace, neither passed him nor tried to pull even. "I'm almost home. What should I do?"

"I'm opening the garage door. You pull right in and close the garage door behind you."

"Okay."

"Can you do that?"

The car hurtled down the street, the words of Rumi in Reza's mind.

Free of who I was, free of presence, free of dangerous fear, hope, free of mountainous wandering . . .

"Reza?"

"Yah. I can do that."

"The garage will be dark. Don't turn on any lights when you get in."

Reza made a hard right on H Street, squealed to a stop near their darkened house, pulled into the driveway too quickly, hit the brakes just as he entered the garage and brought the Benz to a halt by bumping into several tires leaning up against the far wall. The beams shook. Reza shut the engine down, leapt from the car, slapped the electronic switch that began to shut the garage door, and dashed from the garage into the house.

"Lock it," Travis's voice commanded him.

Reza turned and bolted the garage door.

"What the fuck, I can't see a thing in here – "

"Shut up. I'm in the living room, on the front wall, at the side of the window. Crawl over here? Stay low, below the windows."

Reza, on the floor, squirmed along the carpet, smelling and tasting its fibers. What the hell was happening? This is America. Armed thugs don't just bust into people's homes. Do they? He reached Travis's feet and looked up. In the silhouette of the streetlights he found his roommate flush against the wall, a semi-automatic rifle clutched at his chest. With a nod of his head, he motioned Reza to stand against the front wall, behind him. Reza stood and pushed his back hard against the wall, panting from excitement and pumping adrenaline. For several very long minutes, they stood quietly against the wall, looking out the window and ready for an attack that never came. Reza was now breathing normally again. Travis put the rifle to his side, walked away from the wall and turned on the lights. "I didn't see a Jaguar, man."

"I'm telling you, he was following me! He was on my tail the whole way."

"Not the whole way. No one was behind you on H." Travis was already his normal self again, as though the entire episode had never happened.

Reza sat down on the floral couch and looked at his trembling hands. "Seriously, he followed me the whole way."

"Nah, man. Only you turned on H. No one followed you. I was watching."

"I'm telling you, there were two guys in a black Jaguar, with tinted windows, and no number plate! Oh, and this is probably a good time for me ask — when the fuck did you get a machine gun?"

Travis shrugged, engaged the safety mechanism on the rifle, and disappeared briefly into his room. He returned holding a pen and a pad of paper. Reza knew that Travis liked to doodle, sometimes unconsciously, when he needed to relax. Sometimes Travis even drew on walls and furniture. The images were almost always the same — pictures of a small boy with large hair, racing goggles, and a wide, toothy smile, careening around in one sports car or another. Sometimes the car was an outrageous Ferrari, other times it was more of a primitive go-cart. But the features of the boy never changed.

"So where are we going for drinks?" Travis asked without looking up from the pad on which he was sketching feverishly.

CHAPTER SIX

The walls of the rectangular conference room on the eighth floor of Henderson & Humphries were lined with brown boxes, stacked as high as the head of the tallest office services staff in the firm. A long, mahogany table and its eight matching black chairs were occupied by attorneys, hemmed in by the boxes and squeezed together by the few more chairs some paralegals managed to fit in. The view out of the windows to Pennsylvania Avenue was blocked; similarly, because of the stacked boxes, there was no way to see through the glass wall that normally looked out into a carpeted hall. A detritus of crumpled paper, plastic, aluminum foil and cans from ordered-in breakfasts, lunches, dinners and snacks overflowed the trash containers and littered the corners of the room. Reams of white paper had slid from their neat piles and cascaded, like snow drifts, over the table. Each was numbered, though, starting with GAM0000001, so they could easily be reordered and put neatly back into place. Reza sat near the center of the table. Outside, it was a warm, April afternoon. Inside, his coffee was cold.

"Okay, let's go over it one more time," he said.

A junior associate, Katie Baldinger, rolled her eyes and handed him a red-weld binder with several heavily stuffed manila folders. She was cute but frumpy, with red hair and freckles. Reza had been her mentor when she was a summer associate at the firm four years earlier, between her second and third years of law school at Yale University.

She was smart, eager, and naïve, but in an earnest, Midwestern way. "The first folder has incorporation papers for the fifty master-feeder, on-shore and off-shore investment vehicles. The second folder has registration forms for the twelve new advisers and sub-advisers. The third folder has draft risk disclosure language that will have to be customized for all of the prospectuses."

"Okay. Let me look through them. While I'm thinking of it — are we still on schedule to get the investment advisers fully licensed in all fifty states?"

"I think so, but I'll double-check with Liu." Liu was a tall, thin paralegal who previously had worked for over two decades as a corporate lawyer in his native China. While his failure to master the English language had prevented him from passing the bar exam and becoming a practicing lawyer in the U.S., his experience made him an invaluable resource to the corporate practice group at Double H.

Reza gulped his sweet, cold coffee. "Please do. And next time, don't wait for me to ask first. It's your job to monitor the work flows and to let me know if anything is off-schedule."

She shook her head yes.

"Why are we taking the time to register in all fifty states, anyway?" she asked. "What are the chances GAM is going to be doing business in North Dakota?"

"Good question, Katie. Let's just call Mr. Gibran and ask him which states he does and does not expect to do business in. Or maybe I'll just tell him to avoid raising money from anyone in North Dakota because Katie doesn't think it's worth his time to register there." His coal-black eyes burned into hers, a sign that she was far out of line. Reza knew that he had been harsh in his delivery, but the point was valid. Still, he was tired and stressed. "Can somebody get me some hot coffee?"

Liu appeared from behind a stack of boxes at the far end of the room. "I'll go. I need some myself."

"Folks, the point of all this," Reza said, assuming the posture and

tone of an upset parent, "is to provide the client with maximum flexibil-
ity, so they can take full advantage of all the business opportunities and
tax inefficiencies that become available to them, right?"

The other attorneys nodded along.

"So it's our job to make sure the client is and remains fully compliant
no matter what they choose to do. We need to set them up so they can
be nimble, so they can raise money where they want, and from who
they want. To invest their money where they want, and in what they
want. The last thing we need is to have the client be hamstrung and to
lose out on a business opportunity a year from now because we didn't
do our job right today. That's why we've brought all this talent into this
room, right? This isn't simply a matter of corporate law or securities
law. It involves investment management, tax, labor and employment,
immigration. Who else is here, anyway?"

"Litigation," said an attorney slouched against a pile of cardboard
bankers boxes in the corner of the conference room.

"Right. That too. And remember, this client has not restricted us in
any way by imposing cost limitations on us. All they've asked us to do is
our job, and to do it well. So let's please do it." Not the best pep talk in
the world, Reza thought, but he hoped that it would do the trick.

"Maybe now is a good time to discuss some of what we're seeing in
the due diligence," the litigation attorney, a middle-aged partner named
Daniel Montefusco, said.

Liu walked back into the room and handed a small, paper cup to Reza.

Reza thanked him, and peeled open the Styrofoam top. "You're not
done with your review Dan, are you?"

"Not yet. But I have a pretty good sense of what's there. Enough to
have an informed discussion anyway."

Reza sipped his coffee and looked over at Montefusco. He was short,
compact and muscular with close-cropped brown hair. He had the look
of a street kid, but to be a partner at Double H he had to have book
smarts too. Reza didn't see the need to have any litigators on the team,

but Burlington had insisted – for due diligence purposes, he had argued. The firm, like a famished crow, was feasting on the Gibran matter, which generated fees up and down the building's floors and across all the major practice groups. Of course, Reza thought, the firm had assigned a partner of Montefusco's seniority to the matter because the litigators at the firm weren't that busy. He wondered how Montefusco, fifteen years out of Harvard Law School, felt about working under Reza's supervision. "So what did you find?"

"Let's just talk between us for a bit."

"All right, take a break, guys." Everyone stood and stretched and started to exit the stuffy room.

"I'm going to order dinner for the team. You want anything?" Katie asked.

Reza hesitated. "No, go ahead, I'm not sure when I'm going to eat."

She shrugged. "Suit yourself."

Reza held out to Liu the file that Katie had handed him moments earlier. "Take a first pass at this please."

Liu nodded and relieved Reza of the red-weld.

Montefusco looked up from his Blackberry. "I don't really like what I see."

This, Reza thought, is precisely the problem that occurs when too many lawyers are involved with one, lucrative client. Everyone sticks his fingers in the pie. Everyone tries to wrest control of the matter to his own practice group. Suddenly, a straightforward corporate matter becomes a litigation concern. Reza would not have any of it. "Really? What's not to like?"

Montefusco helped himself to the unoccupied chair opposite Reza. He opened a file and handed a clipped set of documents to him. "Look at these."

Reza noticed that the litigator had affixed his own numbering system to the bottom of this new bundle of papers – a clear breach of Reza's express instructions to the team. He debated whether to raise that with

Montefusco, but decided to leave that battle for another time.

"All I see is a bunch of bank wires. From a lot of different banks."

"Yep. Mostly Middle-Eastern banks."

Reza felt a spurt of adrenalin shoot through him. "So? What's your point?"

"Look, I'll cut to the chase. I think you need to make sure you don't have a money-laundering problem. What you have is a pattern of regular wire activity between GAM accounts in Europe and unknown accounts that are opened in a variety of high-risk jurisdictions, odd jurisdictions given the nature of the business that we're looking at. It's very hard to tie the wire activity to some legitimate, GAM business purpose. Any investigator worth his salt would question these transactions from an AML standpoint."

Reza handed the folder to back Montefusco. "Anti money laundering, huh? Is that it?"

Montefusco opened another folder. "Not quite. Another thing for you to consider when you investigate all of this, as I'm sure you will." He didn't wait for Reza to respond. "There is a small group of individuals who are not obviously tied to the business, either as GAM employees or investors. Anyway, these people seem to be behind a lot of the wires that you were just looking at. Next time you speak with the client, you might want to ask who is Majid Abdul-Fattar, and why is he getting a substantial sum wired to him every month at Al-Faisal Bank in Dubai?"

Reza stared at a grainy copy of a standing wire agreement between one of GAM's business accounts in Zurich and an Al-Faisal account bearing Abdul-Fattar's name. "Okay. I'll find out. He must be one of GAM's finders. Funds like GAM often employ finders to connect them with potential investors in other regions."

"Well, this Abdul-Fattar, he must be one connected guy. He's got bank accounts all over the place, and they've all received wires from a GAM account at one point or another over the last five years" Montefusco said, handing papers to Reza one by one. "Banco Agricola de

Venezuela. Cyprus National Bank. Frankfurtbank AG. Unocredit Bank. That one's in Algeria."

"I know."

Reza didn't care for Montefusco's heavy Bronx accent. It seemed to amplify his condescending tone.

"It's not always easy to piece together. Let me show you one particular series of transactions that I found highly interesting," Montefusco continued. "Here's a deposit by GAM into a Galenplex AG account at Frankfurtbank. The same amount then goes, the very next day, from Frankfurtbank to Cyprus. I don't recognize the entity owning this account. It says Devlin LLC. Then the next day, the same amount goes from Devlin to an Abdul-Fattar account in Kuwait."

Reza shrugged. "Galenplex is a real business. I'm sure the wire from GAM to Galenplex had a legitimate business purpose."

"I guess it could have. I guess there could be some legitimate reason a Slovakian fertilizer company is receiving a $1.5 million wire from GAM." Montefusco smiled.

"Don't say it, Dan."

Montefusco did. "That's a lot of shit, man!" Montefusco laughed as Katie returned to the conference room.

"All right, funny man," Reza said to the litigator. "Thanks for doing all this, I guess. I'll look into it."

"No problem, pal." Montefusco rose to leave the room, his rumpled, white shirt now untucked. "Just remember, I'm not telling you there's anything improper happening here. I'm just saying, these are questions that somebody's going to ask along the way and you're better off getting the answers now. You know?"

"Yup," Reza replied glumly. Montefusco packed his belongings and made his way out of the conference room. Reza watched him exit and swiveled in his chair to face Katie. "I hate it when other lawyers look over your shoulder."

She laughed but then bit her bottom lip. "You do that to me all the time."

"Right, good point."

"Plus, Daniel's a partner."

"Don't rub it in."

Reza had played cool, but he had heard Montefusco loud and clear. He didn't at all think that what the litigator found was a waste of time. In fact, if they had any merit – any merit at all, even one iota – then there would be a big question mark hanging over the very large project that Reza had just brought in. That would mean a question mark hanging over his partnership prospects, and, probably, a question mark hanging over his ability to help his mother and his sister. He had to stay cool, and to find some good answers, quickly, to the questions that Montefusco had raised. "How is your work going?"

Katie's freckled face smiled. "Okaaaaaaay."

He liked her, he thought. The red hair, the blue eyes, the endless optimism and cheer: in many ways, she embodied the image of America that he'd carried around in his head for years. "What's with the long okay? I don't like how that sounds."

"I don't want to pile on."

"Bring it. I've got big shoulders."

She smiled again. "There seems to be a common theme to the inquiry letters that GAM has gotten from European regulators. They all want to know how he seems to always buy and sell stocks at precisely the right time, often before some major event or transaction. I could never figure that out, and apparently, the European regulators can't figure that out either."

"Which is a problem."

"Exactly. You know better than me how the regulators are. If they can't figure something out, they just keep digging."

"Naturally, the European regulators can't help but be suspicious of a smart Lebanese trader. I'm sure they think no Arab can be that smart. And more than that, they're extra suspicious of anyone sending profits back overseas, to the Middle-East, and not to more typical tax havens like the Caribbean."

She interrupted him. "Which is why he hired us, I mean you, to help explain all that."

"Yes, thank you." Reza's coffee was cold again. "I need some time to think through all this. And please, let's not talk about this Abdul-Fattar guy any more until I've had a chance to do some homework."

"Who?"

He realized she hadn't been in the room for that part of the conversation. "Never mind. I need to get back to my office. Keep me posted on the progress the team makes tonight. I'd like an update every three hours. Can you do that?"

"Yes," she replied, still cheery.

Reza left the room, slipped into an internal stairwell and took the three flights up, two steps at a time. Moving quickly, and lost in thought, he barreled into Vargas as he prepared to take the last flight. Vargas had seen Reza coming, but had been unable to avoid him given the large number of files he had been carrying, all of which were now strewn on the stairs.

"Sorry, man, I didn't see you," Reza panted as he helped Vargas collect his files.

"No worries. All good. Actually, I'm glad I bumped into you. Literally. Been meaning to ask you – what do you know about day trading?" Vargas asked.

"As opposed to night trading?"

"You know, it's when you buy and sell stocks on the same day," Vargas continued, not picking up on Reza's joke. "You just need some liquidity and volatility."

"You have liquidity?"

"Nah. Right now I only got volatility. But I'm working on the liquidity part."

"How are you figuring out what to buy?"

"That's the cool part. I got turned on to these free stock websites. These dudes, they tell you what's going up or down."

"You're not supposed to rely on those the free sites, Gil."

"Why not?"

"Because they lie. They're purposely telling you to buy so they can sell. They're day traders themselves, not researchers. They're just setting you up."

"Really? They can do that?"

"Not really. But they do."

"Damn. Thanks man. I guess I got to sell some shit right now."

That worked out fine for Reza. He left Vargas in the stairwell and hurried back to his office. He had a lot to sort through. But before he dug into the issues that Montefusco and Katie had flagged, Reza ordered up a nice, hot dinner for himself: lobster tails over rice, with a side of broccoli, a half ear of buttered corn and a thick slice of strawberry cheesecake. Small consolation given the evening's developments, but consolation nonetheless. Reza had not quite gotten to his dessert when, at exactly 8:00 p.m., his phone rang. There were plenty of attorneys still at work, many, like him, having dinner at their desks, and so Reza a few minutes before had taken the precaution to close his office door. Maryam was on the other end of the call.

"Reza, I have incredible news — we have been granted a meeting Rashid Agha Khan! He's back from Kabul, and he has miraculously agreed to meet us! I know he can get us green cards, if we can only get him the money. Isn't it wonderful? Have you been able to make any progress on the money?"

"Wow, slow down. How is mother?"

"She's fine, she's right here next to me."

"I'd like to speak with her, to hear her voice."

"Okay, I will put her on in a minute. Please just tell me that you can help with the money. We'll get the green cards, we'll finally be able to come and join you in America, and I'll pay you back the money in no time!"

"I told you Maryam, I don't need you to pay me back."

"Does that mean you have the money?"

"I'm working on it. If it helps, I can send a deposit. Maybe as a sign of good faith? I can wire fifty thousand dollars tomorrow. Plus, we need to make sure we've checked this guy out anyway, before we give him half a million dollars."

"Reza, this isn't America. I can't do a background check on him. You just have to trust us. You have to trust me. I know what I'm doing and I know I can get us to America if you can just loan us the money."

A loan. It drove Reza mad. Why did she continue to imply that the problem in this equation was his unwillingness to part with the money? Didn't she understand that he simply didn't have five hundred thousand dollars to give? Maybe she really didn't understand. His only memories of Maryam were as a child.

"*Maryam joon*, this isn't *Dallas* or *Dynasty*, I don't have unlimited funds to send you. I'm doing my best. I have a plan to get hold of the money, but it's not coming in the next few days."

"So what do you suggest? That I cancel the meeting with Rashid Agha Khan? I can't show up with nothing, and he's our last hope."

"No, don't cancel the meeting. I'll wire you fifty thousand tomorrow. Use it as a deposit with the guy. In the meantime, I'll see what I can do to come up with the rest more quickly."

"*Merci,* I really appreciate it."

There was a long pause. Reza wasn't sure if he could hear Maryam crying. "Put mother on, please."

His mother came on the line. "*Salam, Reza, khoobee pesaram.*"

"Yes, thanks, I am well. How are you holding up?"

She switched to English, a broken English which she spoke with a lilting, thick Persian accent. "I'm so sorry, Reza, that we are a burden to you."

"Stop, mother, you know you have never been a burden to me. I'm sorry I can't seem to do more to help you."

"This will all work itself out, my son, as Allah sees fit. Please don't worry yourself. Are you eating well?"

He smiled as he looked down at his cheesecake. "Yes, mother, *mamnoon*, I am eating well. And I hope to be eating with you soon, here in Washington."

"*In sha'Allah*, Reza jan, *in sha'Allah*."

Maryam jumped back on the phone. "Mother has a poem she wants to read you. She made me write it out in English for you."

Reza brightened. "Tell me, please."

His mother, now again on the line, cleared her throat.

I had a dream,
Someone will come,
Someone is coming,
Someone who walks with me,
Someone who is in my heart,
Someone who hears me breathing,
Someone who sees me dreaming of him,
Someone who hears me talking, talking about him.
I know, nobody can catch him,
I know, nobody can jail him.
I feel that he is growing on the other side of the fence,
I feel that he is singing with all the drops of rain, and the falling of
leaves.
Someone will come,
Someone is coming,
I had a dream.

Her words, perhaps more so because she struggled to say them, penetrated into his bones. He stayed silent.

"Reza?" It was Maryam.

"It's Forough," he mumbled.

"I have to go," his sister said, gently. "Let's talk again tomorrow. These calls get very expensive."

Reza had an old friend from Double H, Michael Greenfeld, who now worked for the Department of Defense General Counsel's Office. He owed Reza several favors from their days together as junior associates. Most prominently, Michael was indebted to Reza for having helped him rewrite an appellate brief that had been chewed-up by one of the most difficult partners at Double H. Reza had stayed up all night to help bail Michael out, and he had not even billed his time so Michael could receive full credit for the revised product. He called Michael's cell and reached him at home. "I need to talk to you off-the-record."

"Off-the-record or deep background?" Greenfeld asked. "There's a difference, you know," he chuckled.

"Whichever. I want to ask you about something that should stay between us."

"Shoot."

"You're involved with what's going on in Afghanistan, right?"

"Yeah, why?"

"What do you know about a guy named Rashid Agha Khan?"

Silence. Then, "why would you ask me about him?"

Reza hedged. "I have a client that might have to do some business with him."

"Well, they should think very hard about that."

"Why?"

"He's a dangerous, man. And I don't mean that by our cossetted standards here in the States. I mean it by their crazy standards there. He is a very dangerous man."

Reza bit the nail on his pinky. "Dangerous how?"

"Look, what I'm saying is that there is nothing he won't do if he thinks that he's in the right. There's no violence that he won't perpetrate if he believes that it advances some just cause. Which of course is why he's valuable to us."

"Who is we?"

Greenfeld ignored him. "The point, Reza, is that if your client does business with this guy, and he decides for some reason that you've wronged him, or that you've broken some sacrosanct code that only he understands, well, you're in big trouble. You do not want to be on this guy's bad side. Not if you're in Afghanistan anyway."

"What else can you tell me about him? Is he a man of his word?"

"Yes. Unless he thinks you've fucked him. Then all bets are off."

Silence.

"Is this helpful, Reza?"

"I think so."

"Okay, so two things," Greenfeld said. "First, we're even now. And second, this conversation never happened."

And with that, Greenfeld hung up the phone.

CHAPTER SEVEN

That Friday morning, April 9th, at shortly before nine a.m., Reza e-mailed a revised draft of the Private Placement Memorandum – the PPM – to the working group of twenty-three attorneys formed to assist Gibran Asset Management in the establishment of its U.S. businesses. It had been a long night, and Reza was up for every minute of it.

It was barely a few weeks since he'd met Gibran that first time, with Clara, of all people, by his side. The timing of that meeting was, in retrospect, a blessing for Reza's career. Over the course of the past two months, Reza had more than a dozen times spoken by phone with Gibran and Clara, as well as with GAM's Chief Financial Officer, Francois Kling. He also had met on several occasions with GAM's top staff in the large suites they habitually took at Washington's Ritz Carlton hotel. He had walked Gibran through all of the corporate and regulatory issues that GAM would face in establishing a U.S. presence, and Gibran had encouraged Reza, to Burlington's great delight, to spend what it would take to get it done quickly and correctly. Gibran had also been sure, at every turn, to highlight Reza's pivotal role in their decision to work with Double H.

From Reza's perspective, he had now demonstrated his ability to generate business and develop the types of assignments the firm wanted and, according to Burlington, desperately needed. Reza was certain that his handling of this matter, and the development of this client, would lock down his prospects to make partner later in the year.

A new e-mail pinged: "Thanks. Come see me as soon as you're free."

It was from Burlington, in response to the PPM that Reza had distributed moments earlier. Reza went to the bathroom, washed his face and brushed his teeth, and made his way down the hall to the big corner office. John's door was closed, but Jane smiled and motioned for him to go right in.

But first, he remembered something he had forgotten to tell Jane. "By the way, I saw you coming out of Cafe Milano's on Valentine's Day. I guess I shouldn't be surprised that you were at the hippest place in town on a big day like that." He flashed a coy smile.

"What do you mean, Reza? It's only hip if I go there!"

"Of course. Still, a funny coincidence that we were there at the same time. Too bad we didn't see each other inside."

"Just because you didn't see me doesn't mean I didn't see you."

Odd, Reza thought. She had seen him but had not said hello? Before Reza could reply, he heard John's voice boom from inside the office. "Reza? Come on in here." Jane waved goodbye as he opened the door.

"I can't overstate how great this is for you," John said. "There are partners at Double H who have gone years – heck, decades — without generating an assignment like this. This has been brilliant."

Reza stood in the threshold, as if nervous, although pleased to hear that his mentor was so happy.

"Don't just stand there, come in, have a seat. Just before I got your e-mail I was looking at our group's Work in Progress Report. There's well over two million dollars of time billed to Gibran this month! I hope you realize how terrific that is."

Reza slumped on Burlington's couch. "Thanks. I had a sense it was turning into a fairly big assignment, but I wasn't tracking the numbers."

"Well I've been tracking them, and they are large indeed."

So why wasn't Reza happy? His mind wandered briefly to Afghanistan, and his still unresolved need to raise a substantial sum of money. He snapped out of it and refocused his attention. "There are some issues we've come across in preparing the PPM that I haven't been able to resolve yet. I'd like to run them by you. "

"Sure. We'll get to that. But first, let me tell you, that your candidacy for partnership will be a difficult one to ignore when you come to the table with these kinds of numbers. And your timing couldn't be better. This assignment could very well be the difference," he whispered gravely, "between us hitting or missing our annual revenue targets."

Burlington didn't have to explain the significance of that fact to Reza. The younger attorney understood that if the firm did not hit its revenue targets, then there would be partners who would walk away with lower profits that they had the prior year, after the staff and associates are paid their salaries, and that's never a good thing at a law firm. So if Reza could play any meaningful role in the firm achieving its annual revenue targets in the year in which he was to be considered for partnership, he was well aware of just how valuable that would be. "That's great to hear."

Burlington jammed a pencil into an electric sharpener on his desk, forcing him to shout over the grinding gears. "You look distracted."

"Sleepy is more like it."

"I think you should go home for a few hours, Reza. Get some rest."

But he was more weary than tired. "I don't mean to sound presumptuous, John, but do you think there's any possibility of a partnership appointment coming out of rotation? Like maybe, I don't know, now, or in a couple of weeks? Or do I have to wait until the end of the year, to be considered with everyone else in my class?"

Burlington blew on the pencil's sharp point. "We have to wait."

"I figured as much."

"Be patient, son. You're only, what, thirty-one?"

"Almost thirty-three."

He laughed. "A mere baby."

Reza picked off a thread from his pants leg. "How old were you when you made partner."

"It's not relevant. It was a different time. Really, you couldn't be better positioned, Reza. Where's the fire?" In Afghanistan, Reza thought. Somewhere in Farah province.

Burlington changed the subject. "What're the issues you wanted to run by me?"

"Two things, I guess. One is relatively easy and the second more complicated."

"Okay, let's start with the easy one."

"There are a handful of individuals who seem to be associated with GAM's existing European businesses, and I can't get any meaningful information about who they are or what they do relative to GAM. Of course I've checked the public records, and I've run the names by the deal team. Either nobody knows, which would be odd, or nobody wants to tell me. Unless I know, I can't figure out if and how they should be described in the PPM."

To raise money in the United States, Gibran was mandated by federal law to provide prospective investors with specific information about himself, his company, and what he intended to do with any money that he raised. All of this was required to be laid out in the PPM, and it was Double H's duty as lawyers on the deal to make sure that that PPM was complete and accurate in all material respects.

"Have you asked either Kling or Fournier?"

"Yep, both of them, actually. I get the same answer. No idea exactly what these people do relative to GAM. Actually, Kling only says they have nothing to do with the U.S. businesses and I need to drop the issue. I think I should run the names by Gibran."

Burlington shrugged. "I think I'll leave that judgment to you. Of course, it would be entirely reasonable for you to drop the issue now, especially given that you already ran the names by senior members of the deal team. That's what I'd probably do. But if you think you need to run it by Gibran, then go ahead. I'm sure you'll be tactful in how you do it."

Reza appreciated the deference that John showed him, but he found it odd that John was comfortable with the idea of potentially dropping the issue altogether without completing every avenue of due diligence available to them. "Let me give it a bit more thought. I certainly will be tactful in how I raise it, if I do so."

"Okay, so what's the second issue, the more complicated one?"

"There are some curious wire transfers, patterns of transactions that I can't explain. I'm concerned – Dan Montefusco was concerned – that they need to be addressed from an anti-money laundering standpoint, he's concerned..."

Burlington cut him off with wave of hand. "Why is Montefusco flagging AML issues? What the fuck does he know about AML? I knew I would regret getting the litigators involved. They're like bulls in a china shop."

Reza was taken aback at the strength of Burlington's reaction. "In fairness, Montesfusco wasn't saying that we have an issue, only that he thought it required further scrutiny." Reza walked Burlington through what Montefusco had found.

"He's overreacting," Burlington said. "This is one of the world's largest investment managers. They trade billions of dollars in major market centers all over the world. Of course they sometimes send wires to people we don't know, for things that are not readily apparent to us here. Reza, this issue is one we should just drop." Burlington slapped his open hand on the desk as if to close the debate.

Reza stared out the window. "Should I ask him about it first?"

"Ask who what?"

"Ask Gibran about the transactions."

Jane appeared in Burlington's doorway, and he held up a finger to indicate one more minute. "No Reza, you should not do so. Let me be very clear — you should not ask Gibran whether he has engaged in money laundering. You should consider the issue resolved and you should get some sleep. I will speak with Montefusco."

"Okay, John, sounds good," Reza replied, even though it really did not. "Before I go, there's one more thing I'd like to raise with you. It's not related to GAM."

"I've got to jump on a call in a minute, but shoot."

"John, is it possible for me to get a loan from the firm?"

Burlington sat up slightly and furrowed his brow. "I didn't expect that. Why?"

Reza loathed to reveal so much of his personal business, but he now had no choice. He explained to Burlington about his family's situation in Afghanistan.

Burlington cut him off before he was finished with the story. "I'm speechless."

"I need to come up with five hundred thousand."

"I feel terrible for you, I really do."

Was he sincere? Burlington was very good at faking sincerity.

"Let me say this Reza, you have my word that I will raise it with the management committee of the firm, and I will see what can be done. But you should know, at the outset, that this would be an unprecedented step for the firm to take. I don't believe we have even made a loan, certainly not one of this size, to a partner before."

Reza thought briefly about raising again the revenue that the Gibran matter had generated, revenue that he had brought to the firm. He decided against the idea. "I understand. I know you'll do what you can."

"There's just no pool of funds, or any accounting mechanism, for something like this."

"Right."

"But as I said, I'll look into it. It's a compelling story."

Compelling? It's a complete cluster-fuck, Reza thought.

On the following morning, a Saturday, Reza entered the red-bricked, Colonial-style lobby of the Ritz Carlton Hotel. He was exhausted. The soft lighting and a subtle hint of the fragrance of orchids almost lulled him to sleep – even while walking – but Reza shook it off, and boarded an empty, wood-paneled elevator. He reflexively checked the front of the large binder he held to be sure it bore no identifying information. Sure, it was obsessive, he thought, but that's what lawyers are paid to be. And maintaining client confidences was a primary cannon of the profession. There was never a good excuse for violating that basic rule, not even overwhelming fatigue

Reza was to meet Gibran to review and finalize the PPM. And he was prepared to argue why all the details contained in the draft were necessary, both to comply with the federal securities laws and to protect Gibran and GAM against any future claims. Still, Kling had pushed back so hard against the level of detail that Reza had proposed to include regarding the individuals associated with GAM's European businesses. Hopefully, Reza could show Gibran that the detail was necessary and helpful from a legal standpoint, and the PPM would then be finished. Why should they be so opposed to the disclosures anyway? It didn't make sense.

The elevator stopped on the eleventh floor, the top floor in the building, and Reza got off. He paused momentarily in the hallway to organize his thoughts before turning right toward Gibran's suite. As he approached the suite, he braced himself mentally for the possibility that Clara would be in the suite when he arrived. It certainly would confirm his suspicions regarding her relationship with Gibran if she were in his suite that early on a Saturday morning. He hoped that would not be the case.

He knocked on the door, and Gibran opened it. Fortunately, there was no sign of Clara when he arrived in the large and airy suite. A fireplace to their right had already been lit, and the large living room area boasted a fresh bouquet of birds of paradise, bowls of fruit arrayed on several small tables, finely upholstered couches and chairs, and open double-doors leading to a king-size bed. Reza couldn't judge if anyone had slept in it; it was made.

"Would you like some coffee or juice?" Gibran asked, pointing to the dining area of the suite.

"No, thank you very much, maybe just some water. I've already had too much coffee this morning."

Gibran opened a mini-fridge, removed two purple bottles, unscrewed the tops, and poured the water into crystal tumblers. He handed one to Reza and directed him to the living room.

Reza removed his coat and draped it over a dining room chair. He followed Gibran into the living room, toward the fire.

Gibran, as he was when they first met, was dressed impeccably – a custom fitted, monogrammed, off-white shirt made of pure Egyptian cotton, a sky-blue Charvet tie, perfectly coiffed hair, an understated but – as Reza knew – outrageously expensive Patek Philippe watch, and a heavy gold ring. He seemed as refreshed as Reza was tired.

"How was your flight?" Reza asked, sitting with his host at small, round table.

Gibran looked at him blankly, as if the question itself made no sense. "Very comfortable. Have you flown Emirates upper class?"

He had not. "Some time ago, I think."

"It's quite nice. A private cabin with a flat bed, personal mini-bar at your seat, and a flat-screen TV. I relaxed and slept most of the way, although Clara occasionally interrupted with work matters. But I don't mind. That is after all why I pay her."

Reza forced a smile. "Ah, Clara is with you?"

"She usually travels with me."

He scanned the suite again, but it appeared that Gibran was there alone. "I see."

"I've received wonderful reports from her, and from Kling as well, mind you, about your hard work. Your excellence has not gone unnoticed."

"Thank you."

"I've made a point, by the way, to share that thought with John Burlington, as well as my recommendation that you deserve a promotion and bonus."

Reza was flattered. "That's very kind of you." A bonus sure would be well-timed.

"Nonsense. Someone like you may easily be plucked by someone like me should you not feel sufficiently appreciated."

Was that the beginnings of a job offer? "Thank you. Double H has been very good to me."

Gibran's smile remained unchanged, but he paused for a beat. "Quite so."

Reza wiped a sweaty palm on his leg and placed the binder on the mirrored top of their coffee table. "Shall we begin?"

Gibran checked his watch. "Yes, please. What is it that we need to work through this morning?" His easy smile disappeared and was replaced by a stern expression of focus — pursed lips, furrowed brow and forward-leaning posture.

Reza, determined to keep pace, also turned his focus to the files in the binder and red-weld he had brought with him. "All we really need to do is to finalize the PPM. There is one section in particular where we need your input, and that's it."

"This is something that you've already reviewed with Clara and Francois, correct?"

"Exactly. And the consensus view was that your opinion is necessary to finalize and resolve the matter."

"Very well, then." Gibran straightened his already straight tie.

"Okay, it's in this section. Here, where we provide some basic background information on the GAM's existing European operations. We drafted this using information that we gleaned from the files that Clara provided, but Francois in particular objected to the level of detail we included."

He leaned over Reza. "What precisely did Francois object to?" Reza tapped the highlighted paragraphs in the middle of the page to which he had turned. "The description of these associated individuals and entities."

Gibran sat close to Reza and quietly read the highlighted language. It identified three individuals as shareholders in one or more of GAM's European based investment advisors: George Gibran, Ahmed ibn Ibrahim, and Samir Khambarzahi.

"Where did this come from?"

"Like I said, it's a combination of the materials in your European offering documents and information that we pulled from the documents that Clara and Francois sent us. Is any of it incorrect?"

Gibran turned his attention slowly from the page he had been reading and fixed his gaze on Reza. "The issue is not if it is correct. The issue is that this is highly confidential and proprietary information. We don't just advertise such things. Our backers are not people who expect their holdings to be publicly laid out. These are important people, whose lives would be negatively affected by this type of public disclosure. It's out of the question."

Reza was unprepared for the vehemence of Gibran's reaction. "The fact that they're important people makes it even more relevant to an investor, doesn't it?"

Gibran snapped the binder shut. "Bullshit. How is it relevant to an investor in the U.S. if these people are shareholders in an adviser in Europe? It's not as though they have any role in running the activities of Gibran Asset Management. I understand that Americans can have an almost insatiable appetite for the type of personal information that the rest of the world handles with basic discretion, but this is ridiculous."

Reza had hoped that Gibran would be more understanding that Kling had been on this subject. In fact, Gibran was even more opposed to the proposed disclosures. Oddly, on virtually every other point, Francois, Clara and Gibran, had all been fully on board with the strategy of over-disclosure. Why, on this issue, would Gibran and Kling push back so hard? It bothered him. Nevertheless, recognizing that he would not be able to convince Gibran at that moment, Reza decided that a tactical retreat was in order. That was certainly what Burlington would have wanted. "I see your point, George. Why don't we table this, and I'll revisit it with John?"

"As will I," Gibran replied. His expression had relaxed almost instantly, and the easy smile was now back in place. "By the way, are you busy tomorrow evening, Reza?"

That was an easy question to answer. It didn't matter if he did or did not have pre-existing plans — the answer would be that, no, he was not otherwise occupied that evening. "Not at all. What do you have in mind?"

Gibran stood. "At Clara's urging, I've provided some support to the Children's Hospital and have purchased a table at their gala tomorrow night. I'd be delighted if you can join as my guest. You deserve the break."

Reza was, for several reasons, thrilled and relieved to hear that. First, he was happy that Gibran had not asked him to work throughout the entire weekend as he really was in need of a break. And second, he was excited to have been invited to a premier Washington social event, especially one at which Clara may be present. "Thank you, George, that's very kind. I'd love to join you."

Gibran started to make his way toward the door, signaling the end of the meeting. "Great. I'll have my office email you the details. I believe it's at 7:00 pm. Is there anything else?"

Reza thought about the money laundering concerns that Montesfusco had raised – concerns that seemed less and less far-fetched given Gibran's absolute reluctance to discuss his backers. One thing was clear, though: Gibran was unlikely to appreciate being asked about Majid Abdul-Fattar. What was Abdul-Fattar's relationship with GAM anyway? And who was Ahmed ibn Ibrahim? What about Samir Khambarzahi? That name sounded quite possibly Iranian. Why was Gibran so unwilling to talk about these folks?

He scooped up his papers. All that remained on the coffee table, in addition to the PPM, were two identical Blackberrys: his and Gibran's.

He picked up Gibran's and slid it into his pocket.

"No, I think that's it, George."

With his heart racing, Reza followed Gibran into the suite's foyer, shook his hand hard, and made his way out the door. The elevator, which couldn't come soon enough, took him straight back to the lobby. Reza walked down the brassy gold carpet and out of the hotel, turning left, to 31st Street. Rounding the corner, he then broke into a run, away from the hotel, to someplace secluded, a place where he could sit privately to contemplate what he had just done, and what he should do next.

After a few blocks, he dashed into the gardens of Dumbarton Oaks, the museum and research center. There, panting, and cursing himself for not getting to the gym enough, he sat on a bench at the side of a lotus pond. He pulled out the Blackberry and, without giving himself a chance to contemplate the matter further, he pushed the power button. The device called for a password he didn't have. What the hell was he doing? He was breaking every ethical code imaginable. And what did he expect to find on the Blackberry anyway?

Reza stood and stared into a lotus blossom. The pond it grew in was muddy and stagnant, but the white flower itself was pristine and clean. Suddenly, he bolted out of the gardens, quickly gave up on trying to find a taxi, and ran home.

Travis, for sure, could crack the Blackberry's code.

CHAPTER EIGHT

Reza arrived home some twenty minutes later, shirttail out, the balls of his feet throbbing from running too hard in his Salvatore Ferragamo wingtip derbies. He dropped his coat to the floor, just inside of the front door, and called out to his roommate.

"Need your help, man!"

Travis did not respond. Reza ran upstairs. "Travis, where are you?"

He was sitting at the desk in his office, with his back to Reza, toggling between the three computer screens that flashed brilliantly before him. He seemed to be jamming to a tune that blared through his ear buds.

"Hey, Travis!"

Again, no response, so Reza tapped him on the shoulder.

Travis ripped the headphones from his ears, shot up, grabbed Reza by his collar and pinned him against the nearest wall. "Don't fucking do that! Don't sneak up on me when I don't know you're here!"

Reza, released from Travis's grip, smoothed down his already-wrinkled shirt.

"Okay, my bad, I should know better by now!"

Travis sat back down at his computer station and placed the ear buds back on his head. "Damn right you should."

Reza tapped him again.

Travis immediately stood. "Motherfucker! What's wrong with you?"

Reza handed him Gibran's Blackberry, told him it was password-protected and asked him to engineer a way to get at the information in the email accounts.

"Well, well, well." Travis was now relaxed and cheerfully focused on Reza. "This is a big moment. You're getting in touch with your dark side. I'm impressed! I almost feel like a proud parent. Actually, I think I'm getting a bit choked up."

"Seriously, save it for later. I don't have much time before he realizes that I have his Blackberry. Can you or can you not get access to his email?"

"That would be an affirmative, Sherlock. You want it on a thumb drive?"

"I guess so. Something mobile like that is a good idea. Please just hurry. I have to get the phone back to him as soon as possible. Oh, and no tracks. He can't ever know that I tried to access his email."

Travis examined the device briefly and flipped it back to Reza. "Sorry, Holmes. That changes things a bit. To get in, I'd have to first reset the password. If I do that, I won't later be able to set it back to what it is now, because, as is obvious, neither of us know what it is now."

Reza's heartbeat recovered from the run, but he was still breathing heavy. "Then he'll know I tried to get in it."

"Yeah."

He tore off his tie. "Never mind. It's probably for the best anyway. I don't what I was thinking, taking the damned thing in the first place."

Travis started typing on one of his keyboards, furiously and almost rhythmically striking the keys. "It is seriously out of character for you."

"Right? I'm the one always lecturing you about morality. Look at me now, asking you to help me crack the code to a client's Blackberry, a Blackberry that I stole for God's sake!"

"Why did you do it, anyway?"

"It's a long story. I think I'm starting to see shadows."

"Well, sometimes boogie men cast shadows." Travis continued to type. "What's his email address?"

"GGibran at GAM dot com."

Reza pressed four numbers on the Blackberry. WRONG PASSWORD. "Damn it."

"You keep messing with that thing and it will wipe itself clean. What's Clara's email address?"

At the sound of her name, and as her image flashed into his mind, Reza's chest felt tight. "CFournier at GAM dot com. Why?"

"Somebody there named Kling?"

He let the Blackberry drop to the couch. "Yeah. Why?"

"I'm in their system."

"What? What're you doing? What system?"

"I hacked their server. Shitty firewall."

Reza rushed over to stare at the computer screen. "I just wanted to get into the phone, for God's sake!"

"That's too complicated. You got to go through REI. Need the model and IMEI numbers. Got to leave a credit card. Provide an email account. Too many tracks. Hacking the server is simpler and safer." Travis turned to Reza and smiled. A piece of chicken was stuck between two of his upper teeth.

"No, no, you shouldn't have done that. You're probably breaking a hundred laws!"

Travis looked hurt. "So it's back to nice Reza now, is it? Look, this is what I do, it's my art."

Reza almost whined. "But I just really wanted a quick look at his phone."

"You have a thumb drive?"

"No."

Travis slithered out from under Reza's shadow and grabbed a beat-up, black leather bag. "I have to do everything myself."

"Let's just stop. I'm sorry I started this, it was a really bad idea."

Travis sat back down, inserted the thumb drive and placed his fingers, as if on tiny starting blocks, on the keyboard. "Only Gibran's or Clara's too?"

Reza hesitated. "Just Gibran."

Travis began to type in an impetuous and energetic fortissimo until a bar across his screen indicated a download in progress. The Blackberry chimed. They both stared at it.

Then Reza looked at Travis. "I should answer it."

Travis shrugged.

"Hello?"

"Ah, Reza, dear boy, I thought it would be you. We've accidentally switched phones. You're holding mine, I believe, and I have yours sitting across from me."

"Yes, how strange. I wonder how that happened — "

"No matter. I'll have someone swing by to make the exchange. You're at home? Five or ten minutes okay?"

"Of course, though I hate to inconvenience you. I'd be happy to stop back by your hotel, to deliver it. I have to head back into Georgetown later this evening anyway."

"No, no. No trouble at all. Just stay where you are. Five minutes. And I will see you tomorrow evening, right?"

"Yes, of course."

The line disconnected. Then the computer pinged, indicating that the download was complete. Travis, who had turned to listen in on Reza's call, swiveled around and removed the thumb drive from the computer. He exited the program he used to hack the GAM website. Reza took the drive from his roommate and placed it in his shirt pocket. Travis shook his head, opened a closet, kicked away the single shoes and shirts and jackets that refused to stay hung, and motioned with his forefinger to the small safe that revealed itself.

"Put the drive in there, with my shit."

By his "shit," Reza knew, Travis meant the electronic and paper files that he zealously guarded in his safe. Reza never knew what the files

contained, but he knew that they were the fruit of Travis's anti-terror-
ism surveillance. Once a month, Travis emptied the safe, placed the
contents in his leather bag, and made a day trip out to Northern Virginia. Reza knew not to ask where.

"That's not necessary. You're getting carried away."

Travis bristled. "Trust me, you're playing in my world now. How did he
know where you are?"

"It's Saturday. He guessed I was at home."

"What about the address? Did you give him the address?"

Reza was contemplating that point when the doorbell rang.

"Suit yourself," Travis said. "I'm staying up here to work. Just scream
with that little, high-pitched voice of yours if you need help."

Reza shook his head, hurried back down the steps, tucked the Blackberry into his pants pocket, and opened the front door.

"Clara?"

She looked him up and down and then over his shoulder. "You were
expecting someone else?"

"Well, I didn't really know who to expect. George said he was sending
someone. And I... ah..."

She tilted her head to the side so that her long, blonde hair flapped in
the wind. "May I come in?"

"Yes, yes, of course," he stammered. "Come on in. Apologies for the
mess. I could blame my housemate but it wouldn't be true."

She looked for a place to sit, and so Reza quickly cleared off the sofa.
"Thank you."

"Can I get you something to drink?" he asked.

Clara turned toward him – her thin body framed in a black leather
jacket, black leather pants and perfectly polished shiny black boots. "I'll
take a glass of wine, if you have any handy."

Reza dashed into the kitchen and rummaged through its cabinets for
clean wine glasses. He threw open the nearly empty refrigerator to grab
the one cold bottle of Champagne that Travis had been saving for some

special occasion that never came.

This was a special occasion.

He popped the cork.

Reza then snuck out of the other side of the kitchen and darted into the bathroom to quickly wash his face and straighten his hair. When he returned to the living room he found Clara thumbing through the pile of English Premier League soccer magazines that Reza had stacked on the coffee table.

She had a peculiar way of speaking to him through an unbroken smile. "You still find time to read all of this?"

He laughed, a little uncomfortably. "Not like I used to. But it's a good escape, when I need one. From work, that is. Is Champagne okay?"

"Yes, of course, that's perfect."

He handed her a glass. "I haven't tried this Champagne before, but my housemate swears by it."

They toasted and both sat on the couch, sinking naturally into its cushions and each other. Her smile shrunk but her pale, blue eyes widened. Reza stared into them, remembering how beautiful they really were, accented by thick, dark natural eyebrows. "It's amazing, you haven't changed bit since school," Reza said sincerely.

"Ah, were that true, cher Reza, were that true!" Clara chuckled, took a large sip of champagne, and slid her glass onto the coffee table. "Those days seem like a lifetime ago."

"Not to me. It seems like just yesterday. Remember the late night study sessions at my place in Alphabet City, on the Lower East Side? We could barely hear ourselves think over the pipes when when the heat came on. I mean if the heat came on, of course!"

Clara laughed and turned her head so that the scent of her perfume mingled with the evaporating smell of champagne.

"Yes, I remember that well. It was so cold that I had to wear gloves so I could maintain the feeling in my fingers." For the next several minutes, they laughed and reminisced over their days as poor law students:

how neither could afford a comfortable bed or a matching set of pil-
lows, how Reza had bought her a pair of fake sapphire earrings that
he had promised to replace with real ones one day, and how they had
dreamed of spending a carefree weekend in the George V hotel in Paris. It seemed to Reza that despite the years, they were picking back up
right where they had left off. The Champagne was sipped away, until
the bottle was halfway full, almost empty and then gone. Reza soon
felt that there was a palpable buzz or hum between them – not from
the wine but from the sympathetic energy, or the physical harmony,
that comes from two people who are truly in synch with each other.
Reza hadn't felt it, or even remembered it, since he last sat alone somewhere with Clara, some time years ago, with nothing better to do. And
what could be better than this?

She was quiet, with an empty wineglass balanced on her leathered
thigh. Suddenly, she laughed: "The phone?"

"Oh my God, we forgot to exchange phones!" He pulled George's
from out of his pants pocket.

Clara's delicate arm slipped down to her ankle, and she lifted up to
her lap a diminutive Armani bag. She opened it, gave Reza back his
phone and tucked George's into a soft purse. She then leaned over to
Reza and pointed at his shirt pocket. "What's in there?"

"What? This? Nothing."

Her long fingernails, painted a palatial gold, slid slowly across his
chest. "Oh, I think it's something."

He straightened his back and tensed so that his chest muscles were
hard below her touch. "It's just work."

She draped her leg over his lap and flipped herself up to face him.
They were face to face, her lips so close to his nose that he could inhale
her breath. His hands dropped down to her small waist, and he held
her there. She slipped her fingers into his shirt pocket and removed the
thumb drive. He jumped, and she slid off of his lap.

"I need that."

"This?"

"Give it to me please."

"I knew it, I knew it was something," she teased. "I wonder what?"

"It's just work," he said in the coolest tone he could muster.

"My work? You can't be doing other work!"

He was starting to sweat. "No, really. It belongs to another client. It's very confidential. Can I have it back please?"

She handed it back and pushed him down onto the couch, again facing him, sitting on his lap. "God, Reza, don't be so damned serious all the time."

She continued to lean and hover over him, smiling, with her lips slightly parted. He placed his arms around her waist, stroked her back, and kissed her. She kissed him back, gently at first, and then more passionately as he ran his fingers over the once-familiar terrain of her hair and scalp. He could feel, rising through him, the same raw energy that she had generated so often, many years before. And yet he pulled away, stared into her eyes and smiled.

She returned the gaze.

"Look," he said, "I have to ask. Well, actually, I guess I don't have to, but I feel like I need to — what's the story between you and George?"

She spoke through her smile. "He's my boss."

"That's all?"

This time, just the smile.

"I see."

"No. You think you see. He's treated me very well over the years."

"Has he?"

She removed her arms from around his neck. "Professionally."

"I'm sorry. It's none of my business. I should never have brought it up."

"Do you have more Champagne?"

"Unfortunately not."

The smile returned. "I never could count on you, Reza."

He winced. "Let me see if I have any other wine in the kitchen. It will only take a moment."

He ran to the kitchen, rummaged again through the cabinets, and was delighted to find a warm but unopened bottle of Chardonnay. When he returned to the living room with the bottle and corkscrew in hand, only moments later, she had vanished. Instead, Travis was sitting on the couch.

"Where's Clara?" Reza asked.

"Gone."

"Fuck. Did you scare her away?"

"Nah, I heard the door slam so I came out. You ought to be impressed with how long I could sit up there listening to your weak game."

Reza smiled. "There's only one person I'm impressed with right now, and that's me." And while he was indeed pleased with himself, he was more than a bit disappointed that Clara had left so abruptly, without saying goodbye. Did she regret what had happened?

"You still got the thumb drive?"

Panicked, Reza seized the pocket on his shirt. "Still here."

"Hmmph. I was sure that she had lifted it off of you. You better check to make sure it's the one I gave you, that she didn't swap it out."

Reza, his eyes half-closed and glazed, turned to his friend. "You're too suspicious. She's not like that."

Travis raised his eyebrow but did not reply. Instead, he bopped his head and shoulders to an imaginary hip hop tune, and then he started to rap:

> *Got a skinny ass bitch like Marie Antoinette*
> *Bang her in your crib makes you think she's your pet*
> *Yo, let 'em eat cake, then the king lost his head*
> *Four words from that bitch, and then the king he was dead.*

Reza, in typical fashion after hearing Travis's original lyrics, stared at him incredulously. Then he closed his jaw enough to speak: "I don't know whether you suck more at rapping or at history."

"You don't know art from shit."

"Maybe. But suffice it to say that I do know shit when I see, I mean hear it."

Travis walked to the kitchen and grabbed a Red Bull from the fridge.

"Get one for me too please," Reza asked.

"You owe me already for the Champagne. That was good stuff, I think I dropped twenty bucks on that."

Reza flipped open his laptop. "Put it on the tab."

Travis threw him the drink. "I'm going back to my office to work."

"Catch some bad guys for me."

Travis paused. "So why did you lift Gibran's phone anyway?"

That was a difficult question. Without doubt, Reza was committing the most extreme ethical breach of his career – one that would, if discovered, lead to disbarment, if not worse. Then again, it was Travis who had hacked Gibran's email. Technically, Travis committed the act but had no real intent to benefit from the information he pulled. Reza had the intent but didn't himself commit the act. If he simply walked away from it right now then there would be, on Reza's part, no *actus reus* – no overt fraud. And Travis, well, no one was coming after him. He inserted the thumb drive into his laptop. "I suppose I'll find out soon enough."

Travis shrugged and disappeared into his office, into the sanctity of his electronic lair. A folder appeared on Reza's screen, and he opened it to reveal subfolders for the inbox, outbox, notes and calendar entries Travis had copied from Gibran's email account. He downed the Red Bull.

Earlier in his career, as a young associate, Reza had worked on several matters in which he helped to defend white-collar criminals. The clients all profiled the same way: intelligent, wildly successful, charismatic and totally shocked that for the first time in their lives they were in trouble. There had been a moment for each of them, Reza knew, where they had made a little mistake. That was usually not the problem. No, the problem was that they could not own up to the mistake. Instead, the mistake was covered up. And the cover up was almost always the larger mistake, one which could only be remedied by a yet bigger breach, and on and on, until the original, little mistake was the least consequential brick in the edifice that towered over them – the structure of deceit that would eventually come crashing down.

Reza hesitated before clicking open the subfolders. Except for the wildly successful part, he was just like them. He had made a little mistake – he had taken Gibran's phone. It was not too late to stop the chain reaction right there. All he had to do was to destroy the thumb drive, and pretend that Travis had never downloaded Gibran's email. He was perched at the precipice of his little mistake moment, looking down, and equivocating. If Gibran wasn't doing anything wrong, he rationalized, then there would be no harm, no foul, in Reza reviewing his email. But if he was in fact engaged in criminal conduct, then Reza had a responsibility, morally and legally, to do something about it, didn't he?

He clicked open the folder containing Gibran's inbox. Three thousand, one hundred and twenty eight emails. The sent folder had almost as many – 2,731. He grabbed another Red Bull from the refrigerator, which, besides the case of that beverage now contained nothing more than a bag of carrots. The sun had set long ago, but the energy drinks curbed his hunger. He searched at first for Ahmed ibn Ibrahim and Samir Khambarzahi, but neither came up. There were a lot of emails, however, from both Clara and Francois Kling. Reza started with Kling.

Most of Kling's communications to Gibran concerned reports of simple transactions – summaries of the respective day's trades and profits on various exchanges. Gibran never seemed to answer those. Others, however, at intervals of several days apart, were sent from outside of the GAM system – from a Yahoo address – by someone named Alan Krogman. Each of the emails contained attachments with specific reports about the activities of listed, public companies, and each was delivered to Gibran, Kling and someone at a hushmail address referred to only as Sheik. As the night wore on into early morning, and as he tired reading of Gibran's various appointments, chit chats and simple trade orders, Reza began to separate out each of these almost 200 attached reports into a distinct folder. Sometime after three a.m. he focused on reading them.

Krogman's reports lacked emotion or opinion but were presented, in numbered lists, as seemingly objective statements of corporate news gathered by people referred to as "our research analysts." Nothing unusual here, Reza figured. Every billion-dollar fund has teams of analysts carefully tracking specific industry trends that might affect the share prices of respective industry-related public companies. It's market news, for example, if test trials for a new drug fail; that, in turn, could cause a pharmaceutical company's share price to plummet. Greater or lower earnings will precipitate the rise or fall of a stock. Krogman's memos were so chock full of commentaries on price/earnings ratios, Chaikin oscillators, and moving average convergence divergence that by morning, just before sunrise, despite the consumption of two Red Bulls, Reza's throbbing head had fallen back into one of those semi-R.E.M.-semi-still-awake sleeps.

As the morning sun streamed golden into the room, however, Reza awoke with a start. He went back into the last Krogman report he'd read. Gibran's research analysts were reporting the anticipated purchase by GloboPharma of Coaguline Technologies, a huge biotech company, for some £700 million. He googled Coaguline. Indeed, the purchase was announced by GloboPharma at the close of the market on February 11th. He switched back to the Krogman document, but it wasn't dated. Cursing, Reza backtracked through Gibran's inbox to find the original email with the relevant Krogman memo. It was dated January 29th – some two weeks before the GloboPharma deal was made public.

Awake now, despite a complete lack of sleep, Reza isolated the Kling emails to track the trade reports he'd ignored all night. On January 30th, GAM took a small position in GloboPharma. In fact, during each subsequent day of trading, GAM purchased on the London exchange larger and larger amounts of GloboPharma shares at prices holding steady at about 2,600 pence. On the morning of February 12th, following the previous evening's market news announcement, the stock quickly climbed to 3,100. And on that day, GAM sold off most of its position.

Travis was up now, barefoot and in his ratty plaid pajama bottoms, staring inside of the empty refrigerator but settling instead for breakfast on a dry bowl of Cap'n Crunch cereal. He popped the crusty sugar cubes in his mouth one by one and sat on the couch next to Reza. "You been here all night?"

Reza stared at the computer screen. "Yep."

Travis raised an eyebrow. "Must be some interesting reading."

"It is. I think he's insider trading." Reza turned to Travis. "He's a criminal."

"Only when he's convicted of that, right Mr. Shirvani, esquire?"

"Right. Now you're the lawyer. Tell me again, exactly who do you work for?"

"I told you, MYFBB. The mind your fucking business bureau." Travis smiled and dropped several cereal pieces into his mouth.

Reza closed his files and shut down the laptop. "I can't even hear you over that crunching."

"Hmmm? What makes you think they're inside trading anyway?"

An orange morsel of cereal flew from Travis's mouth onto Reza's shoulder. He wiped it off. "They seem to know about a number of market events before the rest of the world does, and they trade on the information. Looks like they have a team of research analysts that get their hands on this information, and GAM buys or sells stocks in the market based on how they think the market will react to the information when it's out."

"Like betting on a horse you know is going to win."

Reza rubbed his eyes. "Exactly. But in this case it's more than one horse."

"How many?" Travis asked.

"I haven't finished going through everything."

"So how do the research analysts get this information?"

"I don't know."

"Sounds like a quick way to make a lot of money."

Reza agreed – it was a very fast way to make a whole lot of money, but it was also, clearly, illegal. Fortunately, it didn't look like Clara was involved.

CHAPTER NINE

At ten a.m. sharp on Wednesday morning, Reza knocked on John Burlington's office door. Reza had decided to tell him everything. Almost everything, anyway – while he didn't get into the details of how the cell phones were switched, or how he had managed to get access to Gibran's email account, he did tell John that he'd found strong evidence of insider trading. Burlington listened patiently. At one point, he stood, walked around his desk, told Jane to hold his calls and closed and locked his door – something Reza never saw him do. Reza handed Burlington a folder of key emails recommending particular buys or sells that he had matched to trading records. For each of the fifteen recommended trades, GAM had turned over the shares within one week, after the public announcement of key news – and profited substantially. After close to thirty minutes, Burlington raised his hand and interrupted his associate. "That'll do, Reza." They looked across at each other in silence. Burlington opened a file drawer and removed a different folder. He opened it on his otherwise bare, neat desk. It contained one piece of paper. "This is a recommendation to the firm's management committee that Reza Shirvani be made a partner, out of cycle, at the very next committee meeting."

A half-opened smile flashed and froze across Reza's face – what exactly was happening? Was he being rewarded for years of diligent and valuable service? Was Burlington recognizing the fantastic job Reza had just done watchdogging the firm's ethical obligations? Or could it possibly be that he was being bought off? But this was John Burlington, the legend – that couldn't possibly be the case. "I'm . . . thank you. I'm stunned. I thought, based on our last conversation, that this couldn't even be considered before next year. But thank you, I hope you know how much that means to me."

"I know, Reza, and you're welcome. Of course, I can't guarantee anything, you understand. The management committee still needs to meet and approve this. But if there ever was a special case, Reza, you're it." He winked and smiled broadly. They both knew that John Burlington could get anything done at Double H if he set his mind to it.

"Yes, of course."

"Now I'm not sure yet when the next management committee meeting is, but I'll keep you posted. In the interim, please keep this conversation to yourself. As you can imagine, it wouldn't help our cause to have this leak out before it's finalized."

"Understood. Thank you again."

Was this how it went down? Was it always so matter of fact when associates were told that they would be made partners? Somehow, in Reza's fantasies, there was always more romance or glory attached to the moment. In his mind, there was lots of backslapping, perhaps a cigar or a sip of champagne shared over dinner. But this seemed muted and contrived.

Burlington stood up and extended his hand to Reza. It seemed to Reza to signal congratulations as well the end of the meeting. Reza stood and shook his hand warmly.

"Before I leave, John, I want to make sure I have your thoughts on the thing that brought me here in the first place, the GAM emails and trading. I'm not sure how you think we should handle that."

Burlington's expression grew grave as he sat back down. "Reza, let me begin by saying that I appreciate how seriously you're taking your ethical obligations. But it seems to me, and I don't mean to be at all pejorative, that you're making a mountain out of a molehill. George Gibran is one of the leading investors in the world, and he is now one of our largest clients. You've been working hard and you are understandably tired. So it's not at all surprising that your sense of perspective might be skewed. In short, the handful of emails that you found doesn't show me anything. Who knows what they mean when taken in complete context? I think you should forget the matter, have a tall scotch, and get a good night's sleep. You drink scotch, right? I never trust a man who doesn't drink scotch!"

Reza was tired, but he also knew that the emails were more than nothing. He had built his entire professional career on interpreting precisely these types of emails, this sort of trading. Why was Burlington dismissing the matter so perfunctorily? "Far be it from me to question your judgment, John, but isn't it worth at least raising this with the GAM folks?"

Burlington leaned forward, halfway across his desk. "Raise what, Reza? What would you like me to do, ask Gibran if his business is in fact a criminal enterprise? No, it's not worth raising. I appreciate that you've expressed these concerns. You did your job. Now it's with me, and my judgment is that you walk out of here, have a tall drink, and get some rest. Check into a spa if that's what you like. I hear the Mandarin Oriental is very nice. And please, charge my account."

"Right. Thanks, John. I appreciate it."

"I know you do."

"Maybe you're right, maybe I'm misreading this." Of course, Reza knew in his heart of hearts that he was not.

Burlington sat back and smiled. "And remember, mums on the partnership consideration."

"Yes, mums it is." For a moment, Reza thought about raising the loan. Burlington had not said anything at all about his request for a loan from the partnership. But this was not the time, he decided, to ask about that. "Hope you get some time off this weekend, John."

The Embassy of Finland on Massachusetts Avenue is minimalist: lots of black, gray and silver, with tasteful green ivy climbing its skeletal skin. It's down the street from the former Iranian embassy – mosque-like, blue-domed and now abandoned. Reza walked slowly past the shell of that embassy, a fossil of a country and a reminder of a time that no longer exists. He stopped abruptly, faced it and said a silent prayer for his mother and sister. And then he ducked into the Finnish Embassy, as a guest of George Gibran, for the Children's Hospital Ball.

He looked around, checked his coat and patted down his gray suit and black tie. The building's airy, interior lobby must have been designed specifically, he figured, for grand galas and receptions. Reza sloped his way down a curved, copper and wood staircase and offered a receptionist, at its bottom, his name. She checked him in.

He made his way straight to a small, black bar. The scotch selection was disappointingly limited to generic blends. "Black Label. Lots of water and ice."

A short, mustachioed bartender struggled to hear him over the din of the crowd. "Got it."

Burlington had been right about one thing – Reza was tired, and he wanted nothing more right now than to turn off the thinking part of his brain. It was getting harder and harder for him to synthesize the events of the prior forty-eight hours. He kicked back a healthy sip of the whiskey, which went down his throat like a bolt of warm, peaty iodine. He drained the glass. "Another. Same way, please."

The bartender obliged.

At least with partnership seemingly achieved, Reza reasoned, he could turn his attention fully to raising the money his mother and sister needed to exit Afghanistan. Yes, that is what he should focus on now. The GAM issues were now with Burlington, and Reza should just leave it at that. Reza was now protected if things went sideways. Just keep your nose down, he told himself, and ride Burlington's coattails straight to the partnership. No one died and made it your job, he told himself, to walk around and police the world's capital markets. Secure your career, take care of your family, and mind your business.

Reza removed the card from his chest pocket, the one he received from the receptionist. Table 7. He scanned the room until he spied the back of a slight, fit woman with long blonde hair chatting with an older, graying couple. Clara. It wasn't so much that the woman was the right height, or that she had the right hair. It was really more the way she stood, how she carried herself. It was the way she held her elbow in one hand while gesturing with the other; the way she tilted her head ever so slightly to the right when she had had a bit to drink.

Reza, feeling relaxed but not quite out of control, ambled over to what must be Table 7. Perhaps it was the fact that he had lost himself in those recollections, but Reza casually placed his arm around the woman's waist and kissed her cheek. "Hello Clara, I was wondering where you'd disappeared to," he said.

She turned to her left while in mid-sentence, slightly startled but still composed.

"Oh, so sorry to interrupt," Reza quickly added as he collected his senses. "I just wanted to let you know I'm here."

"Reza, I was hoping I would see you. George said you would be coming." If she had in fact been unnerved by Reza's approach, then she was cool enough not to show any evidence of it.

Reza smiled at her, for perhaps a moment too long, and then turned to look at the couple to whom she had been speaking.

"Please let me introduce you," she said without missing a beat. "This is Ambassador Virtanen, and his wife Inari. This is my very old friend, Reza Shirvani. We studied together in law school. He is also our lead lawyer here in the U.S." They shook hands.

"It's very good to meet you, Mr. and Mrs. Ambassador. And thank you for hosting this wonderful event in your home."

"It's really our pleasure," the Ambassador replied smoothly "There is hardly a better cause."

"And thanks for inviting me to your table, Clara. Is Mr. Gibran here this evening?"

"No," she said, "the Ambassador had just asked the same question. He's otherwise occupied."

"The Asian markets are open," the Ambassador offered, cheerfully.

"But I trust he'll rush right down here as soon as he can," Clara said.

The four of them stood silently, fake smiles pasted on their faces.

"So what's the news in Helsinki?" Reza asked.

The Ambassador didn't miss a beat. "The usual. Our fishermen are caught in Baltic Sea ice floes, and we've commissioned a new study to prove that work, indeed, doubles the risk of heart failure."

Was he kidding? "Interesting."

"Mr. Shirvani, Ms. Fournier, a pleasure. Allow me please," he said, moving on to the next table. "Enjoy your evening."

Clara turned to him. "The news in Helsinki?"

"Yeah. That's their capitol, isn't it?"

They sat down at Table 7, which was half-empty. A young account executive from a public relations firm GAM had hired joined them, along with a quiet, older couple from Beirut. Clara spoke to them in French. Reza talked English Premier League soccer with the public relations executive and stared at his butter lettuce salad. He got up to order another Black Label before the prime rib was served. Clara joined him. "George isn't coming tonight, by the way."

"Oh. So you mean we can just have fun?"

She chuckled. "Yes, theoretically."

"Excellent."

"Do you want to get out of here?"

He did.

They left the party and walked down the wide, tree-lined sidewalk along Massachusetts Avenue, eastward towards DuPont Circle. They stopped at the historic Fairfax Hotel, just west of DuPont, and took a small table with tawny, leather seats in the lobby bar, the old Jockey Club. Reza was now on his fourth Black Label and Clara her second glass of wine.

"I've heard that President Kennedy loved to come here," Reza offered.

"Oh, that's interesting," Clara replied, not very convincingly.

Reza leaned in toward her. "I guess I shouldn't be surprised that you left without saying goodbye the other day."

"You are right," she giggled, "you shouldn't be surprised."

He took another sip of his drink. "Does it mean that you regret what happened between us?"

She exhaled. "I regret nothing in life, ever."

He paused. "I'm glad to hear it. You know, I've thought about you often over the last few years. Wondered where you were, and if you found what you were looking for."

As if in reflex, she reached for her purse. "I hate that I can't smoke in bars here. You would think that tobacco and alcohol are so natural together."

Like us, he wanted to say. But he didn't. "As slow suicide techniques, I suppose," he said.

"Oh, don't be slow melodramatic." She pulled her telephone from her purse, scrolled through some messages, and then dropped the device on the table.

She was avoiding any serious discussion of their prior life together, he knew.

"Tell me about your life now," she said after several quiet moments. "Tell me something exciting that I don't already know." Reza ran through the list of options in his head. He could share with her what he thought about Gibran's illegal trading, but that would certainly be the end of the evening and, perhaps, his newfound relationship with Clara. Plus, he reminded himself, he was going to keep his nose down and take care of his own business. He could tell her about his struggle to raise the money he needed to buy green cards for his mother and sister, but she might mistake that as ploy for pity. "Well, I think I'm about to make partner at Double H."

"That's wonderful news! *A votre santé!*" They clinked glasses. "And it's certainly well deserved."

"Thanks. But of course, please don't repeat that to anyone," he added. "It's not been finalized. Probably months away."

"Don't worry. I'm very good with secrets." She sipped her drink. "Tell me, do you do anything besides GAM work these days? What kinds of other things do you work on?"

"Very little else," he replied. "But I do have a couple of other things, mostly enforcement investigations, that I still attend to."

She flashed a half-smile. "Very cool. I've always wanted to know more about how those investigations actually work. Tell me about one of them. What's the most challenging thing you're doing?"

Reza took another sip of his scotch and chewed the last cube of ice that remained in the glass. "Well, right now I have to convince the S.E.C. that the C.E.O. of one of my clients did not mean to say exactly what he appears to have said in an email that we've just produced to the S.E.C."

"Fascinating. And how to do you propose to do that?" Clara caressed his arm.

"I'm not sure yet." Reza felt happy. Maybe there was a bond after all that could be rekindled between them. "The problem is that even if I come up with a credible explanation, they will eventually take his testimony and see for themselves that he's a pathological liar."

"Not a good trait in a C.E.O." She shook her head in an exaggerated manner, causing her hair to wash over her bare shoulders. And even though he was drunk by now, he could sense the purposeful manner in which she placed her hand lightly on his knee. "You'll have to tell me the company's name, so I can make sure that it's not in GAM's portfolio."

"Microtrade. But don't worry, I know they won't ever be in your portfolio."

"No, they won't be." She bestowed on him another ambiguous smile.

Reza knew almost immediately that he had said too much and that he had breached a serious client confidence by mentioning Microtrade by name. Even though it was only Clara, and she could certainly be trusted not to repeat this personal conversation, he should've known better. Was he too drunk? Yes, he decided, he should leave before he said or did anything else that he'd later regret. As much as he hated the idea of leaving Clara behind, he knew it was the right call. No part of the conversation was going the way he'd hoped.

"Look, I better be getting home. I think I'll walk, and get some air."

She shrugged, as if she had no opinion whatsoever on the matter. "Okay. You go ahead. I'm going to call for a driver. I can't walk very far in these shoes."

Reza worked hard to maintain his balance as he exited the hotel and labored home, down Massachusetts Avenue, past the stately row of embassies that gilded the lush road. As soon as he had left the hotel, Clara picked her phone back up from the table. She turned off its recording feature and confirmed she had recorded the last five minutes and eleven seconds of their conversation. That should certainly be long enough to do the job. She then finished her wine and called for a driver to take her to George's hotel.

CHAPTER TEN

Like most office buildings in Washington after 9/11, access to the twelve-story building that Double H calls its home was tightly restricted. To enter the building from the open, lobby area, visitors must first pass electronic turnstiles that are activated and opened by building access cards or digitally coded visitor passes. Past the turnstiles, the approach to the two elevator banks is guarded by a rotating team of blue-jacketed security guards. One Friday, the last Friday in May, Reza's building access card failed to activate and open the electronic turnstiles. After several attempts, Reza called out to the large security guard positioned by the elevator, with his back to Reza.

"Excuse me," Reza called out, "my card's not working. Is there something wrong with the machine?"

The guard, who turned and approached Reza, was not someone who Reza had seen previously at Double H. He had a hairy and unfriendly face, with large black mole on the left side of his nose. "No, sir," the new guard muttered through a barely open mouth. "The machine is working just fine. Must be your card."

Reza detected a hint of an accent in the guard's voice, one which he could not quite recognize. It seemed to be an amalgamation of European and North African accents. He looked at the guard's name badge. It read Abdullah. Servant of Allah.

"I haven't seen you here before," Reza said. "Are you new?"

"Yes, sir," Abdullah replied curtly. "Can I see your card?" He inspected it, looking closely at the almost boyish picture of Reza affixed to its front, and then confirmed that it did in fact fail to open the turnstile. "Something is wrong. Maybe it's expired."

"That can't be," Reza said. "They don't have expiration dates."

"Why don't I buzz you up with my card, sir, and I keep yours so I can look into it for you?"

It seemed to Reza that Abdullah spit out the word sir. And then he stared too long at the large, black mole on the security guard's nose. "Okay, but when can I have it back?"

"I'll have it sent up to you this morning, as soon as we figure out what's wrong with it." Reza agreed, and Abdullah opened the turnstile for Reza using his own badge.

True to his word, Abdullah did have Reza's ID sent up later that morning, and there were no further problems with his card or the turnstile after that. But every morning thereafter, Abdullah would be positioned at the elevators when Reza arrived. He would always be near Reza, without saying a word, not even so much as hello. On top of this, Reza had the distinct impression he was seeing Abdullah at a random assortment of places: at Starbuck's when Reza purchased his morning coffee, outside Granville Moore's bar, on the same Metro platform. It felt to him as if he were being observed. But why? Was it all in his imagination? Travis seemed to think so, but it still struck Reza as peculiar.

Back at work, it was business as usual for Reza. Just as Burlington had advised, Reza had pushed aside his concerns about Gibran's trading and had focused instead on servicing GAM's legal needs efficiently and effectively. In fact, Reza now spent virtually all of his hours servicing what had become the firm's most lucrative client, making him the toast of Double H. What other choice did Reza have, anyway? Doing anything else would have been professional suicide. Plus there was the big, fat, burdensome matter of the money — the additional four hundred and fifty thousand dollars his mother and sister needed to buy their way out of Afghanistan and into the United States. Every two weeks Maryam would call and ask about the money. Every two weeks he'd tell her to be patient. He peeked at his watch, sighed, and then looked at his phone. It rang.

She didn't waste a second.

"Have you been able to gather the rest of the money for Rashid? He told us that he doesn't want the rest in dribs and drabs, he wants the remaining four hundred fifty thousand dollars all at once."

"What do you mean dribs and drabs? I sent over five ten-thousand dollar wires. That's neither a drib nor a drab."

"Reza, he says that the paperwork is ready. All we need is to produce the money and he will pick it up for us from the Americans! I know it's a lot of money, but please, do your best. I don't know what will happen to us if this doesn't work. I promise, I will pay you back for every penny." There it was again, the promise to pay him back. He was preparing to respond when someone started knocking on his door. "*Yek lahzeh lotfan*. What is it?"

"Reza?" she asked.

"Not you, Maryam."

Gil opened the door, wheeled in his mail cart, and shut the door behind him. "You ever hear of Clearway? We sell these cleaning products all through the firm, and then I get some of my people in the other firms to sell under me, it's like a pyramid scheme, only legal. Soon we don't have to do nothin', the money rolls in because those people under us, they the ones doing the work. And what the fuck? Why won't the law firms buy this from us, they don't care. All I need to get started is for you to convince the maintenance people here at Double H to buy from me. You know how much they go through in cleaning supplies? Naturally, I'd be happy to cut you in on the action, as reward for your efforts. What do you say?"

Reza pointed to his phone. "Not now."

"Oh snap, sorry." He raised a bottle of Clearway Green Meadows air freshener and spritzed Reza's office. "Kinda stinky in here, bro. Let me know when you're ready to do some business. Later."

"Maryam?"

"Are you talking with someone there?"

"Sorry. Look, I've asked my law firm for a loan. They've said they're working on it. I will check again today. I know the predicament you're in and I'm doing everything I can. I don't know what else to say right now."

"He gave us several months to deliver the money. There's about three weeks left. After that, the deal is off."

"What about the fifty thousand you gave him?"

"That's the least of our concerns. If we can't buy our papers from Rashid, I have to think start thinking of a way back to Tehran. We're out of options."

Reza loosened his tie and undid the top button. "I understand. I have one other option here that I haven't tried yet. I'll work on that too."

"I leave it to you to do what you can. We have until June 18th."

"How is mother?"

"She says she's fine. Of course, she would never say otherwise. Please, Reza, do whatever you can to get us the four hundred fifty thousand before then."

"I will, I promise." He hung up the phone, removed from his drawer a bottle of Tom Ford Extreme cologne and sprayed it around the office to cover up the Green Meadows scent. His inbox pinged. Clara:

> George wants to see you today at 1:00 pm at the
> Four Seasons. He has comments on the marketing ma-
> terials. Please confirm. C.

He wrote back:

> I'll be there. Reza.

With Maryam's call on his mind, Reza left his office early on his way to the meeting with Gibran to stop at a downtown First Metro Bank branch. He walked through the brass doors and was welcomed by a smiling, young bank officer in a black business suit, with straight black hair, red pouty lips and gleaming white teeth. "Welcome to First Metro. How can I help you, sir?"

"I'd like to speak to someone about a loan."

"I'd be happy to help with that. I'm Sonia Jimenez." She held out her hand, which Reza shook. "Come right this way."

Ms. Jimenez led him through a labyrinth of desks, all separated by monochromatic partitions, and each bearing nameplates announcing the occupant's name and position at the bank. Invariably, the positions were either vice president, assistant vice president or associate vice president. Ms. Jimenez swept into her empty cubicle, its desk bare but for a computer screen and keyboard. A glass paperweight bearing the First Metro logo was pushed against the wall, tangled in the computer wiring. If not for her name on the glass, Ms. Jimenez's office, as it were, could very well have been a spare. "Are you looking for a personal loan or a business loan?"

"A personal loan."

"And do you have an account with us?"

"Yes, I do." Reza provided her with his information: his social security number, his address, and a brief description of his accounts.

"Here we are," she said as she leaned in toward the computer screen, appearing to scrutinize the accounts. "I see there have been five transfers in the past few weeks out of your money market account to an account at Banke Mellie Afghanistan."

"That's right. Fifty thousand in total. My mother and sister are in Afghanistan."

"Ooh. I'm so sorry. I have a brother in the Army, and we're worried sick about him getting deployed to Iraq."

"No, mine aren't in the military. They live there."

"In Afghanistan?"

"Yes. I'm working on getting them out."

She smiled. "So how much are you looking to borrow?"

"I'd like to borrow five hundred thousand dollars."

Her fingers clicked rapidly on the keyboard. "All right, then, let's see what we can do here."

Reza sat back, less nervous and more satisfied that the process may not be as difficult as he'd worried.

More clicking. "I see your credit is in very good standing, and you have about twelve thousand in savings."

Reza noticed her long, orange nails and wondered how she could type so efficiently. "Yes."

"Annual salary?"

"Around two-fifty."

Her fingers kept flying across the keyboard. "And what sort of collateral do you have?"

"You mean besides what's in my First Metro accounts?"

"Yes. For example, do you own your home?"

"No."

"Any stocks or other investments, outside your accounts here?"

"No."

"A car?"

"No."

She stopped typing.

"Anything else? Promissory notes, annuities, outside income?"

"No, but I'm about to become a partner in my law firm and I was hoping I could secure a loan against my future income there. I expect that my income will increase substantially in the near future. Probably by about fifty-percent."

"To three hundred seventy five thousand?"

Reza leaned forward. "No. To four hundred thousand."

"No matter, sir. We don't lend against future income," Ms. Jimenez chirped. "We need immediate collateral that can secure the loan. It's going to be very difficult to extend hundreds of thousands of dollars to you without any security. A hundred thousand in an unsecured line, perhaps. But not five hundred thousand."

"I see. Well, maybe we should go ahead and apply anyway, just to see what happens?"

"It won't work, sir. It's not even a close call."

"Do you think I can speak with your manager?"

"I am the manager, sir." She continued to smile through the awkward silence that followed.

"Okay, thanks anyway for your time."

"Happy to be of service. Can I interest you in another low-interest credit card from First Metro?"

Only if I can get a five hundred thousand dollar limit on it, he thought. "No, thanks."

Reza exited the bank and grabbed a cab to the Four Seasons. He rested his head on the taxi's cold window, but it banged against the glass as the dilapidated vehicle rumbled down the pot-holed streets. How, in three weeks, would he raise the four-fifty his mother and sister needed? What was the point of having worked all these years as a successful lawyer in the U.S. if he could not even get his mother and sister into the country? But who knew that he'd one day have to bribe their way to safety? Until recently, they had never even expressed a desire to come to the U.S. It was probably Maryam who drove her to it. But who could blame her? They couldn't go west, like he did as a boy, because Iraq was exploding and the Turkish borders now were sealed. And the Iranians wouldn't have let any family members of Colonel Shirvani to simply fly to Paris, to leave at their own free will. In any case, he was an idiot not to have prepared, not to have saved something more substantial. Maybe the law firm would come through, he thought. Maybe Burlington would convince the management committee to lend him the money. He watched the cars on either side of him pass by and recede like waves on a beach. Deep down, he knew he'd just as soon win the lottery.

The cab dropped him at the Four Seasons five minutes before one. François Kling, Gibran's slender, almost waifish CFO, awaited him in the lobby, and they proceeded to Gibran's penthouse suite.

"Are you well?" Kling asked.

"Yes, I am. And you?"

"You seem tired." Kling's voice, with a German inflection, was relatively high-pitched.

Reza laughed. "Part of the uniform. But don't worry, I don't charge extra for that effect. You're not staying at the Ritz Carlton this time?"

"No, Mr. Gibran wanted to give the Four Seasons a fair chance to make their case." His hand fluttered over the lush orchid arrangements that adorned the otherwise monotone lobby. "Funny story, I should say," Kling added, "about Mr. Gibran's phone."

Not really, Reza thought. "Yes, very embarrassing. They were identical, it was a silly oversight on my part."

"Oversights can be dangerous things, especially for lawyers." It was hard to determine whether Kling was being serious or sarcastic. Did he know more than he was letting on?

The elevator opened. Kling led Reza down the hall and produced an electronic key to Gibran's room. He let himself in, and Reza followed. Gibran was seated at a rectangular, glass table in the suite's dining room. A Lebanese spread of hummus, baba ghannouj, tabouleh, salads, kafta, and various other delicacies crowded the table. Gibran took Reza's hand and led him to a seat. "Let's eat!" he said firmly, and they all sat down.

Normally, Reza would be polite and not eat, but he was becoming more familiar with Gibran – and he was hungry, having not eaten all day. So he piled his plate high with the various dips and salads, and decided this day to dig right in.

George poured him a glass of sparkling water. "Have you ever wondered, Reza, what makes me so successful?"

Why was he asking that? "The question hadn't really crossed my mind."

"Kling, don't you think that most ambitious people would have considered the matter further?"

Kling sipped his flat water. "I do indeed. But perhaps Mr. Shirvani is less ambitious?"

Gibran laughed. "He's a successful, young lawyer, of course he's ambitious."

Reza's collar suddenly felt tight. The conversation seemed artificial, even rehearsed. "I like to think I'm ambitious enough. Though too much ambition can certainly be dangerous too."

"Indeed," Gibran said. "Reza, what do you think the top lawyers at your firm earn – someone like John Burlington?"

"Hard for me to know."

"Come now, you have to have a guess. Three million? Five?"

Reza wiped a shred of parsley from the side of his mouth. "Five would be in the high side. Probably more like two or three in a normal year."

The table was silent for a minute.

"That is an awful lot of talent and work for a relatively small return," Gibran finally chimed in.

Reza chuckled. "Oh, I'll take that. Two to three million sounds just fine to me."

"We made twenty-five million on one trade yesterday," Kling said, flatly.

Where was this going? "Right. Well, lawyering is certainly not as profitable as trading," Reza said. "But the practice of law can be intellectually and personally rewarding."

Gibran and Kling both turned to stare at him, as though he had been speaking a different language.

Reza continued: "What I mean is, I enjoy the intellectual challenge that it can present. It's fun, tackling difficult problems that require real analytical thinking."

"Yes, yes, I can imagine," Gibran mused. "It must not be easy, for example, to convince the S.E.C. that your client knows nothing about a matter which he clearly addressed by email." Reza shifted in his seat. Was he talking about Microtrade? How would he know about that? Unless, of course, he had heard about it from Clara. How stupid Reza had been, he thought, to tell her about that case. And why would she have repeated it to Gibran? If Microtrade ever learned that Reza had breached their confidence in that way, it would be the end of Reza's legal career.

"Still," Gibran continued without awaiting a response, "every man has financial needs and concerns, no? At least that's been my experience."

"Mine too," Kling agreed.

"Life is difficult. Sure, things may go well for a while, maybe for decades even, but things don't go well forever. I mean, look at what happened to your father."

His father? Why would he be talking about his father? Reza tossed his napkin on his plate. "Well, George, I didn't get to know him as well as I would have liked."

"Right, of course not, Reza. Colonel Shirvani was a great man, a brave man. Truly a shame what happened to him. Revolutions are a messy business."

"I appreciate the sentiment, George, I really do, but I don't think my father is relevant to this conversation."

"What I'm getting at, my dear, is that at some point in life, things get bumpy. And when they do, it is inevitably the case that money helps." Gibran put his fork down and turned toward Reza. "Every person will find himself, at some point, in a difficult or compromised position, one in which they have some need. I guess the key to my success, Reza, is that I have knack for being there when that happens. Someone more jaded than you might view that as exploitation. I like to think of it as a heightened awareness when it comes to my fellow man."

"I can see how that would be a useful skill," Reza replied.

Gibran slapped the table and laughed out loud. "You're damned right it is, son. It is a useful skill indeed."

Reza didn't like Gibran calling him son.

"Let me ask you this, Reza, are there bumps in your life now that could be assuaged by money? Are there problems you have that might simply go away if you had a small fortune at your disposal?"

Had Clara also told Gibran about Reza's need for money, to help his mother and sister in Afghanistan? Or maybe Gibran heard it from Burlington. Either way, Gibran certainly knew more about Reza's life than he needed to know and it was making Reza increasingly uncomfortable. He sipped some iced water. "I'm not sure I'm alone in that regard, George. And I must say, I'm not sure I know what the point of all this is." Reza was reaching the end of his patient ability to play along, and he tried hard to sound less exasperated than he actually felt.

Kling coughed, and then cleared his throat. "Mr. Gibran would like to offer you a position at GAM, Reza. He would like to make you the Chief Operating Officer of the newly formed U.S. business. We realize, of course, that you are a committed and valuable member of Henderson & Humphries, but we think you are uniquely suited to manage the operations of the U.S. business, which you yourself have largely set up. Of course, we would compensate you in a manner that is commensurate with this substantial role. Your base salary would $500,000, but, more importantly, you also would be given stock in a variety of GAM's European entities. There would also be a sizeable signing bonus, which we can discuss and negotiate."

"You would work directly with me to build something for the future," Gibran said as he raised his index finger. "I know you appreciate the value of that proposition, and I'm sure you will consider this seriously."

Reza sipped his water as the two men stared at him with closed smiles. "Of course I will, and I'm flattered by your offer. Can I have some time to think about this?"

"Of course, take your time," Kling said. "Inform us whenever you're ready."

Gibran stood. "In the meantime, dear boy, let's just keep this between us, shall we? No need to give old man Burlington any unnecessary heartburn," he chuckled.

"Yes, understood." Reza also rose from the table and flicked some stray hummus from his pants.

"And no need to tell your other clients, either," Gibran added matter-of-factly as he walked away, with his back to Reza. "Poor Jessica Blount and her anxious C.E.O. don't need to hear about your deliberations any sooner than is absolutely necessary."

Damn it, Reza thought, Clara had indeed shared his indiscretion about Microtrade with Gibran. And Gibran was now using it to blackmail him.

"I know you'll make the right decision, dear boy."

The right decision? He no longer felt he could tell right from wrong.

CHAPTER ELEVEN

Reza had been in his office scanning scores from the English Premier League when Jane Erlich called to summon him to see John Burlington. It's not that he didn't have a lot of work to do, or that he was being lazy. It was simply that he was trying not to think. He needed to create a calm, open space in his head. If he could do that, he reasoned, he might be able to figure out the correct answers to the difficult decisions he needed to make.

Today, instead of rushing to see Burlington, as he usually did, he looked first to see whether Arsenal had recruited any decent goal scorers. They had not. He could have spent all day on the BBC Sports Football web site, but he knew that was not an option. Finally, he tore himself away, knotted his green, Jay Kos tie and made his way down the hall, walking slowly and trying to refocus on his immediate surroundings.

He flashed Jane a big, toothy smile when he was near Burlington's door, and she returned his smile. "You look happy today, Reza!"

He stopped. "You know, I've heard that if you can only pretend to be happy, you can eventually fool yourself into actually being happy."

"Well, it looks like you're the fool then!" Jane laughed as she glanced down at her phone bank. "He's free. Go ahead in."

He thanked her, and began to make his way in to see Burlington.

"Oh, Reza?"

Jane had called him back. "Yeah?"

"Don't overdo the smiling. It can be creepy."

Reza paused in the doorway, unsure, staring at her as Burlington shouted in his direction. "Shirvani! Are you in or out?"

He was in, and so he closed the door behind him. "You wanted to see me?"

Burlington motioned for him to sit on the sofa. "Good news. I think we can lend you the money."

Reza sat up. "What? You mean the loan for my mother and sister?"

Burlington opened his palms and raised his eyebrows, as if to say that's just what I said. "That's who you need it for, isn't it?"

"Yes, of course."

Burlington placed a dish of pistachio nuts between them, something he had never done before. Was it Burlington's new snack interest, or an awkward and unnecessary attempt at Persian hospitality? "It wasn't easy. I had to persuade the management committee that you're all but a lock for partner and that you will be a part of this firm for years to come. I went into a bit about your family's background, how your father was a freedom fighter against the Islamists, your mother's struggles, the danger she and your sister are facing in Afghanistan."

"My dad wasn't a freedom fighter."

Burlington shifted in his chair. "Right. Well, my knowledge of the region is obviously not as strong as yours. But no matter, that's not the critical point. The crux of the matter is that you need a substantial loan for a noble purpose, that you are a dedicated member of the Double H family, and Double H is prepared to do something completely unprecedented in order to recognize that."

"I don't know what to say. Truly, I'm speechless."

"It's easy. Start by saying thanks. Then say that you will return that gesture by redoubling your commitment to the firm. And then get back to billing hours!"

Reza was overcome by a sense of relief and happiness that he had not felt in quite some time. A cool sensation raced up from his legs, swept through his torso and splashed across his face. While Burlington had assured Reza that he was working on the possibility of a loan, Reza had become less and less optimistic every day that Burlington would be able to deliver. Now that he had, Reza no longer needed to either abandon his mother and sister, or throw his lot in with Gibran. There was a third option now, one that appeared far better than the two he had been unsuccessfully grappling with. He was relieved he hadn't told anyone about Gibran's offer. "I'll do just that, John. Thank you. And please convey my gratitude to the entire management committee. I can't believe you were able to arrange this!"

"Ha! Did you have so little faith in my abilities?"

Reza stood and went over to hug Burlington. He held him, perhaps a bit too long, but it was a sincere embrace, and Burlington – patting him on the back now as if to say that's enough – returned the gesture. "There, there. Enough sentimentality. Now back to billing hours, young man," he said.

"Thank you, again, John. You won't regret this. I promise to reward your faith in me."

"I know Reza. I have no doubt."

Burlington retreated back behind the safety of his desk. He raised an eyebrow. "The check will take a couple of weeks because we have to move some funds between accounts. Probably June 14th. Let me know if you need me to speed that up for any reason."

"Will do, John."

Reza floated back to his office, determined to contain his obvious joy and to channel the excitement that he felt into some productive task. He looked at the menacing pile of GAM-related documents that rose up from the right side of his desk. Yes, he would begin by tackling the prime brokerage agreements that the newly formed GAM entities needed to enter into with the largest brokerage firms in order to trade here in the U.S. He had avoided that task for days, but he now felt more than ready to tackle it, and he jumped right in. Hours later, he turned to two letters to the S.E.C. that he needed to edit for another client. His energy seemed limitless, and it was well after ten p.m. that he turned off his computer and returned home.

The house on H Street was pitch black. Reza opened the creaky gate, the one he kept promising to treat with WD-40, and walked across the broken pavement to his front door. He opened it with his key and stepped inside. Travis was obviously out. Reza turned on the hallway light, kicked off his shoes and walked into the burnished glow of a partially lit living room. He sunk into the sofa, put his feet up, and exhaled deeply. There were two telephone calls that he needed to make, and he now looked forward to both. He began with Maryam.

"Good morning, sister."

"Do you have good news for us?"

"Of course I do. I have the money. The loan from my firm came through."

"*Khodaye man!*"

He laughed to himself. "Did you have such little faith in me?"

"Yes."

"Did mother?"

"No, never."

"I can wire the remaining four hundred fifty thousand to Mr. Rashid as soon as he's ready. But make sure, first, that you get the green cards secured. No money until you get the green cards."

"You know it doesn't work like that. He needs the money to get the green cards."

"This is our only shot, Maryam. What if he takes the money and doesn't deliver? Who will we turn to then? Will you sue him for it in Kabul?"

"I trust him, Reza, I really do. And I guess I really have no choice anyway, but to trust him. Things here don't work the way they do over there. What am I going to do, ask him for a receipt."

Reza lowered his voice. "Look, Maryam, friends of mine know about this guy. I probably know more about him than I should. He's not considered to be, what's the right word, predictable. We need to make sure we're protected."

"I understand the risks and difficulties. You'll just have to trust me to handle this the right way."

Reza heard his mother in the background. Maryam covered the receiver, so he couldn't hear exactly what was going on, but clearly they were arguing. Perhaps his mother sensed the risk in the plan? Maybe if he could talk with her, he could get her to agree to his perspective and influence Maryam to do the right thing?

His sister returned to the line. "She wants to speak to you."

Of course, he thought.

"I'm sorry we've become such a burden to you, Reza," his mother, Laleh, stuttered in a mix of Farsi and English. "I hate that you're borrowing money to help us. I told Maryam that we should just go back to Tehran. We had a modest but respectable life there, and we didn't need to burden you this way – "

He knew she couldn't go back. "Mother – "

"I can wait. We will eventually get a visa through normal channels."

"No. Please. Stop it," he insisted. "We're getting you both out of there, and we're bringing you to America. It's been too long already. I want to see and sit with you. The money is nothing."

"Thank you, my son. I'll leave my fate in your hands, and those of God. May the right thing come to pass."

He leapt from the couch, and searched through the bookshelf for a dog-eared volume of Rumi. It had been so, so long, and while his father was nothing but an abstract, distant memory, his mother was real. His mother's presence in his life, even at a great distance, had provided him with a secure foundation all those years he was alone. That he might actually see her again made all the risks worthwhile. He found the book: "But you are absent and I desolate – in my earthen abode. Either return home or I vacate my house, taking on the road!"

"What the hell are you talking about?"

Maryam had been back on the line. "Ah. It's you. Never mind. It was Rumi," Reza said.

"Where do you find the time for all this poetry anyway?"

He changed the subject. "When are you meeting with him?"

"We'll go there next week. Now that we have something to tell him, I'm certain we can get an audience. When will you be ready to transfer the money?"

"As soon as everything is arranged."

"You're sure you have it?"

"Of course I do. Well, I don't have it yet, but it's only a matter of time. It's on its way to me."

"Are you sure?"

"Of course. I wouldn't tell you to go and promise the money to an Afghan warlord if I wasn't sure I had the money."

He thought about it some more and then sat up, realizing for the first time the risks that they were all undertaking. "You'll just have to trust me too, Maryam."

It was now past eleven p.m., and far too late for the second call that he needed to make. So Reza turned and lay down on the couch, where he slept until the sun broke, at about six a.m. He showered, changed, and returned to Double H, walking perhaps even more quickly than he normally did. Before turning on his computer, before grabbing a cup of coffee, he made the second call, to Kling. In an ideal world, he would have called and discussed the matter with Clara, but that was clearly not an option.

"Good morning, Francois, I hope I'm not catching you too early."

"No, of course not," Kling replied as if slighted by the suggestion. "What can I do for you?"

"I want to let you know that I've given it a lot of thought, and, as flattered as I am by Mr. Gibran's confidence and generosity, I've decided to decline his offer and to stay with Double H." A brief silence lay heavy over the line.

"I'm sure you have your reasons, but I must say that I am surprised to hear it. Not many people are fortunate enough to be afforded an opportunity like the one that Mr. Gibran has offered you."

"I totally understand, and I know that to be true. It's just that I need to see my commitment to Double H all the way through. I'm sure you understand."

"Yes. I must say, though, that Mr. Gibran will be very sorry to hear this."

"Do you think I need to call him myself directly or will you pass all of this on?"

"I'll pass it on to him later this morning. He insists on hearing bad news quickly."

Kling seemed more jarred by the call than Reza had expected, and he hung up without saying goodbye. Would Gibran be so upset that he would seek to punish Reza, perhaps by revealing Reza's ethical violation to Burlington or, worse yet, to Jessica Blount? The professional repercussions of that could be catastrophic. That was simply a risk he'd have to take. In fact, Reza was even more sure now that he had made the right decision. The loan from Double H had allowed him to make it with a clear conscience.

The worst time to be in Washington, if one has to be in Washington, is during the summer months. The snowflake blossoms of the city's famous cherry trees have, by then, long since fallen, and the muggy, stifling humidity that once made this part of the world a swamp blankets the Potomac Basin. Reza returned from work early on a Friday afternoon in June to find Travis outside, with his head bent under the hood of the Benz. Two buckets filled with sponges and soapy water were positioned on either side of the front wheels.

"What's going on?" he asked.

Travis bolted up ramrod straight. He spoke fast: "What does it look like? I'm checking the fluid levels." He bent down again.

"Why?"

"Someone's coming to buy it," he cried out from under the hood.

"Really?"

He stood up again. "Yeah. This guy at the BP station told me that his friend has been looking for exactly this car, and that he'd be willing to pay fifty grand."

"It's not worth nearly that much."

He wiped his hands on his shirt. "I know. But if he pays me that much, I can pocket 30 or 35, and still buy another ride just like this. I might even buy you dinner at a burger joint of your choosing. Now grab a bucket."

The two of them washed the car – Reza on the passenger side, and Travis on the other. A film of dust built up along the edge of the thick, yellow sponge, and Reza wrung it out after almost every swipe. "Why would this guy's friend pay you so much for this heap anyway?"

"There's no heap here, man. This is a classic. Just scrub."

"I'm scrubbing."

By three, the car was as clean as it ever was. Reza went back into the house to change while Travis stood outside in the sun, admiring his work. The blue-green exterior glinted and, with its front wheels turned a hard right, the car appeared as if it would growl if approached. By the time Reza stepped back outside, the gas station attendant and his friend had arrived. Travis was expounding on the benefits of their prospective purchase.

"Really, it's been decades since anyone has made a car like this. The design is timeless. In fact, it's more a work of art than a car, it's an expression of one's ethos." Travis was on a roll, Reza thought. "But you gentlemen understand that, which is why you're here and not at the Ford dealership."

The two men turned to Reza. One held out his hand. "Ghulam."

The other followed. "Zarbakhat."

Reza greeted them. He wasn't sure but he thought he recognized the second man as the BP station employee. The first must be the friend and potential purchaser.

Travis looked at Reza but continued speaking to his guests. "Now I gotta be honest with you, I wasn't even planning to sell this beauty. But Zar Bucket here assures me that you are the kind of man who will truly appreciate and take care of her. That's the only reason I'm even willing to contemplate parting with her."

"Have it ever been in accident?" Zarbakhat asked. He was probably southeast Asian, Reza figured, tall, with a full head of black hair piled high on his head and friendly, chestnut brown eyes. His friend, Ghulam, was shorter and stockier, with curly ribbons of chest hair poking out of his V-neck t-shirt. His head was shaved, and he wore a gold stud in his left ear.

"Not since I've had her, and not before that either. My father was the original owner."

"No problem. I can inspect body myself."

Zarbakhat lay prone on the ground and peeked at the chassis underneath. Ghulam, too, went to work, checking the wear on each tire. Travis nodded his head. "Take your time, gentlemen, an educated consumer is a good consumer."

Zarbakhat stood back up and slapped the dust from his now dirty pants. "Who drives car? You ever drive?" He pointed with his chin toward Reza.

"Sometimes. Why?"

"I see you in the station sometimes."

Reza shrugged. "Maybe. Can't remember if I've driven it there before but it's possible."

The two prospective buyers stood and walked around the vehicle, continuing their inspection. They looked at the rubber window moldings and tapped with their knuckles around the doors, hood and trunk.

"Original paint?" Ghulam asked.

"Like the day it was born," Travis smiled proudly.

"Good. That's important. Do you normally keep in garage or outside?" Ghulam asked.

"Usually outside, in the driveway," Travis said.

"Can we take her for drive?"

"Of course, just leave me your license.» Travis pulled out and handed the keys to Ghulam.

Ghulam turned and handed the keys to Zarbakhat. "You drive since you're the expert." He then turned back to Travis. "Do you have bathroom I can use before we go?"

"Sure. There's one to the left, down the hall when you walk in," he pointed toward the front door.

Ghulam ambled into the house while Zarbakhat sat inside the car and started the eight-cylinder engine. It turned right away and then hummed into a steady purr. Zarbakhat tested the wipers, lights, radio and air conditioner.

Reza, recognizing that his services were no longer necessary, made his way back up to the house. He noticed, immediately upon entering, that the door leading to the bathroom that Ghulam had gone to was wide open. But there was no sign of Ghulam. Had he gotten lost in the house? "Hello," Reza cried out.

"There you are," Ghulam replied, as he turned into the hall from the living room area. "I lost my way." He smiled, walked past Reza, and sauntered back down to the driveway, as Reza wondered how he could possibly have gotten lost in a house like theirs.

About thirty minutes later, a dejected Travis made his way came back into the house. "They're not buying the car."

"Really? I thought they were loving it," Reza said, looking up from When Saturday Comes, a soccer magazine.

"I did too. But when they came back from their drive, they started complaining that she was pulling a bit to the right, that she might need new brake calipers, all this other bullshit. I'm telling you, something's not right in the state of Denmark."

"Did you just quote Hamlet?"

"Yah, why do you look surprised?"

"Huh. I guess I shouldn't be. So how did you leave things?" Reza asked, as he turned back to his article.

"They said," and then Travis imitated Zarbakhat's accent, "'Make sure, drive safe.'"

Later that night, in the midst of one of those anxious yet deep sleeps, Reza dreamt about cats and dogs. As he lay in his bed, several cats of different colors kept jumping up to swipe at him. One was a large cat, like a Maine Coon, with long, shaggy hair, and Reza, in the dream, struggled to push and bat it away. At the same time, an orange tabby and a few other black and white cats prowled around his bed, threatening him with loud growls and gurgling meows. Reza tried to scream for help, but his voice was completely gone. Suddenly, in the dream, his bedroom door burst open, and the most beautiful turquoise-colored dog bounded in. Like a friendly Labrador, albeit a blue one, it snuggled up to Reza in his dream-bed and smiled at Reza. Finally, he thought, now I'm safe! It was then that his cell phone rang. An international number that he didn't recognize.

"Hello?"

"Reza! It's me. We're at Rashid's compound and we're stuck here! I don't know what to do! Reza, *komak*!"

"What? Is that you, Maryam?"

"Yes, of course it's me."

He looked at his clock. "Do you know it's four in the morning here?"

"I know what time it is. Did you hear what I just said? We're stuck in Rashid's compound! We can't leave!"

Reza was now fully awake. *"Yavash tar,* Maryam. What do you mean you're stuck there?"

"We came to see Rashid, and all of a sudden he says there is fighting going on and we can't leave until it's more safe. I told him we don't care, and that we want to leave, but he says no, we absolutely can't go anywhere until it's safe!"

Reza sat up in the bed. "Start from the beginning. Tell me exactly what happened?"

"Mother and I called on Rashid this morning, like we had discussed. I told him that we would soon have the rest of the money, the four-hundred fifty thousand, and that we wanted to buy the green cards. He got a very grave look on his face, and said things have gotten more difficult with the Americans, that five hundred thousand is no longer enough to buy two green cards. He said it's a lot more expensive now."

"How much more expensive?"

"Five million."

Reza tore off the covers and jumped out of bed. "What? Five million? Are you kidding me? Who does this guy think we are?"

"I don't know Reza. I told him that we don't have that kind of money, and that you had worked so hard to come up with the five hundred thousand. He said that that was fine, but we should understand that he can only do this for us if we pay him five million by Wednesday, June 30th. After that, his contact in the U.S. military is being reassigned and the possibility of a deal is completely over."

It was the morning of Saturday, June 12th. "Okay, so why are you still there?"

"So mother and I start to pack our things to leave, and one of his men comes in, whispers something in his ear, and he says we can't leave now because there's a lot of fighting in the area. He says we have to stay as his guests until the fighting has died down."

"And how long is that going to take?"

"Who knows? He says that it's going to be the case until he notifies us otherwise. He says it could be days or weeks. We told him we don't care, and we want to leave now, whatever the risks, and he says that that's not possible. He says that he is responsible for our safety since we came to his house as guests, and we can't leave until he is able to assure our safety."

"Are you safe there? Are they mistreating you in any way?"

"No, thank God. They have actually given us very nice quarters, with Rashid's wives and kids, and they are being very respectful to us, but we just can't leave."

"And where is mother?"

"She is praying right now. She says we are fine and we should just be patient, that Rashid is an honorable man who is interested in our welfare and protection."

"This sounds more like extortion to me, not protection. I don't like the sound of it at all."

"I agree. In fact, at the very end of our meeting with him, Rashid said we should speak with you again to see if there is any way you can come up with the five million as soon as you can. He said there are sometimes obvious avenues open right under our noses that we don't notice until we're forced to look for them. It was like he was hinting at something but didn't want to say it explicitly. What is he talking about?"

"How should I know, Maryam, I've never even seen or spoken with the man."

"All I know is that we have eighteen days left to pay him."

After a lengthy pause, Reza finally broke the silence. "Are you sure you're safe?"

"Yes, but I just want to get out of here."

To America, somehow. "I don't blame you. Let me see what I can do."

They said goodbye, and Reza sat back on his bed, in a slight stupor. There was no sense in trying to go back to sleep. He now had to find a way to come up with five million dollars. Fast.

CHAPTER TWELVE

As unpalatable as it seemed, it was clear to Reza that his only real option was to go hat-in-hand to Gibran. There was no one else who could potentially deliver to Reza five million dollars. Of course, if he did do so, Gibran would own Reza, probably for the rest of Reza's professional career. And Reza would certainly be implicated in whatever money laundering and insider trading Gibran and his cronies had been up to. But at least he would be able to save his mother and sister, and bring them to safety in the U.S. That seemed a worthwhile trade to him.

For a brief moment, before that early morning call from Maryam, Reza thought that he had actually pulled it off. It all seemed plausible when Burlington, despite the odds, had come up with the loan. Reza was going to get the money he needed to bring his mother and sister over to the U.S., and he was going to become a partner at Double H. But then some warlord somewhere in the high desert of Asia somehow thwarted all of that. The tables were turned on him in an instant. Now he needed five million dollars, and there was only one place to get it, whatever the cost.

But before going through with the decision – which he knew would be irreversible – Reza needed a second opinion. And not just from anyone, but from someone who really knew and understood Reza, someone who would have only Reza's best interests at heart, and someone who knew how the world worked. The only person who fit those criteria was Travis.

"So let me get this right," Travis said, as he considered Reza's proposed plan of action, "you are going to throw away your career; you're going to borrow five million dollars from the man that you know to be a criminal, the man who tried to blackmail you into working with him? And you are going to use that money to pay off a warlord in Afghanistan against whom you have no recourse?"

"It does sound stupid when you say it like that."

"How would you say it better?"

Reza sighed. "I can't say it better. And as bad a move as this may be, I can't think of any better options right now."

Travis stood up from the couch in their dimly lit living room, walked to a window, and drew the curtains open. An avalanche of bright morning sunlight burst into the room, causing even the fibers of the worn carpeting to sparkle. Reza squinted to see him clearly, standing as he was in the center of this shimmering explosion of light. "There's a link you're not connecting."

"What's that?" Reza asked.

"Don't you think it's strange Rashid raised his price astronomically after you told Gibran you wouldn't work for him?"

"What does one have to do with the other?"

"Let's say Gibran suspects that you're on to his criminality. That's likely, no?"

Reza's heart skipped a beat. "I guess, yeah."

"So what would a smart man like him do in that position? Keep his enemies close. That's why Gibran offered you a job in the first place. Get it? He protects and insures himself by hiring you. You're never going to turn on him if you work for him. You with me?"

Reza looked up and shrugged. "Let's say I'm with you so far."

Travis paced across the room, in and out of the sunlight. "But then you surprise him by saying no. You won't work for him. So now he's exposed again."

"You're suggesting that Gibran convinced Rashid to raise his price to an incredible number, one that I couldn't possibly hit without his help? Maybe you've spent too much time with your crazy CIA friends."

"What part of this strikes you as wrong?"

"For one thing, we don't know that Rashid knows Gibran."

"Is it such a big leap to assume a man of Gibran's means could connect with Rashid if he wanted to?"

"Even if he did, how would Gibran know that my mother and sister are there, and that they're trying to get green cards...." As he trailed off, Reza realized that he himself had said more than enough to Gibran and to Clara to allow Gibran to make that connection.

Travis's eyes opened wide, as if in recognition that Reza finally got it. "Don't worry, I can help you with this. But I need some coffee first."

They changed and stepped out to Morning Joe, the gourmet coffee shop that had recently opened in Foggy Bottom to cater to Washington's affluent professional class. Reza ordered a skim cappuccino, and Travis, a large, triple-shot Americano. They then walked, in relative quiet, to the Washington Harbor. There were very few people, other than the occasional joggers, who came on Saturday mornings to the ornate boardwalk that lazily straddled the Potomac River. They found an empty bench that provided an unobstructed view of the Kennedy Center for the Performing Arts. The white bricks and gold columns of the hundred-foot high landmark glimmered in the bright sun.

"You need to start with this proposition," Travis said. "Neither Double H nor George Gibran is going to get you out of this mess, at least not without creating an even bigger mess."

"I know. One can't help me now and the other comes with too many strings attached." Reza looked up to the tree-line on the Virginia side of the river and observed a USAir jet approach the National Airport runway located nearby. "I guess I can call Mike Green again. Maybe someone at the Defense Department can get involved and help out. Maybe if we get the government behind it, and then maybe leak the story to the press, that will put pressure on Rashid."

Travis shook his head. "Bad play. That could back-fire and really put your mother and sister at risk. Who knows how a guy like Rashid would react to that kind of pressure, to a story in the *Washington Post*."

"I suppose you're right about that." Reza ran his hands through his matted hair.

"Plus, your mother and sister are not even American citizens. Why would the government get involved?"

Another plane, this one a Delta flight, followed the path taken by the USAir jet, toward National Airport. It really was a pretty place to spend the day, Reza thought, if only under better circumstances. "So the conclusion is what, besides the fact that I'm totally fucked?"

"Not yet you're not," Travis interjected as he shot up from the bench. "You still got two weeks."

"To do what, raise five million? I don't even have enough organs to sell."

"What about that four-fifty you're getting from Double H? When's that hitting your account?"

"Monday, why?"

"Simple, we take the four-fifty and turn it into five mil."

Reza couldn't see the humor in Travis's suggestion. "Right, an Atlantic City trip is a great idea right now."

"Who said anything about AC? Vegas, maybe."

"So what are you suggesting?"

Travis jammed his knuckles into his eye sockets and exhaled loudly. "Why does everyone make me spell everything out? We bet on a sure thing. That is how we turn the four-fifty into five mil. What sure thing do you know of, man? Please tell me you understand what I'm saying!"

Reza did in fact understand. And it was brilliant. It was illegal, it was unethical, and yet — it was spectacular. Reza and Travis both smiled, as Reza also rose from the bench.

"We piggy-back on Gibran's trades," Reza whispered to Travis.

"Exactly. No one gets hurt, and something good comes from his criminal enterprise. What could be better?"

"Gibran is always right, he always wins with his trades. We just have to follow his lead and bet big. Why didn't I think of that?"

"Because I'm smarter than you, and because you're too ethical. By the way, why are you whispering? There's no one around!"

"I don't know. I can't help it." Reza was still whispering.

"You have access to his accounts, right?"

"Yes, of course."

Travis looked at the calendar on his Blackberry. "Okay, there's twelve trading days between Monday and June 30th. That should give a brilliant lawyer like you more than enough time to turn four-fifty into five mil."

As his fear subsided, Reza's voice gained strength, and his analytical mind began to formulate a plan. "We're going to have to trade in multiple classes of securities and derivatives — stocks, options, swaps. We need to emulate his results, but our trading has to look different enough that no one will notice the correlation between our trading and his."

"Our trading, kemosabe?"

"Of course. You're doing this with me. I'll direct the trading, but you execute it. I can't do this by myself. Plus, it's a helpful layer of separation if the trading is done under your name rather than mine. And, besides, if we do this right, I'll get my mother and sister out of Afghanistan and you'll still have enough money left to buy that bar in St. Maarten. What was it, Le Coloniale?"

Travis nodded his head. "Okay, now you're talking."

"I'll start finding a CDS or two that correlate with the stocks he tends to trade."

"The what? CDS?"

Another plane roared in, and so Reza was forced to shout: "Credit default swaps. They're like insurance contracts that someone enters into to protect against the possibility of a bond going into default. But the swap is it's own freestanding instrument, and the value of the swap is inversely correlated with the underlying bond it's tied to."

"What does that have to do with the stocks that Gibran's trading?"

"Easy. Say Gibran has figured out that IBM is doing poorly and the price of IBM stock is going to go down. Well that means that IBM bonds will also do worse, and the price of swaps tied to IBM bonds are going to go up. Get it?"

"I think so," Travis said. "But I don't really need to get it. You be in charge of that part of the plan."

"Agreed. You just get down to First Metro and make sure you're authorized to trade the full range of securities and derivatives online come Tuesday. You're going to be busy."

"Yes, boss." Travis saluted him.

Reza rubbed his eyes. "The only other part of this that I have to figure out is how you and I can communicate safely about the trading, in a way that can't be detected or traced."

"Well, that's my area. The only way to do that is to go low tech. No phones, email, or text messages of any kind. It's not always efficient, but that's how we make sure we're never compromised."

Reza thought for a moment and then rose from the bench. "We probably need someone else, someone we can trust, who can be runner."

Travis smirked. "Problem is we only trust each other."

Reza looked into his eyes. "Vargas. He works in our mailroom. He's a reliable guy, he owes me, and he'd make a great messenger.

"I don't know, man, is it safe to bring him into all this?"

"No, no, I'm not talking about bringing him into all this. He's just going to help us pass messages. He doesn't need to know what he's passing along or why. And if he's paid for his efforts, he'll be more than happy to assist."

Travis chuckled. "I think you're going to make a great criminal."

He was right — Reza was about to become a criminal. However he analyzed it, that conclusion was inevitable. But he really had no other choice – it was for a noble and selfless cause, one that he had promised to fulfill since he was a boy. It's a narrow boundary into the world of criminality, he now realized, one that's easily crossed, depending on need, circumstance and the ability to self-deceive. If he ever had another chance to represent a white-collar criminal, he'd have a lot more sympathy and understanding. "I think I now know how Robin Hood felt."

"Tally-ho, motherfuckers," Travis yelled into the open sky.

CHAPTER THIRTEEN

Tareek Abdul-Majeed gently pushed his cart off the service elevator and into the modern, executive offices housed on the 41st floor of the World Tower in London's Canary Wharf. The elderly, Pakistani janitor was not surprised to find that everyone else appeared to have already left for the weekend. He looked at his gold-plated Timex watch and thought to himself that he too could leave by about 8:30 p.m. if he used his time efficiently. There were a total of twenty-seven offices on the floor, and he had long ago calculated that it would take him an average of about one minute to clean each office. *Insha-allah*, he thought, he would be back at his home in Finsbury Park in time to enjoy a lamb supper with his sons.

His routine in each office was similar. First, he would empty the two trash cans in each office — a blue, plastic one for paper that could be recycled, and a silver tin one for all other trash — into the two large bins that formed the bulk of his cart. Next, he would wipe the empty surfaces in each office. And finally, he would look for and move to the kitchen any dirty plates or cups that had been left behind. It always surprised him, particularly given the importance that he gave to cleanliness, the mess that the owners of these offices created and then ignored. Half-eaten sandwiches and coffee-stained mugs were the most common and least offensive examples. "Animals," Tareek muttered as he shuffled into the first office. At least he no longer had the task of vacuuming these offices late into the morning hours. That was reserved for the less reliable and experienced members of the janitorial staff – usually, as he would sometimes confide to his fellow, veteran cleaners, the lazy Africans.

Indeed, by 8:28 p.m., Tareek had completed his tasks and was prepared to leave the 41st floor. Before walking out of the last office assigned to him, he glanced thoughtfully at the silver framed photograph that sat on the desk, beside the keyboard. It was picture of an apparently happy family of four. A smiling and proud father, a beaming mother and two playful little girls – both with curly blonde hair that resembled their mother's. Did they have any clue, Tareek wondered, what atrocities their government perpetrated in their names throughout the globe? Did they care how many Iraqi and Palestinian children were being slaughtered at that very moment by their troops? Of course not. All they cared about was the materialistic cocoon in which they had ensconced themselves here in London – their cars, their clothes, and their lavish meals. Soon enough, Tareek thought, they would learn the errors of their ways. They would learn that the happiness that they had achieved was an illusion. It was only a matter of time.

Moments later, Tareek was back on the elevator with his cart, now full of trash, heading down to level G3. He glanced at the bin that contained the recyclable paper and noted that it was full. Weeks earlier, he would have found that to be a daunting sight. But now, after all his experience and training, he was not at all worried. He knew precisely what needed to be done, and how it needed to be done. He gazed again at his watch and observed that it was exactly 8:30 p.m. Absent any glitches, he would soon be in the tube, heading home.

Once on G3, Tareek headed down the long and brightly lit hallway that led to the trash dumpsters. As he walked, he could hear the voices and laughter of other members of the janitorial staff from the locker room located at the opposite end of the hallway. That, too, may have once concerned him, but not so now. About two-thirds of the way down the hallway, Tareek stopped his cart in front of a single-stall bathroom. He turned the knob and confirmed that the bathroom was unoccupied, as it almost always was at this time of night. He glanced around, removed the recycling bin from his cart, and walked with it into the small room.

Inside, after the door latched closed, Tareek performed the same tasks, in the same sequence, that he did every night. First he locked the door. Then he placed the bin on the floor and removed the light blue overalls that constituted his uniform. Underneath the overalls, he wore a faded brown blazer, which his wife Amina had carefully sewn for him. It was the same brown blazer that he wore to and from work every night. In fact, Tareek's co-workers often made fun of the fact that he never removed the jacket, regardless of the summer weather and the increasingly haggard condition of the fabric. One day, they had jokingly offered to pool their funds to buy him a new one. Tareek had laughed and played along — they would never find another jacket equally nice he had replied.

Next, Tareek removed the blazer and reached inside the lapel for the two small buttons that Amina had sewn into the lining. It had become harder and harder for him to open and close the buttons as his eyesight weakened — he would soon need Amina to replace them with bigger buttons. Once he opened them, Tareek was able to reach into the space that existed between the outer fabric and the lining of the jacket. It was into this space that he proceeded to insert ten documents from the recycling bin that he had brought with him.

At first, after receiving his mission from Sheik Ahmed, Tareek had spent a great deal of time trying to identify and remove the most important papers in the bin. Over the months, however, he learned that he was very unlikely to know which papers were or were not important. And that made taking the extra time to try to identify the important papers an unnecessary risk. So now, he just selected ten to twelve pages at random, driven only by the desire to select paper that had not been torn or crumpled. He figured out quickly that torn papers were less informative to the reader, and crumpled papers were more likely to change the form of his jacket when they were placed inside the lining.

Minutes later, Tareek exited the bathroom looking as he had when he'd entered it. He casually placed the recycling bin back in his cart and resumed his trek toward the dumpsters. The hallway was still empty. The only sounds that could now be heard were the squeaking wheels of Tareek's cart and the dragging of his canvas sandals across the linoleum floor.

At his locker, Tareek changed his shoes and packed away his personal supplies, ready for the next day. He said his goodbyes to the few fellow janitors that remained and made his way out onto the street and into the Canary Wharf Underground. He rode west on the Jubilee Line to Green Park, where he transferred to the northbound Victoria Line before exiting at Finsbury Park. Out onto Wells Terrace, it was but a ten-minute walk to his small home. Tareek enjoyed the time alone, especially in the summer, away from his job, strolling past the silo-like minaret of the Finsbury Park mosque, and finally to his broken street with brown row houses, each one the same as all the others on the block. His was the last on the street, and unlike the others, to his pride, it had a green roof. He opened the gate to his box of a tidy lawn and then stepped inside his front door. Here, he was king, and the aroma of dinner greeted him.

It was close to 9:30 at night, but Tareek's family, of course, had waited for him before eating. Amina whisked to the dining room table large platters of lamb and long grain rice. His three sons sat quietly, awaiting their father's prayer: "*Allahomma barik lana fima razaqtana waqina athaban-nar. Bismillah.*"

Then they tore into their food. It was a Friday, the night all his papers for the week would be picked up, so Tareek, too, ate quickly. Then he retired to his bedroom, opened a small safe in his closet and set forth on his bed everything he had gathered that week. He unbuttoned, again with some difficulty, the interior pocket of his worn jacket and added today's batch to the pile. Aasim, the messenger – the next level in Sheik Ahmed's operation – would arrive soon. Tareek, as always, would invite him in and ask him to stay for tea, and perhaps a smoke, but Aasim would beg off, citing all the other many addresses at which he still had to stop. Maybe one day Tareek would be last on the list, and Aasim could accept his hospitality. They had known each other for eight months now, and despite the lack of time together Tareek had great admiration for him. Every other week, of course, Aasim would also drop off Tareek's payment. Tonight was also that night. Perhaps that's why Amina prepared a particularly sumptuous meal.

A Ford Fiesta pulled up and stopped in front of Tareek's home. Tareek, who had been waiting at the front window, was surprised. Aasim always drove a Peugot. A figure soon emerged from the car, seemed to squint at the address above Tareek's door and made his way past the gate. Tareek opened the door without waiting for the man to buzz: this man was not Aasim.

"*Salam Alekum!*" the man said, in an accent Tareek determined was more South London than Cockney.

"*Alekum-Salam,*" Tareek replied, welcoming him into his home and sizing him up as either Egyptian or Palestinian. "Where is Aasim?"

The man looked down toward the ground. "I've replaced him."

Tareek stifled a harrumph. "I would think the sheik would have mentioned that to me."

The man mumbled, looking distracted. "The sheik is so very busy, I apologize for any confusion. My name is Masum."

Innocent, infallible.

"It seems irregular," Tareek said. "Maybe I should call the sheik."

"Please," Masum said, "go right ahead, but he is, as you know, very busy."

Tareek hesitated. He would hate to bother the sheik with his own stupid fears. Clearly, Masum knew where he was and what he was here for.

Tareek led the man to a desk, just by the front window, and handed him a yellow envelope containing all of documents he had gathered that week. "You will stay for some tea?"

"Thank you so much for your kindness and your hospitality. Unfortunately, I have so many more errands to run that, with deepest regrets, I must decline."

Same as Aasim, Tareek thought, smiling. "And when you are greeted with a greeting, greet with a better greeting than it or return it."

"Surely Allah takes account of all things."

Tareek was pleased – the famous couplet was among his favorite passages from the Qur'an.

Masum gathered the papers and swiftly made his way toward the door. Then he turned to shake Tareek's hand. Tareek, seeming to have something more to say, did not let go. "A good word is like a good tree whose root is firmly fixed and whose top is in the sky."

Masum seemed to search for the right thing to say. "I was told you are a profound learner of the noble Qur'an. The verses you quote are among my favorites, and this last one even wiser than the first. As the Prophet said, 'the ink of a scholar and the blood of a martyr are of equal value in heaven.'"

Tareek accepted a white envelope, containing his cash payment, or contribution, as Sheik Ahmed would call it. Still, he gripped Masum's hand. "Amina, bring me the pastries from the kitchen counter! You must accept a small gift from me, an expression of our new friendship."

The man stammered. "I really must go."

Amina, smiling, as always, came to her husband's side and handed him a paper bag. "I insist, these are from Mehbobi."

Masum eyed the bag. "I do very much love that place."

"Take it, take it!" Tareek pushed the bag into Masum's hands and watched as he started his Ford Fiesta and pulled away.

"Tareek, the pastries are from Mahal," Amina said.

"I know."

"Why did you tell him Mehbobi? I never go there. Everyone knows they're not *halal*."

Tareek didn't answer her. Instead, he returned to his bedroom, picked up the phone and placed a call to Sheik Ahmed.

CHAPTER FOURTEEN

On the morning of Monday, June 14th, Reza sat still behind a highly polished, mahogany conference table at Double H, trying his very best not to stare at the plain white envelope in front of John Burlington. The partner's large and veiny hands framed the envelope, and one of them shook just a little bit. Reza focused instead on Burlington's familiar and lined face. Every muscle in Reza's his body was taut, as if he were a gun about to fire. Burlington apparently felt that the moment demanded a speech of sorts, because he droned on and on and on. What could Reza do? The man was about to hand over four hundred and fifty thousand dollars to him. The least he could do was listen.

"Back when I joined the firm in 1974, there were four of us, and I was paid a princely sum of twenty thousand dollars a year. And believe me, that was plenty for a young, single guy. I had a terrific little apartment in a townhouse near Dupont Circle. What a time that was! Even Henderson was a young man! We were constantly up on the Hill, Watergate and all of that coming down, it was a very heady time. Little did I think how we'd grow. More than five hundred associates now, Reza, it's quite an operation to manage."

"I can only imagine, John."

"I hope you can. I have big plans for you, Reza, and I think you know that. Even putting aside my great personal affection for you, which is genuine and deep. You've always been a talented lawyer and a terrifically hard worker, and your partnership here is inevitable as far as I'm concerned. And we're going to get it done this year. I don't think the management committee would've approved this loan if they weren't prepared to support your partnership consideration."

Reza couldn't help but wonder what speech he would be receiving from Burlington around this same time if he had not brought in the Gibran account months earlier. Would John still think his partnership to be inevitable? "Thank you for those kind words."

"I mean what I say, Reza."

Reza watched Burlington smooth the surface of the envelope with the side of his hand. It was almost as if he were loathe to let it go.

"This is a lot of money, and it represents our belief in you. Clearly, it will have to be paid back, and I think you'll need to come forward with a payment schedule that's reasonable, one that makes sense for both you and the firm."

"Of course."

"We'll also have to charge some interest on the loan – obviously we'd be making money on this money if you weren't spending it. Something like prime, or prime plus one. How about four percent per annum?"

"That's fair."

"It'll be compounded, of course. The accounting department will be in touch with you about all this, so come up with a payment plan and have something ready to submit to them."

"I certainly will," he said sincerely.

"A partnership is largely based on trust and personal commitment. We trust you, and we are committed to you. We hope and expect that that sentiment is mutual. That's why no one is asking you to sign a contract of any sort."

"I do understand and appreciate that."

"And you can only imagine," Burlington chuckled, "how hard it is for Double H lawyers to hand over money without a lengthy written contract."

Reza forced himself to laugh along with Burlington. Inside, however, he felt desperate to get his hands on the envelope. It was now 11:20 a.m. – only five hours left until the market closed for the day, and of course the check would still have to clear. "It's a testament to you, John, that you were able to arrange this, and to pull it off in such short order."

"Very well, then. On behalf of the firm, I'm extending to you this loan for four hundred and fifty dollars, to be used exclusively toward helping you secure your mother's and sister's freedom. The term of repayment is four years at a four percent interest rate, compounded quarterly."

"Four hundred fifty thousand, you mean."

"Yes, of course," Burlington laughed loudly. "We wouldn't be here wasting each other's time over four hundred and fifty dollars, would we?"

"No, I don't think our hourly rates would support that."

"Certainly not." And with that, Burlington handed Reza the envelope. Then he rose, exited the conference room, and left Reza there with the check in his hands. After a couple of minutes, Reza also stood, slipped out of the conference room and made his way downstairs and out of the building. Travis was waiting for him, as promised, on the sidewalk immediately in front. He looked relaxed, leaning against a lamppost and basking in the hot, summer sun.

"Hey man," Reza chimed as casually as he could, "how're you doing?"

"All good, brother," Travis replied breezily as he separated himself from the lamppost.

Reza placed his hand into Travis', and they shook briefly. When Reza withdrew his hand, a folded check was left in Travis's palm. Travis smiled, nodded and slid the check into his front pants pocket. "Always nice to see you, pal," he said, turning and walking away. "I gotta run now and see a man about a thing."

Reza quickly made his way back into the building. There was lot of work to be done and time was limited. As he approached the elevator, he noticed Abdullah watching him, with the same grave expression that was always on his face. "Back already, sir?"

"Yes, I am," Reza replied, trying hard not to stare at the large mole. "Too hot out there for me." Did Abdullah keep such close tabs on the comings and goings of all the buildings residents?

Back in his office, Reza began to survey Gibran's trades over the previous days, both those that had settled and those that had been executed but not yet settled. There was nothing nefarious about that – Reza often tracked GAM's trades, or asked one of his associates to do it. In fact, Reza made sure to leave his office door open while he worked, to avoid the impression that he had anything to hide. Fairly quickly, Reza identified three companies whose stock Gibran appeared to be accumulating. Reza then wrote the names of the companies in pencil, on a small yellow post-it. Next to each company's name, he wrote a short, cryptic instruction: "ChemTechno, buy stock and call options, sell put options; AMP, buy stock and sell CDS; Veloce, buy stock and sell put options." Reza then closed the screen he had been studying, and he turned his attention to other, unrelated client matters. It was hard, but important that he at least maintain the appearance of productivity during the day.

At a little before one p.m., Vargas abruptly entered Reza's office. "What's up, bro? Am I interrupting?" Vargas bobbed and weaved, like a boxer in a ring.

"Not at all." Reza stood, walked around his desk, and extended his hand. He and Vargas shook hands briefly, and when Reza pulled his hand away, only the small yellow post-it remained in Vargas's possession.

"Your cousin feeling any better?"

Vargas stared quietly and uncomfortably at Reza for a moment before placing the yellow post-it in his pocket. "My cousin? Yah, he's doing much better, thanks for askin'. I think he'll be home from the hospital real soon."

"Good. Glad to hear it. Be sure to give him my regards."

"Will do."

"Okay then," Reza said as he pointed with his thumb back to his computer. "I better get back to work."

"Yah, and I gotta run, take care of a few things." Vargas had started to exit Reza's office before he completed that sentence, and he was well down the hallway before Reza had made his way back around his desk to his computer. Occasionally during the afternoon, he checked on the three stocks to ensure that they were all performing as well as expected – they were, and each stock was up substantially by the time the markets closed at 4:00 p.m. A little after five p.m., Reza turned off his computer and prepared to leave to meet Travis by the Washington Harbor. He had just finished packing his briefcase when Jane poked her head in from the hallway.

"Hey handsome. You working a half day today?" She smiled and peered at Reza from above her reading glasses.

"Not at all," Reza replied somewhat nervously. "I'm taking some files home. I decided it was time for a change of venue. What are you doing, slumming around these parts anyway?"

"Oh, I just like to keep tabs on you, that's all." She chuckled and walked away. Was that a joke? Was she — was Burlington — on to him?

About thirty minutes later, Reza found Travis at an outdoor table at Sequoia's Restaurant. It was still warm and bright out, and Travis, judging from the number of bottles on the table, appeared to be on his fourth beer. The restaurant was marginally crowded, but it was not yet overflowing with the happy hour crowd that would invariably invade its grounds by six p.m.

"You better slow down, cowboy, I need you sober," Reza said as he sat at Travis's table.

"Don't worry about me, I can handle my alcohol."

Reza knew that he could. "How did the day go?"

"Exactly as planned."

"No glitches?" Reza hoped that he sounded less anxious than he felt.

"Nah, man, none at all. I created all the positions you wanted, and you can check them over when we get home. The only unexpected event was that your man Vargas almost threw up when he ate the post-it. I can't believe you made him do that!"

"It's a good precaution. Plus, I wrote in pencil so it's all organic," Reza smiled.

"You're a sick bastard. But I like it." Travis raised his bottle as if to toast Reza before taking a large sip. "Now go get yourself a beer so I don't have to drink alone." Reza walked to the large rectangular bar at the center of the patio and purchased two beers so he could try and catch up with Travis. When he returned, Travis seemed more fidgety and less comfortable. He was holding a pen, and he had clearly been doodling while Reza was gone — Reza could see etched on the tablecloth the image of Travis' typical cartoon boy driving what looked like an old Aston Martin. He also had a large envelope on the table in front of him, one that wasn't there when Reza left moments earlier.

"What's this?"

"This, my friend, is a few of my most important papers. I want you to hang on to them for me, just in case."

"Just in case what?"

"Just in case. Period." Travis sat up straight in his chair and looked around before leaning in closer to Reza. "You're playing in the major leagues now," he whispered. "We're dealing with bad people, and big stakes. Things can happen. Things that no one can anticipate. All I'm asking is that you take this file and hang on to it — but not at home, somewhere else, like at your office. If for any reason something bad or unexpected were to happen, then I want you to have what's inside. If everything goes down like we planned, then you just return that to me unopened."

"What exactly is in it?"

"Nothing you need to know about unless things go south. Cool?"

"Yeah, cool," Reza replied stoically. "But you're overreacting."

"Maybe I am. And maybe I'm not. We'll see. In the meantime, cheers." Travis lifted his bottle and swallowed the remainder of his beer in one very large gulp.

"Cheers to you, too," Reza replied as he finished off the entire Heineken with the biggest sip of his life.

George Gibran listened politely to Sheik Ahmed's exhortations but declined his invitation to immediately make a trip to Jeddah. "Surely, Ahmed, it can wait. I'm up to my neck in business here in Washington."

"It's important we speak. If you can't come now, I'm sending someone to see you."

"Who?"

"I have people where you are."

"You're a many-tentacled spider, my sheik."

"As soon as I knew you were serious about this American adventure I called a few friends."

"Rather hospitable of you."

"It's very serious. You will see that my concerns were not unfounded after all. And, there's an issue in London as well. I'm not sure if they're connected. But I'd rather not get into all of this by telephone."

"Of course. That is never an ideal venue. Who would you like me to meet?"

"A reliable friend. His name is Zarbakhat Haq. He can be there within the hour."

Gibran hung up the phone. "Clara, darling," he said with customary aplomb, "I'm about to have a guest, an unexpected one. Perhaps it's best now for you to be on your way?"

She emerged from the bathroom and breezed past him, her scent lingering in her wake. She placed a few folders in her case and stood before him. "Of course."

He wrapped an arm around and tried to pull her into a kiss, but she smiled and wriggled away before slipping out of the hotel suite.

Some thirty minutes later, Gibran received a call from the lobby desk. A man wearing a filthy, green overall, covered with oil and grease, appeared at his room. Gibran let him in but did not offer his hand. Haq stood in the foyer and proceeded to tell Gibran everything that Ahmed had instructed him to say: their concerns about Reza Shirvani's motives, something about piggyback trading on GAM trades, and the strange appearance in London of a man named Masum who had since disappeared with a week's worth of janitor files.

"Where do you work, Zarbakhat?" Gibran asked, looking down his nose at a man to whom he had not yet offered a seat.

"British Petroleum."

"I presume not at the St. James Square offices?"

Haq stared at him, indecisive. "No, H Street."

"Indeed. And where exactly did you get all of this information?"

"Sheik Ahmed received phone call from a man named Tareek, who was suspicious about the man named Masum who picked up his papers last Friday evening. The man named Tareek thought that the man named Masum wasn't actually Muslim."

As if that were the litmus test for reliability. "How so?"

"Something about pastries that aren't *halal*."

Gibran puffed out his cheeks. "Please tell me your anxiety is fueled by more than *baklava*, my good man! What's all this nonsense about Shirvani?"

"We follow him for weeks."

"We?"

Haq shifted his feet, as if he wanted to sit down. "There are several of us, working for Sheik Ahmed."

"Charming."

"We install devices in his house, to listen. Nanobots."

"I'm familiar with the technology."

"We listen to many of his conversations, with his roommate."

"And?"

"He and his roommate are trying to copy GAM trades. We can't be sure, but we think a third person is also involved. He's American. He curses a lot. They seem to be racing to raise money for something, but we don't know what."

"His mother," Gibran muttered.

"Excuse me?"

"I said motherfucker."

"Yes."

Gibran poured himself spring water out of a purple bottle and into a glass. "Anything else?"

Haq put his hand on the back of a dining room chair but removed it immediately after Gibran, with a look of disapproval, turned toward him. "Nothing, really. Only that they are very bad people, non-believers who live unclean lives."

Gibran walked up close to Haq's face and stood there, nose to nose. "You work for Sheik Ahmed, and Sheik Ahmed works for me. Therefore, you will do what I say, do you understand?"

"I am here to serve you in any way that I can."

He gripped the man's strong arm, hard. "Listen carefully to me, then. I want you to give Reza Shirvani the scare of his life. I don't want him hurt, yet, but I want him to be very frightened. Do you think you can manage that?"

Zarbarkhat grinned. "Yes, yes. I manage. With happiness."

The janitor operation came to an immediate halt. Tareek and his peers stopped pilfering documents, and no one came to their homes on the following Friday night to collect. GAM's trades, too, conspicuously slowed down. Reza noticed the changes in trading, but it didn't concern him. There was enough trading happening in the accounts that he could still decipher meaningful trends. And if there were fewer trading opportunities, then Reza and Travis would just have to increase the size of their bets when the opportunities did present themselves. Within a week they already had managed to generate over two million dollars in trading profits, so he felt comfortable pressing down on the gas a bit. ChemTechno seemed like the perfect opportunity.

GAM had been building a position in ChemTechno for weeks. And it was clear to Reza, that it was a likely takeover target. GAM's interest in the stock confirmed for Reza the rumors that were milling about in the marketplace. ChemTechno was likely to be bought by one of its larger competitors soon, and its price would likely rise by twenty to thirty percent immediately upon the announcement of the acquisition. For a couple of days, Reza had been instructing Travis to buy ChemTechno stock, to sell put options on the company, in anticipation of a price hike. Reza knew in his gut that it was time to bet big. He pulled out the pad of post-its that sat in his top desk drawer and scrawled in pencil, "Chem-Techno – sell as many puts as you can. Go all out." He then placed the post-it note in his pocket and looked at his watch. It was 9:25 a.m., on Monday, June 28th, and he would have to focus on client work until Vargas came by. It was useful that business started to slow down as July and August approached, and many of the partners, like Burlington, would be away with their families on summer holidays.

About ten minutes had passed when Vargas came careening into Reza's office. Once inside, he straightened up his frame and worked hard to catch his breath. "Sorry I'm a minute or two late, man, I had to deliver some paper to the copy room, and the elevator took forever!"

"No worries, Gil. I'm glad you were able to stop by. I just wanted to know how things are going at home. With your cousin." Reza flashed his palms skyward, opened mouth wide, and raised his brows in a stunned expression, as if to say "what the fuck?" Reza had reminded Vargas countless times to maintain an air of normalcy and casualness around their interactions.

"Yeah, right, man. Things are good." Vargas adjusted his tone. "It's real nice that you're keepin' up with me, I mean with my cousin, like this."

"No problem," Reza continued in a relaxed tone. "Don't forget to let me know if I can be of any help." Reza held out his hand.

"Will do," Vargas said, as he shook Reza's hand and took possession of the folded post-it note. Vargas then turned and sauntered out, and Reza returned to his desk and his legal work.

Several hours later, shortly after two p.m., Reza broke from his research to check the news. To his pleasant surprise, the leading business news story was that ChemTechno's largest competitor, Argo Industries, had launched a hostile takeover bid for ChemTechno's outstanding shares. To Reza's even greater surprise, Argo was offering ChemTechno's shareholders a thirty-five percent premium over the price at which ChemTechno's shares had closed the previous day. This was a windfall that even Reza had not imagined. "Unbelievable," he muttered under his breath. "You are very good, Mr. Gibran, very good indeed."

Reza calculated that based on the stock and options trades that Travis had carried out over the previous days, they likely had made close to 2.3 million dollars. If Travis had been able to act on his note today and to sell a meaningful number of puts before the deal was announced, then they would certainly be sitting on profits of millions more. He might already have made all the money he needed with two days left to spare. Reza decided that he had to speak with Travis directly and quickly, and he could not wait to pass another note through Vargas. He stood up, walked out of the office, and called Travis on his cell phone.

"Hey, it's me."

"I thought you weren't supposed to be calling me, remember?"

"We may be done. Did you get my note about the ChemTechno puts? Please tell me you went big!" Reza closed his eyes and pressed his palm against his forehead as he awaited Travis's reply.

"Of course I did. I know how to do my part."

"Oh my God! Thank you! How big did you go? What were the unrealized profits on the puts?"

"Just shy of three mil."

Reza's eyes grew wide and he almost jumped off the ground with joy. Two tourists walking beside him on the sidewalk, an elderly German couple Reza thought, frowned and shook their heads. Reza apologized for having almost bumped them and returned to the phone. "What's the account value now?"

"You ready?"

"Yes, I'm ready, please, come on, what is it?"

"You promise you won't wet yourself?"

"Please, Travis," Reza yelled, "stop fucking with me. What is it?"

"Say pretty please."

"Pretty motherfucking please with sugar on top!"

"Account value reads 5,995,443," Travis said.

Reza couldn't believe that they had actually pulled it off. Not that he doubted it, but it's one thing to imagine and plan a scheme like this, but quite another to actually realize it. They sat on the phone in silence, before Reza finally spoke. "Cash out. We're done. Get out of every position and settle the trades as quickly as possible."

"Yes sir, captain."

"Travis, we really did it."

"Like taking candy from a baby."

Travis sat at his computer, closed and liquidated all of the positions and instructed that they be settled as fast as possible. He then walked out of the house and made his way to the Benz, which was parked out on the street. He dropped a large duffel bag in the back seat and slipped into the driver's side to turn the key in the ignition. A few moments later the bomb, which had been placed under the car, exploded. Large chunks of asphalt rained down over the road and surrounding homes. Trees lit up like enormous torches. The house adjacent to where the car was parked was on fire. Dogs howled, and car alarms went off throughout the neighborhood.

Nothing was left of the Mercedes Benz collectible but a crater and a twisted carcass of superheated black steel.

CHAPTER FIFTEEN

The first sounds Reza heard, from high up in his office, were the sirens – fire engines, police cars, ambulances – all heading in the same direction. Then Katie, the junior associate in the next office, appeared in his doorway. "Did you hear? A huge explosion on H Street. Don't you live there?"

Reza turned to the NBC Washington website. The shots from a news helicopter, streaming live, were focused on a smoking, mangled wreck in a hole that practically blew away the entire street pavement. It was in front of his house, on the other side of the street, cordoned off with yellow tape. He kicked his chair back, turned off his computer, pushed Katie aside and ran out of the building.

The collection of emergency vehicles started more than four blocks away. Reza fought past the chaos of firemen, policemen, neighbors and bystanders until he was steps from his own home. He peered into the gigantic hollow in the street: a melted but still evident three-pointed star crowned the otherwise twisted steel, poking up above the smoking lip of the void. It was the Mercedes Benz logo.

"Oh God! Travis!"

Reza approached an officer keeping the bystanders away and told him that he lived in the nearest home. And that he thinks he knows the owner of the car.

The officer guided him to a large police department van, more like an

RV, which served as a sort of command center. There he was interviewed by several officers in an attempt to understand what had just occurred.

"Was there anyone targeting Mr. Meadows that you were aware of?" asked one officer, a large, African-American sergeant named Blaine.

"No. Why? What happened?"

"Did you ever drive this car?"

"Yes, once in a while."

"Is there anyone who would want to hurt you?"

Reza stopped breathing for a moment. "No, of course not. Why are you asking?"

"This was a very powerful car bomb. Same kind of thing the military sees in Iraq."

"Oh my God."

"It went off when he turned the ignition."

Reza started to panic. "So he was in the car?"

"It seems that way. Our forensic guys have found personal effects near the vehicle. We're also observing human remains, but we've not yet been able to identify them, given the heat and the extent of damage. Whoever and whatever was in there was burned to a crisp. I'm very sorry."

Reza started to cry. "No, no."

"Did you and Mr. Meadows get along?"

"What? Of course we did! He was my best friend in the world!"

"What sort of name is Shirvani?"

Really? That was relevant now? "Persian. Why are you asking?"

Blaine hitched up his pants. "Just asking. I'm a curious guy."

"I can't believe this is happening." Reza buried his face in his hands and tried to stifle his sobs.

"I'm very sorry, sir. Would you like us to get you a doctor?"

"No. I'm fine," Reza replied as he wiped his face with his sleeve. "I just need some time to digest this."

"Of course. That's very natural. In the meantime, we're going to be

conducting a homicide investigation. When you're ready, we'd appreciate it if you could provide us with access to your home. We need to inspect Mr. Meadows's belongings and personal effects. We can certainly
let ourselves in, but we'd prefer not to do that if we have an alternative."

"Yes, naturally. I can let you in. Let's go now."

"You sure you're up to it now?"

"I'll be fine."

What choice did Reza really have? He had to let them in, and he'd
have to explain why Travis had five computers in his room. Not to mention the guns. Eventually, they may very well find evidence of the trading operation that he and Travis were running. But it didn't really matter at this point. They'd eventually get a warrant and search the place
anyway. Reza figured he'd committed enough criminal acts today – no
sense adding interference with a homicide investigation to the list.

The front door was locked when they reached it. Accompanied by
four police officers and after clearance from a bomb squad, Reza, with
hands shaking, put the key in the door. He took a deep breath and entered. The place, apparently, had been ransacked. Most of the furniture
in the house had been turned over. In Travis' room, the clothes that had
been hanging in the closet were now on the floor, in an unruly pile in
the middle of the room. Travis's computers had vanished completely.
And the safe in his closet was wide open and empty. In fact, all that remained in his bedroom was the bed, the blankets and a heap of clothes.

"What a mess," Blaine said.

"Someone's been here," Reza added.

"No shit. We're gonna have to dust this place and go over everything
with a fine-tooth comb." He turned to his men. "Guys, let's get foren-
sics in here and start going through every inch of this place."

"Am I allowed to stay here?"

"Afraid not, Mr. Shavani."

"It's Shirvani."

"That's what I said. Isn't it?"

"It doesn't matter. Where do I go?"

"Do you have friends you can stay with? Maybe a hotel? Figure we'll be in here for about two days. You can plan to come back on Wednesday. If that's all right."

"I'll figure something out. Can I get my stuff from my room?"

"Sure. Though one of my guys will have to inspect and inventory what you take. I'll also need to take a fuller statement from you when you're feeling up to it. Here's my card in the meantime."

Reza took the card and made his way to his room, still unable to comprehend that Travis was gone. He grabbed some clothes, toiletries and his hidden envelope of ten thousand dollars in cash – remarkably, still there – and dropped them into his overnight bag. Another officer examined and slowly inventoried all that Reza packed. "I'm real sorry for your loss," he said mechanically as Reza left the room. Dozens of people, gathered around the house, gawked at him as he made his way down the steps and back out to the street. He returned to the only other place he would feel comfortable – his office at Double H. It would more than do for two days.

By Wednesday morning, June 30th, Reza was allowed to return to H Street. The home looked more or less as he last saw it – Travis's clothes were piled a bit more neatly but everything else appeared to be in place. He opened a laptop and began to unpack his bag. Reza had had a lot of time to think since Monday afternoon, and he reached the one inevitable conclusion he had hoped to avoid: he had no option now but to turn to the government and tell them all he knew about George Gibran, Ahmed ibn Ibrahim, and the apparent access to inside information that GAM had capitalized on. It would surely be the end of his legal career, and the investigators would eventually piece together the trading operation that he and Travis had run, but it didn't matter. Travis was dead. If he kept playing games, Reza reasoned, he would be next.

The other problem he had concerned the six million dollars they had generated over the past week's trades. Travis had liquidated the positions, but it would take three business days for the trades to settle. And, more importantly, there was no way for Reza to access or move the funds once they cleared into Travis's account – at least not until Travis was declared dead and his estate was settled. God only knew if Travis had a will. No matter how hard Reza thought about it, he couldn't think of a solution to the problem. Rashid was expecting his funds today. Reza had been so close to pulling it all off, to freeing his mother, but it was now so incredibly far away. Fucking Travis! Fucking Gibran! He was sure the businessman, somehow, was involved in Travis's death. Who else would've blown up Travis's car and ransacked his home? The other possibility, of course, was that it was someone who had a score to settle with Travis, someone who Travis had come across during his day job, whatever the hell it was. Reza knew that Travis dealt with some nasty people, and there was that weird car chase a few months earlier, the black Jaguar – for all Reza knew, Travis might have had other enemies.

Reza was contemplating that point when the doorbell rang. It was probably the Metropolitan Police Department investigators. Reza dropped his bag on the bed and opened the door. He was immediately hit on the side of the head by the butt of a rifle and pushed back down onto the floor. Two men started kicking him, but he squirmed away, on hands and knees, and bolted himself inside of the bathroom. The men kicked at the door, and it almost gave way. A small, frosted window on the bathroom wall led straight outside into an alleyway. It was stuck in place and never opened, a problem that Reza had always vowed to fix whenever Travis indulged himself in an extended bathroom visit. Now, more than ever, he wished he had. The bathroom door was secured by a cheap lock, and whoever the goons were that had just invaded his home could shoot it out or kick it in. Whichever way they decided would easily work.

"Shirvani, step back," one said. "We're going to blow this door open, but we don't want you shot."

Apparently they had decided how to do it. Reza leaped away from the door, covered his fist in a towel and punched the window. It gave but didn't break. Still, the intruders had not yet entered the room. He punched at the window a second time, and then a third, and finally the glass gave way and smashed on an asphalt path on the side of the house. Reza muscled his way up onto a narrow windowsill and squeezed his body through the frame. He was halfway out, but his belt got stuck on some glass that hadn't cleared from the bottom of the window. He heard a muffled gunshot, as if from a silenced pistol, and then he knew the bad guys had penetrated the bathroom. Before he was able to free himself and escape, two hands were around each of his legs. They pulled him back into the bathroom, the glass shard gashing his belly and his chest as he slid back inside. He shouted, writhing from the pain. They pushed him back against one of the bathroom walls, and he finally had a good look at his tormentors. He knew each of them: Zarbakhat, Ghulam – and Gibran.

The side of his shirt was bloodied. "What are you doing with these thugs, George? I didn't think you'd allow your manicured hands to get so dirty."

Gibran didn't respond but instead motioned for them to take Reza back out into the living room. Ghulam had a gun to his temple. Zarbakhat grabbed a chair from the kitchen table, placed it in the middle of the living room, and shoved Reza into it. He removed several plastic Speedcuffs and tied each of his ankles to the legs of the chair. He also cuffed Reza's hands behind his back. Gibran lit a cigarette and sat back on the floral couch. He exhaled in Reza's direction.

"No smoking in here," Reza said.

Zarbakhat smacked him across the face.

"Gentlemen," Gibran cautioned his assistants. "Our host isn't going anywhere. Why don't the two of you get some fresh air outside?"

They moved toward front door but instead went into the kitchen, waiting to pounce again at Gibran's command.

"Reza," Gibran suggested, "you need to relax."

"Funny."

"Seriously, chap, you ought to take some deep breaths and contemplate your poor decision-making."

"I'm not in a contemplative mood."

Gibran smiled and put out his cigarette on the carpet. "I don't mind the piggyback trading, I thought that was fairly insightful on your part. But stealing my emails, and sharing my information with the Serious Frauds Office and MI5 – those are rather brazen violations of an attorney's duty, wouldn't you say?"

Reza looked down at the blood still seeping from his chest. "I don't know what you're talking about."

"Come now, you'll be going to jail for a long time my Persian friend. Before the federal agents arrive to arrest you – and yes, you'll be arrested, I'm not planning on killing you – you might as well humor me. How did you discover my methods and my network? How did you stumble on my good friend in London, Tareek?"

Reza looked up at him. "I swear I don't know what you're talking about."

"I so wanted to help you, Reza. If you would have just taken the easy road that I offered you and worked with me, then you'd be in a very different place now, wouldn't you? And you most certainly would have been better able to help your mother and sister, no? I know definitively that you would have found our mutual friend Rashid to be a more flexible negotiating partner."

Reza nearly spat out his words. "So you manufactured it all? You risked my mother's and sister's lives, just to protect your illegal trading and money laundering?"

Gibran pulled on his cigarette and tapped the ashes onto the carpet. "That's such a negative view of the situation. I'd prefer that you look at it in a more positive light. I was simply framing reality in a way that ensured you made the right choices. But you were too stupid or maybe too pigheaded to do that."

Reza strained against the Speedcuffs. "Or maybe I didn't want to be a part of your insider trading, your money laundering, and whatever the hell else you do."

Gibran scoffed. "Tsk, tsk, my boy, look at what all your moralizing and righteousness has brought you. It really is a shame. You had such great potential."

"Where's Clara? Does she know about this?"

"Let's see. I last saw her this morning when she was naked, rolling around in my bed. And in terms of her involvement in this, well, let me explain it to you the following way. I expect that your friend and former lover is wrapping up her meeting this morning with the United States Attorney's Office." Gibran glanced at his diamond-encrusted Rolex. "I expect that by now she's provided all the necessary evidence to show that you and your late but brilliant roommate, Mr. Meadows, stole from me and engaged in insider trading. The FBI will be here very soon, Reza, to arrest you. Haq!"

Zarbakhat and Ghulam stumbled their way back into the room. Have a look at Mr. Shirvani's laptop here, and check his bag too. Let me know if you see anything that relates to me or our operations. Also take whatever paper files you can find."

Reza shouted at him. "You're an idiot. There's nothing here. The police forensic team spent two days here."

Gibran rolled his eyes. "Do you really think, Reza, that you're in a position to be questioning my judgment and intelligence?"

Reza closed his eyes. He was too angry to cry, but he knew now that everything was lost. Travis was dead. He had failed his mother and his sister. His legal career was certainly over. He was probably going to jail.

"Don't feel too badly, Reza," Gibran muttered, passing him by. He placed what, in another context, would have been a fatherly hand on his shoulder. "I've broken men much bigger than you."

The time passed so slowly. Zarbakhat and Ghulam helped themselves to the little food in his refrigerator. Reza felt tired, either from a loss of blood, or from the diminished adrenalin that had seeped through him, relentlessly, over the past two weeks. His head rolled, and for perhaps a minute at a spell he fell into bits of anxious sleep. Tied to the chair, though, he was hardly comfortable. He had no way to judge the passage of time, but he figured that he must have been sitting there for a couple of hours. His chest was on fire. Finally, there was a strong rap at the front door. "FBI. We have a search warrant. Is this the home of Reza Shirvani?"

Gibran motioned for his goons to untie Reza, which they quickly did. "Answer the door," he ordered.

Reza stumbled across the room and opened the door. Several police officers poured in. The largest and oldest of them approached him. "Are you Reza Shirvani?"

"Yes sir."

"Step to the side, please."

The officer then approached Gibran. "Are you George Gibran?"

"Yes."

"Mr. Gibran, you're under arrest."

Gibran's jaw dropped open. "What?"

"You are under arrest for money laundering, wire fraud, bank fraud, false imprisonment and what looks to me like at least assault and battery."

Zarbakhat and Ghulam raced toward the sliding door leading to a back garden but they were tackled by other officers, cuffed, and led out to a black van.

Gibran remained in a stupor as he was handcuffed and read his rights. "That whore," he muttered to no one in particular as the phalanx of police led him out. "That stupid, stupid whore. She's ruined everything!"

One female officer remained with Reza.

"Mr. Shirvani, I think you need some medical attention."

"I'll be fine. I'll get myself to a hospital."

"You sure? We'd be happy to give you a ride."

"No, really, I'll be fine."

"Suit yourself." The last police officer left the house, and Reza watched her disappear down the pavement, past the crater where Travis had been incinerated and into a waiting government car.

Reza composed himself and called Vargas. "Gil, I need your help."

"I heard what happened. I'm sorry, man, I really am."

Vargas, like most of the rest of D.C., had heard about Travis. "I know you are. You're a good friend."

"What I can do?"

"You still have that envelope I asked you to hang on to for me, right?"

"Course."

"Great. Can you bring it to me?"

"For sure, man."

"One other thing," Reza added. "Stop a drugstore and get me a couple of first aid kits."

CHAPTER SIXTEEN

Of all the God-forsaken places in a God-forsaken world, Farah Province, in Afghanistan, is among the worst. The terrain is alternatively dusty and flat, framed by sharp mountains shaped like jagged glass, equally brown and dusty, and devoid of trees or any other sort of life at all. Boulders lay strewn between dry tumbleweeds. Farah City, the capital of the province, rises out of this terrain, as if a town might suddenly appear on Mars, and it is here that the provincial government buildings are found. It is also home to the tribal leader Rashid Agha Khan, the Lion of Farah, the undisputed leader of his people, and, like Gilgamesh of old, the king among kings of a long-neglected desert wasteland.

Sheik Ahmed pulled his *ghutrah*, his head scarf, tightly around his face, as the jeep that carried him from the southern border town of Zaranj approached the outskirts of Farah City. No matter how much he tried, however, he couldn't keep out the dust and the sand. Occasionally he'll cough, sometimes loudly, but the driver – a local he hired at the airport – was oblivious. Onward he drove, too fast at times, and the vehicle sometimes rose off of the road and smashed back down. Ahmed was diabetic and fat. An old back like his can only take so much stress.

As soon as he had received Tareek's phone call more than two weeks before, he made plans for his escape and survival. And of course it was the right move. Already, GAM had been penetrated and Gibran was arrested. MI5, in London, had raided GAM's offices, and his network of janitors had been rounded up too. He could be reasonably sure that Saudi Arabia would not deliver him to either the British or the Americans, but the Sauds couldn't be trusted. On the one hand they support Islamic charities. On the other, they are dogs licking the feet of their American and British masters when they're called. That's why, brothers like Ahmed knew, they will someday fall. There is no God but Allah and Muhammed is His Messenger.

Afghanistan is a no man's land, and a much better place to lay low. As uncomfortable as it might be. Ahmed's home in Jeddah was relatively humble, of course, but at least it had air conditioning. He opened his *ghutrah* and wiped the sweat pouring down his neck and his face. "Driver. Are we almost there?"

The man pointed to a small, white building with peeling paint. "This is the gateway to Sheik Rashid's palace."

A palace? Only in Farah. They drove up to the gate, but the car was stopped by four men carrying rifles. Both he and Ahmed, along with Ahmed's three travel companions, were ordered out of the car. Ahmed addressed the men and identified himself. They treated him with the deference he demanded. The sheik paid the driver, recovered his bags from the jeep and sent him on his way back to Zaranj. Two of the men in the back seat removed a third individual, tied up and now hooded, and lay the tired body on the dirt road. Sheik Ahmed was led to an SUV, a black Land Rover, and he was invited into the back seat. The others were taken to a second Land Rover. Ahmed's driver – one of Rashid's men – packed away the sheik's bags and started the car. The air conditioning whirred and a blast of cool air wafted into the back seat. Ahmed closed his eyes and enjoyed the one luxury he most missed. The security man accelerated toward Rashid's headquarters.

The landscape in Rashid's large complex was as naturally dry as the rest of the province, but the warlord had irrigated large swaths of it to suit his lifestyle. There were two acres of green on which he grew vegetables. An even larger area was devoted to a fruit orchard. Clutches of brown, low-rise buildings housed his chickens, cows and sheep. To the immediate rear of Rashid's main work and living complex was situated a large reservoir, which, Ahmed figured, must be replenished by deep wells because it barely ever rained in Farah. The reservoir must also be the source of all the irrigated water the property demanded. Quite possibly, it provided the drinking water for the property as well.

At the entrance to a plaza bordered on three sides by the main buildings, the sheik was directed inside Rashid's home. A couple of Rashid's men took care of Ahmed's bags. His colleagues, and their prisoner, were directed to an adjacent room. Ahmed entered a bright reception area, surrounded by windows on all sides. The walls were painted yellow, and the floor was covered by several red carpets, printed in simple geometric diamond-like patterns. Cheap brown cushioned chairs were pushed against one wall. A low-rising coffee table was also crammed toward the side of the room, along with some rickety chairs, leaving the rest of the large room open and unadorned. Rashid appeared to be waiting for him, along with other senior leaders of his clan. Each took turns greeting Ahmed. Rashid and his men wore beige summer clothes – long tunics and light cotton pants. Some of the men also sported simple blue vests. Each man also boasted a different colored turban – some were gray, others black. Rashid's was white, even whiter than the whiskers on Ahmed's beard.

Rashid led Ahmed, by hand, to the coffee table, and they took their seats along with three of Rashid's companions. "Sheik Ahmed, welcome to my home in the great western dynasty of Farah. I hope you will make yourself comfortable here. My staff is at your service. May you stay here in health for as many days as you wish."

Ahmed stood and deeply bowed. "Your generosity and hospitality is known all through the lands of the caliphate. I know I would want for nothing here in your home, but I don't at all wish to impose. I don't presume to stay long in your magnificent . . . palace. I am here, mostly, to share some news that is unfortunately not good."

Rashid sat up straighter. "You are aware of the proverb, dear sheik, to open your mouth only if what you are going to say is more beautiful than silence."

Ahmed grinned and looked him back in the eye. "All of my wisdom is of the Prophet, not the poets. Allah sometimes takes us into troubled waters, not to drown us, but to cleanse us."

Rashid sipped his mint tea. "So what troubles from afar do you bring with the intent to cleanse me?"

"Our brothers in London have been apprehended in connection with George Gibran's financial activities. No doubt, you recall Mr. Gibran? The Lebanese financier who has paid you handsomely over the years."

Rashid bristled at Ahmed's impertinence. "I am familiar with the man."

"He also has been taken into custody, in America. Some of my men have been arrested with him."

"And so they are looking for you? Is that why you're here?"

Ahmed laughed heartily. "No, I don't run like a lamb from wolves. I simply thought it prudent to leave Jeddah for a period, but no, I'm not on the run."

"What are you, then?"

"A messenger. I'm hear to tell you that we were betrayed by the son of a bitch Iranian lawyer, the Shi'a, Shirvani, who interrupted our many years of painstaking work. He is to blame!"

Rashid took another sip of tea. "I have heard of the young man. It appears that Mr. Gibran chose his staff poorly." Rashid's men nodded in agreement.

"Very poorly. As you know, the bastard's mother, the woman named Laleh, and her daughter – Shirvani's sister – are in your custody."

"Indeed, they are my guests here."

"They need to be killed."

Rashid raised an eyebrow toward Ahmed.

"An eye for an eye. It is only fair. It must be done."

Rashid rose, and then exploded. "How dare you to come into my home, to indulge my hospitality, and presume you may tell me what to do? I promised to hold the old woman under my protection. I never said I would kill an innocent, half-blind Muslim woman who has been, under my roof, praying to Allah five times a day."

Ahmed also stood, as did all of Rashid's colleagues. "But under these circumstances — "

"In my land, I determine the circumstances!" Rashid now was shouting. "This woman you call Laleh has been teaching my wives to pray more devoutly, and she's taught my children to read and write. She has even taught my youngest daughter poetry that I have not heard since my own mother passed. I am humbled by her presence in my home."

"Pshaw! This is nonsense that you speak." Ahmed's face was red. "Did this mother of a traitorous dog teach you such drivel?"

Rashid slapped him hard, with the back of his hand.

The older man fell to the floor, his face trembling and stinging at Rashid's feet. "We should never have wasted our money arming and training you Afghan dogs. For what? For such nonsense as Hafez?"

Rashid's men pulled weapons from their robes and trained them on Ahmed, still trembling on the floor. He knew now that he had miscalculated — he too brazenly had insulted his proud host. On his knees, he cowered and begged for mercy. "Rashid Khan, I have wronged you. I am deeply sorry. Please, have mercy! Have mercy on me! I have only sought to serve the *ummah*!"

"Stand up you pig. You disgust me. Have you no dignity?"

"I'm deeply sorry, Rashid Khan. It is only your magnificent grace that will permit you to overlook my failings. If you will allow me, I have a plan, yes, an idea that, with your blessing, can achieve both our objectives."

Rashid motioned for his men to stand down. "You strip of foreskin, I need no help from you to achieve my objectives. I can set the mother and her daughter free whenever I like. I'm keeping them as my guests."

"Please, hear me out, there is substantial money in it for you. And your men."

Rashid sat down again. His men remained standing. "I'm listening."

Ahmed stood, rubbed his face and straightened the *ghutrah* on his head. He patted down his robe. "I can offer you a proverbial carrot. I have a prisoner with me who possesses none of the pieties of the woman you talk about. Fine, set the mother and daughter free. Or keep them as your guests, as you please. But please also accept my prisoner as yours as an expression of my regret for causing you so much trouble."

"Who is this prisoner?"

"We grabbed her in Morocco and brought her by ship, thanks be to God for our Somali brothers, through Iran, entering at Chah Bahar, and then past the border at Zaranj into Farah. The tribute I paid to your soldiers upon entry to your province, I should mention, was steep. She is with my men now, in the next room."

"I asked you who she was, not where."

"She is Shirvani's whore. And she is just as responsible for Gibran's downfall, the downfall of our operations, as that dog, Shirvani. He will pay you a king's ransom to free her, which you, as king, deserve. And in the unlikely event that he doesn't, then you will enjoy her, somehow, nonetheless."

Rashid's men snickered but he ignored the comment. "Bring her to me."

A door on the far side of the room opened, and a woman with long, blonde hair was dragged in and dropped in front of them. Ahmed forced himself not to smile – all of what he'd said since he arrived was calculated to place her in the clutches of the Afghan warlord. He hadn't wanted Shirvani's mother to be released, to escape unharmed, but he was sure that this new plan would work just as well in support of his ultimate objective. "Her name is Clara Fournier. A Frenchwoman."

"She looks ill."

Ahmed shrugged. "She doesn't travel especially well."

"What is she worth?"

"Nothing to me. My guess is millions for Shirvani."

"Can he raise millions?"

"I believe he already has – he stole millions from Gibran."

Rashid eyed Ahmed suspiciously. "Your story makes no sense to me. What are you really doing with this girl? Why do you have her?"

"I explained to you Rashid Khan, as a ransom."

"Don't patronize me. I was this close to killing you – " he held his thumb and forefinger before Ahmed's face " — and my anger with you is no less abated."

Ahmed spoke fast. "She knows how Gibran's operations work. She knows everything, where all the money is. I thought, when he was taken down, that she would be invaluable in reestablishing the operations. I though that she could continue to work for me, and that I could run the operations, without Gibran."

"That's ridiculous, you stupid cow."

"Of course, yes, I understand that now, but I was panicked. Still, I thought she would be useful. She has all the inside information! I swear to you that Shirvani will pay for her pretty head! He is only alive because of her, and he will have no choice to but to try and buy her freedom."

Rashid turned to the several men surrounding them. "Take her to the women's quarters, and see if she can be nursed back to some form of health. Have the women try to feed her. No one else is to touch her. If I learn that anyone hereafter lays a hand or other body part on her, I will personally cut it off myself."

"A wise decision," Ahmed said.

"Shut up. The same goes for you. If you so much as touch her, if you haven't already, I will slice off whatever fat and limp organ you have used in the offense."

"Thank you, that is everything I could possibly desire."

"Show this fool to a room."

"Thank you, Rashid Khan, you are most gracious."

"And bring me Mother. I'd like to hear some Hafez."

Ahmed was shown to a room in the main building, with a bath, a bed, and a prayer rug. He bent down to offer his thanks to Allah. Then he turned on the air conditioning and laid back on the bed, imagining what he was sure would be Reza Shirvani's gallant arrival.

CHAPTER SEVENTEEN

Reza spent the days that followed Gibran's arrest healing himself, physically and emotionally. The gash to his torso ultimately required more than twenty stitches. Some were in his belly, and others in his chest. It left an ugly scar, stretching more than a foot and a half down the length of his body. He had to be careful not to jerk his right arm too suddenly or stretch too far in bed. More painful, of course, was getting used to life without Travis. He had packed Travis's belongings in several boxes, all of which he moved to the garage. That was it: that's what a person who dies is reduced to. There wasn't even a body to bury. The police had found some badly charred bones, but, besides Travis's melted wallet, nothing that would be of use even to identify who he was. The pit in the street was filled days after the explosion. The pavement on H Street now was smoother than it had been before. Life, for those who still lived it, went on.

By July 15th, the world looked very different than Reza had anticipated it would only a couple of weeks earlier. Yes, he had miraculously come up with the five million dollars he needed to buy his mother's and sister's freedom, but the money was now sitting in a brokerage account in Travis's name, and Travis was dead. The funds could remain there for a very long time. Reza had no idea if Travis even had a will; Reza didn't. The cash would be tied up in probate and then eventually distributed to Travis's parents, wherever they were. Even the four hundred fifty thousand dollar loan from Double H was locked up there. He knew he couldn't plan on getting access to that money any time soon, if ever.

He also knew now that the likelihood of rescuing his mother and sister from Afghanistan, and gaining them entry to the U.S., was virtually nil. Who knew if Rashid ever even had access to green cards, or what he intended to do with his mother and sister had Reza been able to deliver the five million dollars? Reza would never find out, he thought, and his mother and sister would be fortunate to safely return to their home in Tehran. For all his training, connections, and resources, Reza had not been able to come through for them when it mattered most. Those were the cold facts.

And then there was Clara. He had tried everything he could think of to reach her, all to no avail. None of the individuals left at GAM knew — or perhaps they knew but were unwilling to say — where Clara had gone, and she had not responded to any of his calls or messages. It would have meant so much to Reza if he could speak with her at least once more, to find out why she had done what she done, why she had protected Reza and had instead turned Gibran in to the authorities. Was it because she really did care for Reza after all, or was it simply the moral and right thing to do? Perhaps he would never find out. All he had managed to learn, from one of the FBI agents who had been involved in the raid, was that Clara was going somewhere in North Africa. That made sense – he recalled she had spent summers there years ago.

Finally, there was the matter of his legal career. He had managed to snatch defeat from the jaws of victory virtually overnight. He had gone from having partnership virtually promised to him, to being sent home on administrative leave with no prospect of a return any time soon. Yes, Burlington had "suggested" that he take some personal time to recover from his injuries and to cope with the death of his best friend, but Reza knew what was really at play. The firm's largest client, for which Reza had been singularly responsible, had turned out to be a criminal and a terrorist financier. The revenue stream from GAM was gone, and

Double H was now enmeshed instead in a very public and damaging investigation by the United States Attorney's Office and the FBI. Would Reza try, Burlington probably wondered, to cut a deal for himself and to roll on Double H? It was best to keep him at arm's reach, they had likely concluded.

At exactly 9:00 a.m., his cell phone rang: it was from an international number, and it had to be Maryam.

"*Salam*, Maryam, how are you and mother doing?"

"*Salam*, Reza, we are well, thank God."

"I'm glad to hear it. But I suppose you can guess by now that I haven't been able to come up with the money. I'm really sorry. I did everything I could."

"I know, Reza. It never really seemed possible anyway, to think that you could raise that kind of money, especially in such a short time frame." Reza wished he could correct her, and tell her that he had in fact come up with close to six million dollars and he could not access it because it was sitting in his dead friend's account. But he knew that he couldn't say all of that.

"How are they treating you and mother?"

"They are treating us incredibly well, Reza. We've been living with Rashid's wives and children, and it's like we're part of their family. It's actually the most comfortable we've been in months."

Reza considered the idea of his mother and sister now being part of an Afghan warlord's extended clan. "That's very odd. I'm certainly happy to hear it, but it's still very odd."

"I know it must seem that way. The weirder part is that mother has taken Rashid's youngest wife and his children under her wing. She teaches them how to read and write, and they all act like she's their mother or grandmother."

"I don't know what to say."

"Let me make it weirder for you. Rashid has started calling her Mother."

"What? What does she have to say about all of this?"

"She loves it," Maryam replied. "She loves the attention she gets, particularly from the children, and she says she would be perfectly content never to leave."

Upon hearing that, Reza experienced a very real sense of vertigo.

"Reza, are you there?"

It had been so long since Reza had seen his mother, he could barely remember who that person actually was deep down inside. Perhaps she really was more a part of Rashid's family than his. In many way, she was an abstraction, something he created out of necessity — an old woman in another land — someone who gave his life meaning. "I'm here. I'm just trying to get my head around all of this."

"Me too," Maryam said. "And the hard part is that as nice as they are being to us, and as comfortable and happy as mother is, I can't stay here forever! I do actually want to live a normal life!" She was crying, softly, but loud enough that Reza could hear. "They say we can leave soon, and go back to Iran if we want. But I really was hoping to come to America."

"I know. Of course you were. And I know I haven't exactly come through for you guys, but don't give up on me completely. I have one other avenue I can explore to try and get you and mother over here.

"Thank you, Reza, I'd be lost without you."

They finished the call. Reza walked down to the kitchen, and poured himself a very tall glass of single-malt scotch, neat. He took a large sip, and made his way back to his bedroom. He reached behind his bedroom mirror, and pulled out a large and slightly stained envelope. It was the envelope that Travis had left for him in case things went badly, and which Reza had smartly entrusted to Vargas. There was no doubt that things had in fact gone badly, and Reza was now ready to open it for the first time.

The envelope contained roughly a dozen documents, including letters, memoranda and photographs. Some were in English, and some appeared to be in Arabic. Before examining them, Reza turned to the handwritten note that Travis had affixed to the pile:

> *"Reza, if you're reading this, it means I'm not around anymore. It probably also means that you might be in a bind, and that you may have some nasty folks on your heels. I thought I could do you one last solid by leaving you some of my most valuable documents. These documents identify three Iraqis who are working with U.S. intelligence but who are in fact double-agents with ties to Islamic terrorists. No one in the U.S. government knows about this. Don't ask me how I know – ha, you can't anyway, 'cause I'm dead! Just thank me in the next life for having the wherewithal to save information for you. You're smart enough to know how valuable it is and I'm sure you'll put it to good use.*
>
> *Your friend always,*
>
> *Travis.*
>
> *p.s., don't get too sentimental about me. Life is short; enjoy it. And don't forget – get down to Le Coloniale and have an umbrella drink for me once you've sorted out your problems!*

Reza wiped the tears that had welled in his eyes. He wasn't sure what he would do with the information that Travis had left, but he understood its value.

It wasn't hard to get to the United States Attorney's Office for the District of Columbia – Reza walked down H Street at about 4:30 p.m., hung a right on 4th, and after a few minutes he was there. It was another of those nondescript glass and concrete buildings that choked central Washington, each projecting more authority than the next. He made his way up to the Criminal Division. They had told him, when they called several days earlier to invite him down for an initial meeting, that he could bring a defense lawyer with him. But Reza had chosen not to do so – he wasn't sure he could trust anyone enough, not given the way the last several weeks had played out. An Assistant United States Attorney with an unusually large smile came to greet him in the reception area and then led him to a conference room with a drab, burnt-orange carpet. He was confronted there by ten prosecutors, including the tall and regal Division Chief, Peter J. Goodwin. Suddenly, the projection of authority was not simply an architectural feature.

"Mr. Shirvani, please come in and have a seat," Goodwin said. "My apologies for the small army gathered here, but the information provided to us by Ms. Fournier has led to the opening of several broad-ranging investigations. I'm hoping that you can help us push forward those lines of inquiry."

"I'd certainly be happy to do so. If I can."

"Great. I'm glad to hear that. Before we start, I see that you've chosen not to come with counsel. You do understand that you're entitled to have a lawyer here with you, correct?"

"I do, thank you. I've chosen not to bring one."

"Very well, then. Perhaps we can start with some introductions." The prosecutors took turns identifying themselves as senior representatives of various task forces created to deal with money laundering, insider trading, fraud and terrorism. "As I'm sure you can tell by now," Goodwin added when everyone had been introduced, "we've taken this matter very seriously and have dedicated substantial resources to it."

"Yes, that is quite clear."

"Because of that, and the depth of the documentary information that was provided to us by Ms. Fournier, we think we have a pretty good handle on the basics of the scheme that GAM was perpetrating. We think we know who GAM's sources were, we think we know what information they were getting, and we think we understand how they were leveraging that illicit information in the marketplace."

"Great. It sounds like you're pretty far along in your investigation. So what exactly do you need from me?"

"The biggest question that is left for us right now, Mr. Shirvani, is what the firm of Henderson & Humphries knew about this illegal activity by GAM, and when."

Reza blanched.

"Now we know that you're not a partner there, and that you had limited control over the firm's conduct. But to the extent you do have some insights to share on that subject, that would be very helpful to us."

Reza knew immediately where Goodwin was going. They were asking him to roll on Burlington and Double H. They already had the case locked as to Gibran and his associates, and what they were aiming for now was another headline-grabbing case: a venerable law firm brought to its knees.

"Of course," Goodwin continued, "we would be more than willing to provide you limited immunity from prosecution if you're able to assist us in a meaningful way, if the information that you provide were to otherwise expose you to some form of liability."

Impressive, Reza thought: Goodwin had flashed the carrot and the stick at the same moment.

"Now Henderson & Humphries will be receiving a subpoena from us by no later than – Sheldon?"

"Tomorrow morning," one of the Assistant United States Attorneys replied from the back of the room.

"And I fully anticipate that the firm will retain another top law firm to defend it, and that they will throw up all sorts of defenses."

Reza felt obliged to speak. "I would expect so."

"Some of those defenses will take time for us to work through. I'm sure, for example, that the firm will assert that any of its communications with GAM are protected from production by the attorney-client privilege. We, on the other hand, believe we can show that the communications were carried out in the advancement of a fraud conspiracy and they are therefore not properly subject to a privilege. I'm sure you know that exception to the general rule."

It was hot in the room, which was, unlike the conference rooms at Double H, uncomfortable, probably purposely so, to begin with. "I do, yes, that goes back to law school."

"So that means, as I'm sure you've gathered, that we will eventually get the communications and the records that we need. And we will eventually piece together on our own what Henderson & Humphries knew and when. But what you might be able to do is to help us get there faster. You might be able to save us a lot of time and a lot of resources. That's important to us, Reza. We don't have infinite resources. By the way, may I call you by your first name?"

"Yes, of course."

"Thank you, Reza. So the decision you have to make is this – are you prepared to help us move our investigation forward more quickly? Are you prepared to share with us all that you know about what Henderson & Humphries knew and when?"

Reza remained silent, and the prosecutors stared at him coldly. Reza thought back to his conversations with Burlington, the times he had tried to share with him his concerns about Gibran. Burlington knew exactly what Gibran was up to, Reza thought – he just didn't want to admit it. The billings were simply too high to turn away from. That's why Burlington and his partners at Double H had instead buried their heads in the sand – and purchased Reza's silence along the way.

Goodwin interrupted Reza's train of thought. "I see you're thinking hard about the decision before you. I'm glad, this is a big decision for you. I don't want you to make it quickly. In fact, I want you to go home and think about this for a bit. We're not going anywhere."

Reza was relieved to hear that, and he exhaled audibly.

"Guys," Goodwin turned and asked the assembled group of prosecutors. "Is there anything else we should tell Mr. Shirvani before he leaves to think more about his options?"

"Absolutely," Sheldon replied in a gruff tone. "Two things. First, we should remind Mr. Shirvani that if he chooses not to cooperate with us, and if we learn of any misconduct on his part during the course of our investigation, then he's fair game. No cooperation means no immunity." Reza looked over at Sheldon. He was a paunchy young man, with short red hair. The collar of his buttoned up shirt was too tight. "And second, we should let Mr. Shirvani know that he's not the only game in town. His colleague, Jane Erlich, has already made the wise decision to cooperate fully with our office." Wow. Good for Jane, Reza thought. She always was a smart one.

"Thank you Sheldon," Goodwin said. "Very good points. I'm sure Mr. Shirvani will give them the consideration they deserve."

"Anything you want to ask us, Reza, before you leave?"

Reza thought for a moment. "I'd like to ask a hypothetical question."

"Sure, go for it, we love those," Goodwin replied with a quick laugh.

"Let's say I was able to help you. Do you think you could get the State Department to issue visas and possibly political asylum for my mother and sister?"

"I'm sorry, what?"

Reza proceeded to tell Goodwin and the others about his mother and sister in Afghanistan, carefully leaving out any reference to Rashid.

"Well, we're going to have to look into that, Reza. It's not something that I've dealt with before, and I can't make any promises. But I'm happy to look into it."

"Thank you. Please do. And while you're doing that, please consider one more hypothetical. Would it help my cause in that regard if I were able to share with you certain items of value relating to our foreign intelligence activities?"

All of the prosecutors, including Goodwin, appeared startled.

"Well, it all depends," Goodwin finally said, "on how valuable the information is. But we're certainly interested in hearing more about it." And with that, the meeting adjourned and Reza walked home, indirectly, passing the moonlit Potomac tidal basin along the way.

CHAPTER EIGHTEEN

For the next few days, Reza grappled with the very difficult decision that lay before him. Yes, he needed to see what Goodwin had to offer him, but Reza also needed to decide if he was willing to cooperate with the government in its investigation of Henderson & Humphries. Double H had supported him for years. They had given him a loan to help his mother and sister, and they were prepared until very recently to make him a partner. Plus, any liability that Henderson & Humphries had was probably a direct result of Reza for having brought it and Gibran to their attention. If they came out of it alive, they would certainly destroy him. On the other hand, Reza had tried to warn Double H and Burlington about Gibran, and they had chosen instead to ignore his warnings. And one thing was certain – the partners at Double H would not hesitate to roll on Reza if Goodwin were to give them that chance. So why should Reza behave differently in the pursuit of his self-interest? Even Jane was protecting herself. If he could cut a deal with the government to save himself, and possibly his mother and sister, was he really in a position not to take it?

Reza returned home from a long walk along the Potomac River early one morning to find a yellow package propped up against his front door. It was covered in an excessive amount of packing tape. It bore his name and address, both of which had been written, clearly, by someone whose first language was not English. There was no return address.

He was suspicious about what might be inside, and he thought about bringing the entire package directly to the police, or perhaps to the United States Attorney's Office. But instead he carried it inside and laid it on the kitchen table. Maybe it was something from his Maryam, or possibly his mother? His curiosity got the best of him. He shook it – nothing rattled. He patted it down for wires or other elements that might indicate a bomb. Finally, he found a pair of scissors that Travis, oddly, had used for cutting slices of pizza, and he trimmed off the top crease. Nothing exploded. No powder puffed out of its interior.

He spilled out its contents and discovered a note, together with a photograph. The note was handwritten – in what looked like Clara's script. The photograph depicted a woman with long blonde hair, sitting in a chair with a gun pointed to her head. She was blindfolded, but clearly it was Clara. The note demanded, on behalf of Sheik Rashid Agha Khan, the sum of five million dollars in exchange for her release. An address and a contact was provided for him in Farah Province, Afghanistan. A man named Ismail. A threat was issued to not inform any governmental authority. And a deadline was provided to come up with the payment: July 28th, five days from now, or Clara would be killed.

The same warlord in whose home Reza's mother and sister were living, whose kids were being schooled by Reza's mother, was now threatening to execute Clara.   Who was this guy, Rashid, and how the hell did Clara end up in his grasp? And what did this turn of events mean for the safety of his mother and sister? Maybe Maryam was reading it all wrong — maybe they were simply being lulled by Rashid into a false sense of comfort and safety.

He read the note again: Do not alert any governmental authority. But he had to – didn't he? The State Department at least ought to know, he figured, but they weren't likely to take any action. Clara was a French citizen, and obviously State had more important geopolitical concerns that involved Rashid and more specific American interests. France would be the more natural government to be involved – Reza had a vague idea that they even paid ransoms, in the past, to free their kidnapped citizens. But what if Rashid murdered her in response, as he had promised? And what if his mother and sister were to be jeopardized? He would never be able to live with himself.

He turned back to the picture. Yes, it was definitely Clara, and it looked relatively recent. Something else about the picture caught Reza's eye, something vaguely familiar. He squinted in an attempt to sharpen his focus. Yes, it was the earrings. Clara was wearing the same fake sapphire earrings that Reza had given her so many years earlier, in law school. Could she possibly have held on to them all this time? And why was she wearing them in this picture? Was it a message that only Reza would understand?

He switched on his laptop, searched for the Embassy of France and placed a call. "May I speak please to someone about a criminal matter concerning a citizen of France?"

"For criminal matters, please call the Metropolitan Police Department. I can give you their number."

"No, it's not a D.C. crime, it concerns Afghanistan."

"Ah, *oui*. Then I can direct you to the Embassy of Afghanistan."

"No, you don't understand. I'm calling about a French national in trouble in Afghanistan."

"Are you French?"

"No, I'm American. Can I speak to an assistant to the Ambassador, please?"

"It depends on which section you require."

"What are my choices?"

"Agriculture, science and technology, cultural affairs, customs, nuclear affairs – ."

"Nuclear affairs. Just connect me please to someone."

"*Oui*, thank you, please hold on."

Reza waited. "You have reached the assistant to the third secretary to the Ambassador of France in the Office of Nuclear Affairs. No one is available right now to take your call. Please press zero to return to the operator."

Reza pressed zero. "Embassy of France."

"Yes, I just called before about a French national in Afghanistan who needs to get out of the country."

"You may need to speak to the International Security Assistance Force."

"How do I reach them?"

"They are in Kabul."

"We're going round and round here."

"Sir, I have already directed you to the Embassy of Afghanistan. We have no jurisdiction over that nation."

"Don't you care that a French woman's life is threatened in Afghanistan?"

"There are many French nationals in the line of fire. We at the Embassy support the troops fighting for democracy and freedom."

"When are your hours?"

"The Embassy is open for visitors from 8:45 a.m. to 1 p.m."

"Fine. I'll be there in the morning."

"I'm sorry sir, but you will first need an appointment."

"How do I get an appointment?"

"Is this for a visa?"

"No, damn it, I'm calling about a French national who has been kidnapped in Afghanistan!"

"As I told you before, for matters concerning Afghanistan you have to contact the Embassy of Afghanistan – ."

Reza hung up the phone. He clicked on to Google Earth and typed in the address for the Farah City contact provided in the envelope from Clara. The city was larger than he'd expected after the way that Maryam had described it. The address he entered appeared to be a low-rise dwelling, brown and dusty like the rest of the block on which it sat and the city to which it belonged. Still, it appeared relatively modern.

He tried calling Maryam. No answer. He paced around his living room hoping to identify some obvious solution. He was unable to do so and after several minutes, he collapsed on his couch in a mix of frustration and exhaustion. He closed his eyes and covered his face in his hands. He wished Travis was still there, to help him sort through this. Instead, he reached for Rumi:

How long can I
Beg and bargain
For the things of this world
While love is waiting

How long before
I can rise beyond
How I am and
What I am

It was clear what he needed to do. It was just a matter of having the strength to do it. Reza grabbed his passport and the ten thousand dollars that he had hidden for so long, and then he bolted out the door.

The Embassy of Afghanistan looks like a schoolhouse – worn red bricks, a weathered flagpole out front, and well manicured trees and flowers along its entry path. The gate was open, and Reza walked right in. The front door, however, was locked. He checked his watch: one-thirty in the afternoon. Could they be closed?

He knocked on the door but no one answered. He knocked again, more purposefully – he was determined to be heard. A short and disheveled security guard approached him from around the side of the building. "It's closed. Go away. Come back tomorrow."

"I have an emergency. I need to see someone."

"Tomorrow, I said! Come back tomorrow!"

He studied the man. Definitely an ethnic Afghan, with wrinkled and weathered skin, no moustache and a short but messy beard. "I don't need to see the ambassador, or the first secretary or even the second secretary. The third secretary will do. You have to help me. I'm here on important business and it can't wait until tomorrow."

The guard looked past Reza, to the empty lawn beyond. "Who are you? Are you Afghan?"

"Persian, originally. But I'm an attorney here in Washington. And I have extremely urgent business that I need to discuss with someone inside the embassy. Look, this might affect U.S.-Afghanistan relations. It's very important. Do you want to be responsible for having turned me away?"

The guard appeared nervous. "Why don't you call the ambassador?"

Reza took a risk: "I tried that already. And as you probably already know, he's not in Washington right now. Kindly find someone to let me in. Please!"

"So call someone else. Or, like I said, come back in the morning." The guard turned and began to walk away.

"Wait, wait, I have something to show you." Reza implored. The guard stopped and turned back toward Reza. Reza pulled out his wallet, peeled off a hundred dollar bill, and placed it in the guard's baggy chest pocket. "Bring me, please, a secretary. Just to the door. I assure you that he will want to see me."

"I will ask," the guard said as he patted his chest and stepped away to make a call on his radio. Within minutes, a beautiful, long-haired young woman in a white, buttoned shirt and khakis appeared at the entrance. "Well don't stand there," she said with an easy smile, "come in."

Reza stopped gawking at her and stepped inside. She closed the door behind him but did not invite him any further. "I'm Naima Amirzadeh, an Embassy intern."

"Nice to meet you," Reza said, giving her his name and Double H business card.

Nader Hossain Salehi

"You're Iranian."

"Yes. Persian. Originally."

She smiled. "Like me. Funny. Now, I understand you have some important business?"

"Yes, I need a visa immediately. I need to see a secretary."

She crinkled her nose. "I thought you really had important business. Anyway, you know we stop seeing people for visas at noon, and they usually take at least three days to issue."

"Can I get one right now? I'm heading to the airport tonight. I know it sounds crazy, but it's a matter of life and death."

"Really?" She smiled at him incredulously.

He was going to have to beg. He gauged his audience, with a trained attorney's eye. "Look, my mother is in Farah, and she is very ill. She has an acute, drug-resistant infection, and it's starting to affect her organs. I've just gotten my hands on a new super antibiotic. It's a bit experimental, and we don't know for sure if it will help her, but it's the only chance she has. I have to get a visa as soon as possible so I can take it to her. Every hour counts."

The intern blushed, having clearly believed and been moved by the story. "Okay. I understand. I can't make any promises, but let me see what I can do. You stay here."

She turned and walked quickly down a long hallway, her large hoop earrings bouncing with each step. At the end of the corridor, she opened and disappeared behind an old, creaky door. Reza could barely hear her muffled voice from where he stood. She seemed to be speaking excitedly to a man with a deep voice. Moments later, the door opened and she reappeared in the hallway. She smiled and waved Reza down toward her. "Come, Mr. Hakim will see you."

He thanked her.

"This is Mr. Hakim, the third secretary here," she said, as Reza entered the office. "He has kindly agreed to see you. Good luck." She waved goodbye, left the room, and closed the door behind her, leaving Reza alone with the polished third secretary.

Hakim, a thirty-some year old Afghan with short, brown hair, designer spectacles, and a neatly-pressed, Italian cut suit, invited Reza to sit across from him.

"What can I do for you?" His voice was calm but serious.

"Thank you for your time, Mr. Hakim," Reza said. He then repeated the story that he had told the intern.

"Amazing," the third secretary said. "And where exactly did you get this medicine?"

Clearly, he was not going to be as easy to snow as the intern. "I'm not proud of this," Reza said without hesitation, "but I'm going to be honest with you. I stole it. My roommate works at Georgetown Hospital Center. I learned about the drug from him. They were using it in tests at the hospital. I used his identification, I went to the hospital, and I took it."

"Remarkable, indeed," the third secretary said calmly. Reza maintained his gaze, and neither man said a word for several seconds.

"Do you think you can help me? Please, I beg you." Reza said.

Hakim ran a hand along the lapel of his shiny, trim blue suit as he deliberated. He then pulled some papers from a folder on his large and neat desk. "Fill this out. It's the visa application form. And let me see your passport."

Reza pulled it out of his pocket and handed it to him.

"I'm going to need a two-by-two photo of you as well. Normally we have to send this to another department to be processed, but I perhaps I can take care of it – "

"That's incredibly kind of you," Reza interjected before Hakim was finished with his sentence.

"As I was saying, I think I can take care of it, but you will have to pay an expedited handling fee."

"Of course. How much is that?"

"Let me see," Hakim said. He consulted a loose sheet of paper that he pulled from his drawer. "The normal processing fee is two hundred and fifty dollars, and the expedited fee is two thousand."

"Two thousand!" Reza exclaimed before catching himself. "Of course, no problem."

"And it has to be cash."

Reza removed two thousand dollars from his wallet and handed it to Hakim, who counted the money before placing it in his drawer. "Now I need the pictures."

"I need to catch a flight tonight at nine," Reza said.

"I'm here until five. Fill out the application, get the photos, and come back before then. Your visa will be waiting."

Reza jumped from his chair. "I'll be back. Can I have your cell number in case I can't get back in?"

Hakim gave it to him.

Reza ran out and headed straight to Double H.

He had several photos of himself in his office, photos which he had used for a federal district court application a year or two earlier. But his hopes for a quick entry and exit were dashed when his I.D. card failed at the turnstiles in the Double H lobby. Abdullah, the security guard, called him over. "I'm sorry, Mr. Shirvani. Instructions are to not let you enter."

"What? Why?"

"Instructions came from Mr. Burlington directly."

"Look, I just need to get some personal files from my office. I will be back in two seconds."

"No can do," Abdullah replied with his arms outstretched.

Reza glared at Abdullah and briefly entertained the idea of running around him. Abdullah seemed to read Reza's mind.

"Easy, Mr. Shirvani, let's not make this harder than it has to be."

Reza decide the risk was not worth taking. He turned and headed back out toward the front door. "Fuck you and the bastards you work for, Abdullah, whoever they are," he shouted as he ran out. "And do something about that ugly mole on your face! It gets bigger and uglier every fucking time I see you!"

Reza hailed a cab and made his way through the ever-present traffic around DuPont Circle to a twenty-four hour CVS drugstore. He dashed to the back of the store and found, to his great delight, a photo booth that he had a hunch was there.

He then had to wait anxiously for his turn as two teenage girls took dozens of pictures of themselves while laughing and making silly faces.

Reza jumped into the booth as soon as they stood to leave, and he took six headshots of himself. It was four in the afternoon when he walked out of the CVS with the pictures in his hand. He had an hour to make it back to the embassy, to see Hakim. He decided to run to Wisconsin Avenue.

He arrived just after 4:20 p.m., panting, outside the embassy. This time the front gate was locked. Reza shook it but no one came in response. He pulled out his cell phone and called Hakim. No answer.

He shouted toward the sealed embassy. "Hakim!"

"Mr. Hakim!"

He started to feel like an idiot. People stared at him from across the street. "Mr. Hakim!"

He didn't dare jump over the wall, although he probably could have made it. The people staring at him would have surely called the police and he would have to spend hours explaining himself.

Finally, the Afghan security guard approached.

"Thank God. I'm so glad to see you."

The man was nonplussed. "We're closed, sir. Come back in the morning."

"What? I explained everything to you already, didn't I? Mr. Hakim told me to come back before five. I have an appointment with him."

The guard shrugged and started to walk away. "I wasn't made aware of that."

"Wait!"

The guard turned and patted his chest.

"Un-fucking-believable." Reza peeled off another hundred-dollar bill and slipped it through the gate and into the guard's pocket. A clanging steel chain fell to the ground, and the steel doors squeaked open. Hakim, indeed, was still at his desk and the visa was ready. Reza handed him the application, which he had completed in the back of the taxi to CVS, as well as two of the photos he had just taken.

"Are we set now?"

"Yes, we are," Hakim replied, straightening his yellow Hermes tie. "Safe travels, and good luck with the drug."

"What? Right, the drug. Thank you. I'm very hopeful."

With that, Reza departed the Embassy of Afghanistan two thousand and two hundred dollars lighter, and hailed a cab to Dulles International Airport.

CHAPTER NINETEEN

Reza managed to catch an overnight Air France flight to Istanbul, with a stopover in Paris. At Istanbul, he switched to Turkish Airlines for a nonstop flight to Kabul. It took ten hours to get to Istanbul, an eight-hour layover at Ataturk Airport, and then another five hours to Kabul. He disembarked at Kabul International Airport on Sunday, July 25th, at approximately six in the morning. He called Maryam again, from the airport's transit area, but again there was no answer. Reza approached customs and produced his passport and visa. A female customs officer examined his papers and asked him to wait. She left her station with his passport and visa and disappeared behind a closed door. Not good, Reza knew. She returned two minutes later with a male officer – a large man with no moustache but a whiskered beard – who asked to accompany them into another room. The female returned to her post; the male asked Reza to have a seat.

"You departed from Washington?" he asked.

"Yes."

"Why are you here?"

He looked him straight in the eye. "To see my mother. She's Iranian, and she's in Farah."

The customs officer laughed. "No one comes from Washington to Afghanistan to visit his mother."

"There's a first time for everything."

He examined his papers. "The visa is not in order."

Reza noticed his meaty, fat fingers. "That can't be. I received it personally from the third secretary to the Afghan Ambassador to the United States. Mr. Hakim. I have his personal telephone number, if you'd like, you can call and verify it yourself."

He tossed the visa page toward Reza, and it hit his chest. "Tell your C.I.A. handlers they missed a stamp."

"I am not C.I.A. This visa bears Mr. Hakim's personal signature. Trust me, you could be in a load of trouble if you fail to admit me."

The officer slapped his knee and broke out into a loud laugh. "Is that right? Well, your Mr. Hakim can kiss my hairy ass."

Reza put his face in his hands.

The Afghan official leaned forward. "Tell me again why you're really here."

He looked through his fingers, and then folded his hands on the table. "Fine. I'm here to see Rashid Agha Khan."

That got the customs officer's attention. "What business do you have with him?"

Reza calculated the dynamic. "Do you really think Rashid Agha Khan would want me to be explaining to you what business I have with him? I'm sure this is a very nice position for you and your family. Do you think he couldn't find a way to make you unemployed, at the drop of a hat?"

The customs officer hesitated. "When a man of Rashid Khan's stature has an unusual and important guest, we are alerted to this. But we've heard nothing about your arrival. Usually we're provided for prior to the arrival. Certain gestures typically are made, if you get what I mean."

Reza understood what he meant. He removed five hundred dollar bills from his shirt pocket and pushed them toward the official. "How thoughtless of me. I did hear on my way in that it's your daughter's birthday today. I had no time to bring a present, as I should have, since I left America in such a rush, but I trust that this small gift will be accepted."

The customs man took the money. "Thank you. My daughter will be very happy."

The man rose and motioned for Reza to follow. He led him back to the female customs officer, who stamped his passport for entry and handed all his papers back to him. Reza passed through the customs gate, with the man and woman waving him a kind goodbye. He exited the terminal and stepped outside into a cacophony of human voices and car horns, blowing dust, and blistering heat: he was now in Afghanistan.

Several bearded men in long, white robes and hats eyed him with suspicion. He was dressed in beige pants and a red t-shirt, and he wore white leather Lacoste sneakers. He was too conspicuous – like a tourist stepping off of a cruise ship, all that was missing was a camera hanging from his neck. Several boys selling cheap goods pulled on his arms and surrounded him. He freed himself from their clutches and walked past two green and white commuter buses idling outside. He lost the boys as he turned past the last of the buses and faced a series of jeeps and military trucks in camouflage parked around a dusty, weed-strewn central plaza. Beyond the jeeps he saw what looked to be a taxi stand, or at least an area of cars for hire. A dozen drivers stood outside their vehicles and smoked. Many were older and surprisingly overweight, and none made any gesture toward him to solicit his business. Did everyone here think he was with the C.I.A.?

"Hey English!"

"Hey American!"

Reza looked past the line of smoking drivers, toward a slender, younger man calling his way. "*Francais! Deutsch Mann!*"

He walked over to him, past the stares of the other drivers who seemed more content to smoke instead of work. The kid must have been barely sixteen. "Do you speak English?"

"Little!" He smiled broadly, and his face lit up.

"Okay. Take me to Farah."

"Yes, Farah! Yes, sir – inside!"

Reza slid into his white Toyota Camry. "What's your name?"

"Arman."

Arman drove them into the city center of Kabul, leaning on his horn the entire time. They crept through the traffic of the city, which, in Reza's eyes, was surprisingly green – the parks were well landscaped and the streets were tree-lined. The people, too, were more diverse than what he'd seen at the airport. Some women wore black chadors, but most others sported simple headdresses, with their faces and beautiful dark eyes fully exposed. Men wore the ubiquitous white summer robes with a variety of different colored hats and skullcaps. Younger men, like Arman, wore simple white t-shirts. More than a few even sported reversed baseball caps on their heads. After thirty minutes, Arman pulled the car over in front of a building choked with small markets and stores. "We are here," he announced.

"Where?"

He pointed to a clothing store besides which they had parked. Indeed, the sign above read Farah.

"No. Farah Province. In the west."

Arman smiled again. "First here, come. Come."

He exited the Toyota, and Reza followed. They entered the market, which was filled with stacks of *taqiyahs* of every imaginable color, the caps worn by most Afghan men. Row after row of traditional shirts and pants, *shalwar kameez*, hung on crooked steel racks. An older man emerged from the back and, after exchanging words with Arman in what Reza believed to be Pashto, went again into a back room and emerged with a platter of tea and cookies. "My brother!" Arman said.

"There's a mistake," Reza tried to explain. "I'm going to Farah Province, in the west. To see Rashid Agha Khan."

Arman's brother, who was about to sip his tea, hesitated at the mention of the Rashid's name.

Arman was nonplussed. "I take you! Don't worry. First, clothes."

Arman rifled through the racks of clothes and selected a white *shal-*

war kameez, with a blue vest and a red *taqiyah*. "America, no?"

The red, white and blue motif was, Reza thought, even more conspicuous than his Lacoste shoes, so he agreed on the white robe and red cap but passed on the vest. "Too hot," he said, to the brothers' obvious disappointment.

Arman also brought him black socks and shoes, which Reza squeezed into. He ditched his other clothes – better to blend in than scream American. He paid for the goods with U.S. cash, peeling off another hundred dollar bill, which impressed Arman and his brother. As they prepared to leave, the older brother spoke: "Rashid?"

"Yes, I'm going to see Rashid."

"Bad man."

"So I hear."

Arman's brother took Reza by the arm and led him into the back room. He opened a desk drawer and produced a pistol. "Makarov."

Reza didn't understand. Arman's brother pushed the pistol and a box of 9 mm bullets into his hands. He tried to give them back, but Arman's brother insisted. Then Reza tried to pay him for the weapon, but his brother refused.

"Gift, gift," Arman explained.

"You need," the brother added. "Rashid. Bad man."

After grabbing some *taftan* rolls for breakfast, and filling the Toyota's tank, Arman and Reza headed west out of Kabul toward Farah. The distance was formidable – five hundred miles – but the condition of the road made it seem longer. The route avoided any other major Afghan city and instead cut right through the heart of the fabled Hindu Kush range. The road was often treacherous, with hairpin switchbacks and cliffhanging turns, and sometimes it just petered out, causing Arman to search slowly to pick up the next paved road to the west. The mountains closest to Kabul were tall, uneven and snow-peaked but Reza noticed that the elevations tended to diminish the further west they drove.

After several hours, the sharp, cold peaks receded, and they entered a high desert plain. At around two p.m., Arman pulled over to stretch and eat. He handed Reza a box filled with rice, carrots, cherries, raisins and some sort of meat. They ate in silence, listening to the wind blow through the empty sands and valleys. Reza thought back to his escape from Iran, as a boy so long ago – his fear of animals in mountains, the long journey into the unknown. He looked up. Far above a falcon circled. "*Pedar*," he said, and said a prayer.

Colonel Shirvani, to Reza, had barely existed, and Reza gave him little thought over the twenty years since he had left Iran. What really happened that night? Why had they taken him, and why didn't he even make it until the morning? Was he an enemy to the Islamic Revolution? Or was he like a dolphin, accidentally swept up in an unforgiving and unfeeling tuna net? Reza had spent so much energy over the course of those years in devotion to his mother that he felt badly, right now, to realize he couldn't recall his father at all. Could he ever know him? And what would the Colonel think to see him now?

After they finished their meals, Arman walked back to the car and handed Reza the pistol. "Shoot," he said.

Reza had never before fired a weapon. He held the Makarov in his right hand, aimed into the boundless desert and slowly squeezed the trigger. When it volleyed, Reza's arm jerked up awkwardly and he took several steps backward. Arman howled, eventually falling to the side of the road in laughter.

"Come on, it wasn't that funny," Reza said. Then he emptied the chamber into the Afghan void, shooting with two hands, and then one, as he gained better control over the pistol's recoil.

Arman showed him how to load the weapon and set and unlock the safety. Reza tucked the gun into his waist, cinching the *kameez* tighter, feeling less American but not quite Afghan either: a Persian, perhaps, lost somewhere between two faraway worlds.

By midnight they had reached Farah. Its darkened, low rising dwellings seemed ancient to him and menacing. There was barely any other traffic and no one walking in the streets. Arman drove him past the address he had for Rashid's contact, a man called only Ismail, and then parked the Toyota in an abandoned lot two blocks away. Reza decided not to stay in any of the sketchy hostels they had passed along the way and instead hoped to catch some sleep in the back seat of the car. At dawn, he rose and gave Arman four hundred dollars, which almost brought the young man to tears. Arman got back in his car and turned it east. Reza faced the address for Ismail and his destiny, which would be revealed to him some time this day.

Reza alternatively paced and sat in the street and waited until nine in the morning until approaching the front door of the address he had been provided. It appeared to be a private home, rather than an office – two cats sneaked down from the roof to rub against his ankles, and the few potted plants in the front yard seemed to have been regularly watered. He rapped on the door. He heard footsteps from within and then saw an eye look through a peephole. The mouth connected to that eye muttered something in what Reza took to be Dari. They were close to the border of Iran. His Farsi, he hoped, would help him to communicate.

He decided to identify himself as a friend. "Hey! *Refigh!*"

The door opened. A slight man with a short beard and white taqiyah appeared. "*Mitoonam komaketoon konam?*"

Yes, you can help me. "*Ismail eenjast?*"

The man instinctively turned to look down a short hallway. "*Ba man bia.*"

The man said come, and so he followed. It was dark in the home, and the ceilings seemed unusually low. Reza crouched slightly as he made his way down a narrow hallway that appeared to lean to the right. After some fifteen steps, the man stopped in front of an open door and motioned for him to go in. "Ismail," he said.

Ismail was even slighter than the other man who opened the door. Immediately, Reza calculated that he could take him in a fight if need be. The only problem was that Ismail sat with his feet up on a desk cutting an apple with an unusually long switchblade. Reza looked down to the waist of his *kameez*, where the Makarov was tucked away. Unfortunately, in the next instant, it was gone.

Ismail had casually flicked his wrist, the one holding the knife, and then the other man snuck up from behind and relieved him of the weapon. It was so fast that Reza had no time to react. The man handed the pistol over to Ismail, who had a quick look at it and dropped it into the bottom drawer of his steel desk. Then Ismail, in Dari, asked him who he was.

Reza handed him a copy of the letter he had received from Clara and pointed to the man's name and address.

Ismail smiled. "Shirvani?"

He nodded yes.

"What a surprise," he said in English.

"I'm here to see Rashid."

"You mean Rashid Agha Khan. Do you have the money?"

"That's for me to discuss with Rashid Agha Khan."

Ismail laughed again. "Don't fuck with me." He motioned again toward the other man, and Reza was flipped around, pressed against the wall and searched for any more weapons. The man pulled the wad of cash out of his pocket and tossed it to Ismail. "This is five million?"

"No. I'm not stupid enough to walk around Farah with five million dollars."

This time both Ismail and the other man laughed. Then Ismail and his driver gripped Reza by the back of each arm and led him to a black Mercedes SUV parked in a side yard. They pulled out onto the main street and drove for some twenty minutes to what Reza assumed was the outskirts of the city. There, they approached a concrete and steel gate guarded by four men with Kalashnikovs. Ismail slipped out, lit a cigarette, offered one to each of the guards and chatted with them, casually, as his driver sat with Reza in the SUV, a loaded gun on his lap. A short time after stamping out his butt, Ismail motioned to the car – again, with the slightest flick of his wrist – and the driver slid out, opened the passenger door and wrenched Reza out of the vehicle. Stumbling at first, Reza steadied himself and marched on his own power toward the gate. Three of the men trained their machine guns at him, and a fourth searched through his bag. The guard removed Reza's passport and visa and took them into a small building that appeared to be a guardhouse, or maybe a place to get out of the vicious sun. He heard some chirping, in Dari, through a radio. Before long, another vehicle, in a cloud of dust, headed toward them from the interior of the compound. It pulled up beside them. Ismail opened a rear door and pushed Reza in. Then he went around the front of that car and jumped in. This new driver, a fat man with a different sort of robe, turned to face him. "Greetings, Reza Shirvani. I am Sheik Ahmed ibn Ibrahim. Do you know who I am?"

Reza suddenly felt very tired. "Sounds familiar."

"Good. I'm so pleased! It saves us a lot of time."

"Where are we going? Where's Clara?"

"Who?"

"The woman you kidnapped."

"The whore? You will see her soon."

"Is she with my mother and sister? Are they with Rashid?"

Ahmed laughed, a loud and artificial laugh, as he pressed on the gas pedal. "So many questions! Why don't you just sit back and enjoy the scenery. All will become clear soon enough."

Reza gazed out at the rich fruit orchards, feeling so near to the end. He was in over his head. A securities lawyer from Washington, D.C., negotiating with a murderous Arab and an Afghan warlord in Farah. It made so little sense that it was better not to think about it that way. Plus, what choice did he have? He was at the table now, and he had to play the cards he had as best he could.

The car came to a stop in front of a plaza leading to a low-rise build-ing. Several more men with Kalashnikov rifles stood guard there. Reza was removed from the car and taken through the plaza. Would they stand him up against a wall as they had done to his father when they find out that he doesn't have the five million? Would they shoot him right there, in cold blood? Maybe that's where all this was leading.

But no one asked him about the money. Instead, they shoved him through a door and down a hallway to another, locked door that one of the men opened with a key. He was tossed in, and he fell to the floor. The door was bolted behind. He heard a gasp from the other side of the room, and then his eyes fell on Clara. And she was alive!

"Oh God, what are you doing here?" she asked.

A warmer welcome would have been nice. "I came to save you, naturally."

Reza pushed himself off the floor and surveyed his surroundings as his eyes quickly acclimated to the relative dark of the cell. The walls were made of bare cinder blocks, and the only light in the room streamed in from one open, very small window near the ceiling. The floor was unfinished, an uneven combination of hard and soft mud. The air was heavy and dank, and the only furniture in the room consisted of a large, wooden day bed that carried a thin, balding mattress.

"You're going to save me? How are you going to save me? Did you call the authorities?"

Reza snapped his attention back to Clara. Yes, but she hardly looked like the same person. Her normally silky hair was now matted and tangled. Her skin was visibly chafed and dry, and her soft lips were lightly blistered. Her black, v-neck sweater had several small holes, and her designer jeans were caked in mud. And yet, the same warm glow still emanated from her magnetic blue eyes.

"With all due respect," Reza said, "I think the authorities are a little too busy around these parts to spend a lot of time looking for you."

She nodded in silent agreement.

"Are you okay?" he asked.

"Yes. I'm fine. No one's harmed me."

"Good. What about my mother or sister? Have you seen them?"

"Your mother and sister? I don't think so. Are they here too?"

"Yes, I think so," Reza replied. He slapped and wiped the dust from his pants.

"Look, it's incredible that you've come here, Reza, but you really shouldn't have. You don't owe me anything, especially not after all I put you through, with that bastard Gibran."

"I'm capable of deciding for myself what I do and don't have to do," Reza said as he slid his fingers across the cold cinder block wall. "And we both know that if it wasn't for you, I'd be the one in jail now instead of Gibran. Everything before that is erased as far as I'm concerned."

She grabbed and kissed his hand, squeezing it tightly between hers. "It's good to see you. Thank you for coming."

He gently stroked her cheek and brushed back her hair, revealing her small and delicate ear. Yes, she really was wearing the earrings that he had given her in law school. "Ha! I can't believe you still have these," Reza said as he lifted one earring with his index finger.

"Of course I do." She smiled self-consciously and darted a glance away from Reza. "They're very valuable. Remember that you promised to replace them with real sapphires one day."

"And I will. I'm a man of my word."

"I know I once told you, Reza, that I have no regrets in life. Well, I do. I have one very big regret. I'm so sorry that I was never as good to you as you were to me."

"It's not too late, Clara."

She looked back at him, as tears welled in her eyes, and chuckled. "You know, I always admired your optimism."

"It's going to be okay. Really, I know it will."

She quickly wiped the tears from the corners of her eyes and regained her composure. "See what I mean? Anyway, do you have a plan for getting us out of here? Did you come here with money?"

"Money, no. But yes, I do have a plan. May not be the best plan ever conceived, but it is certainly a plan. And I think it just might work."

"So what is it?"

"I'm going to cut a deal with Rashid, one that sorts all of this out once and for all."

"You're going to negotiate with these people? How are you going to do that? Oh, Reza." The tears again filled her eyes. "That's not a plan. They're going to kill us!"

The door burst open, and two heavily bearded men barged in. They grabbed Reza, warned Clara to stay back and marched him down the hall and out to the plaza. This time they stood him up against a wall of the building and then walked away. Reza counted a dozen men, all armed with rifles, milling around the perimeter of the plaza, waiting, apparently, for an order to be given.

"I am here to see Rashid Agha Khan," he shouted as loudly as he could.

The men glanced and sniggered at each, but no one said a word.

"Do you hear me? I am Reza Shirvani, and I have come here from America to see Rashid Agha Khan on important business," he continued to shout. More glances and chuckles from the armed men, but nothing else.

So was this it? This dull and dusty plaza in Farah is where all his efforts would end? Was he to die alone, without having saved Clara, or his mother or sister? Without even having had a real chance to carry out his grand plan? Maybe his father had also lamented his impotence near the end. Reza always imagined that his father had stood proudly, as proud as he always was, and had taken the fire with righteous indignation. That's how Reza would take it too. If he had to die now, so be it – he would betray no fear – no one would ever say that they saw him cry, whimper or beg at the end. "You cowards, I order you to release me now, or there will be Hell to pay! Do you hear me? I am Reza Shirvani!"

Sheik Ahmed entered the plaza, laughing in an exaggerated fashion, and barked instructions to the men in Arabic. They moved, slowly, without discipline, to the opposite side of the square and lined up, casually checking their rifles. It was late morning, not even noon. The clear, blue sky and the brown and green surroundings shimmered and pulsed with a suddenly sharp and beautiful evanescence. But no comet streaked across the sky to save Reza Shirvani, no divine intervention would be bestowed by Allah. Life was cheap here, and daily it ended with no pomp and circumstance. And so he stood there, the one son of Colonel Shirvani – chin up, chest out – at peace with himself and prepared to scream back with all his might at the volley that was headed towards him.

That's when Rashid appeared from around the open end of the plaza, holding a large, green pear. "What the hell is going on here?"

The men stood down.

"Did I authorize this? Are you executing this man? On my land? Without my permission?"

"This is the American, Shirvani," Ahmed said. "He came here with no money. He can not pay you the ransom you required. Now it's my business alone, Rashid Agha Khan."

Rashid shouted at the men in Dari, and they dropped their weapons to the side. He glared at Ahmed. "Everything in Farah is my business."

Rashid walked up to Reza, who was trembling but still frozen in a position of near-death pride. "Are you Reza Shirvani?"

"Yes."

"Did you bring me the ransom for the girl?"

"I'd like to discuss the matter with you privately, if I may, Rashid Agha Khan."

"Of course he doesn't have it. It's just as I said," Ahmed interjected. "If he did, then he would be screaming yes!"

Rashid took a large bite of the pear, dropped the remainder to the ground and wiped his hand against his shirt sleeve. "I was about to go for my walk," he finally said to Ahmed and Reza. "You two will come with me, and we shall get to the bottom of this matter once and for all." One of Rashid's guards handed him his long walking stick, a staff carved from the native timber of Kunar, with an ornate brass base and a roaring lion's head at its top. Then he, Reza and Ahmed walked silently out of the plaza and back around the rear of the main buildings. Rashid led them several hundred meters along a dusty and well-worm path until they reached the reservoir, a deep lake, placid in the harsh, Afghan desert. They stopped by the water's edge, and Reza and Ahmed waited for some signal from Rashid that he was ready to speak. But, for several long moments, Rashid simply gazed upon the glimmer of the morning sun on the small ripples in the water.

"So," Rashid finally said as he turned to Reza. "Do you or do you not have the money?"

"I do not, but — "

"See, I've been telling you," Ahmed shouted. "Let me kill him now!"

"I have warned you several times, my dear brother," Rashid said, "that this is my house, and I decide who lives and dies. And if someone is to die, I decide when and how. I will not repeat myself again." Ahmed clenched his fist and turned away in frustration.

"Now, what were you about to say? And I warn you not to toy with me or waste my time with silly games."

Reza knew that the critical moment was upon him. This was the one final opportunity he would have to save himself, his mother and sister, and Clara. He summoned every ounce of advocacy within him.

"I was about to say, Rashid Agha Khan, that I am not rude or stupid or simple enough to come to your home without a proposal that is worthy of your interest. And I would certainly not be foolish enough to dream of wasting your time with silly games. It is true that I do not have the money that you've asked for. But I do have something else, something that I think is worth even more than five million dollars, especially in your capable and worthy hands."

"And what is that?"

"Before I describe it, and show it to you, may I be indulged a question?"

"You may."

"If you agree that I am right, and that my proposal suits you, can I have your word as a righteous leader of men that all of us, including the girl, and my mother and sister if they are still here, can leave safely whenever we choose, under the banner of your protection, with the green cards that you had agreed to sell to us?"

"I have already told Mother that she and her daughter can leave any time they wish. They are guests in my home. And I will still provide the green cards, at the right price of course. As to you and the girl — yes, you have my word that you too can leave safely any time that you wish. But I warn you again not to waste my time."

"It is a reflection of your magnanimity, Rashid Khan." Reza then reached into his shirt and pulled out a faded and folded envelope. "What I have here is something that I believe the United States government would pay at least ten million dollars for. Other governments may pay even more. You can decide, of course, when it is in your hands, what you will do with it."

"This is ridiculous drivel," Ahmed interjected, unable to contain himself. "He is playing games with us!"

"I will decide that, Ahmed," Rashid said. "Speak a good word or remain silent."

Rashid then turned back to Reza. "What is in the envelope?"

Reza handed the envelope to Rashid, who looked tentatively at the contents.

"This file identifies three Iraqi agents who are working closely as informants with the United States government. But what makes the file truly valuable, is that these men are in fact double-agents who are lying to the Americans, and this file proves it beyond a doubt." Reza could tell that he had Rashid's interest and attention. "No one has this information. No one in the United States has any idea about any of this. I don't need to tell you, Rashid Khan, how much they might be willing to pay for this information."

"Indeed, you need not tell me."

"Enough of these lies and games," Ahmed stammered. "I will kill this dog now!"

Ahmed pulled a pistol out from beneath his robes and raised his right arm toward Reza. Rashid instantly swung his walking stick up from the ground and struck Ahmed below his outstretched arm. Ahmed's arm flew skyward, and the gun fired harmlessly into the air.

"You son of bitch," Ahmed yelled as he turned back towards Rashid. Before he completed his turn, Rashid raised his stick up into the air and swung back down with all his might, burying the brass base into Ahmed's right shoulder, instantly cracking his collar bone. The pistol fell to the ground, and Ahmed crumpled to his knees, crying in pain as his left hand reached reflexively for his broken right shoulder. Rashid quickly lifted his right knee to his chest, and brought his heel down on Ahmed's grimacing face. Ahmed, unprepared for the blow, was knocked off balance, and he fell backwards into the lapping waves of the reservoir behind him.

"Help! Help! I can't swim," Ahmed yelled as he flailed about trying to grab the concrete barrier that formed the reservoir's lip. "Mercy, I beg you!"

Rashid looked down at him, his upper lip curled and his teeth bared. He pushed down on Ahmed with the walking stick, leaning his full weight on the lion's head. Ahmed started to sink in a billow of white robes and bubbles. Rashid continued to press down until he lost his grip on the staff. Ahmed, however, had already ceased to struggle. The water closed in over the Saudi sheik, and his last bits of breath sizzled and popped on the surface. The lion's head was the last to sink, and down it went as well into the artificial lake.

Rashid wiped his hands on his shalwar and turned to Reza.

"If what you say is true, then I am interested in your proposal. If any word of it is false, you shall meet a fate far worse than the late sheik."

What could be worse, Reza thought? "It is all true," he said.

Rashid then looked toward the two guards who had come running up the path behind them, probably in response to the gunshot. "Let everyone know that the water is not potable today," Rashid told them. "And fetch my staff when it comes up, and the body too, whenever it manages to surface."

He took Reza's shaking hand in his, and led him to the chicken coop further down the road.

CHAPTER TWENTY

Strange as it was, it took a few moments before Reza realized that the old woman waiting patiently by the chicken coops, dressed head to toe in a floral chador, was his mother. Rashid eventually left them alone, to be with each other, and Reza held his mother closely. He cried, at times loudly. She, in return, smiled and kissed his head benevolently. What struck him most, once the emotional rush had subsided, was the degree to which his mother had changed. The Laleh he now held, after twenty-five long years, was not the Laleh who placed him in Barzani's hands long ago. Yes, there were physical changes — he had expected that. Her eyesight, for example was so bad that she had to squint to make out the outlines of Reza's face. But the bigger changes seemed to Reza to be emotional. Of course she was delighted to see and hold him, but her expressiveness was tempered by a certain formality. The years had forged in her a resilience and stoicism that seemed to shut off an entire spectrum of human feeling. Who could blame her? Like a stone, she was impervious to gain or loss, victory or defeat. And so, after all this time, after the journey of the past few days, Reza held in his arms a mother who truly was as much Rashid's as his own. She no longer belonged only to him. Time had taken her away.

Maryam, on the other hand, was precisely the person that he had imagined in his mind's eye all these years. She was tall, slightly taller than Reza, with a lanky frame and short brown hair. Her skin was fair and lightly freckled. She smiled and laughed often, lighting up her beautiful, almond-shaped face. Reza thought that he could still see in her signs of the endless, positive energy that had characterized her as little girl. It was no wonder, he thought, that she had refused to give up and go back to Tehran.

Reza stayed in Rashid's compound for the next five days. He, Laleh and Maryam laughed, shared stories about their lives and occasionally cried again. Eventually they began to think and talk about what they would do next. And to Reza's continuing astonishment, his mother did in fact want to stay in Rashid's home. She had become very close to Rashid's wives and children, and she felt more useful and needed by them than by Reza and Maryam. And Rashid's children seemed to clutch at her in loving reciprocity. Maryam, on the other hand, wanted to come to America to build a future for herself. And Rashid, to her great joy, did indeed provide her with the long-promised green card. It turned out that Reza's file – Travis' papers – had been worth much more to Rashid and the American government than even Reza had imagined.

And then there was Clara. Reza was permitted to spend a little time with her, alone, before she left Rashid's compound for the French embassy in Kabul. They held hands, laughed, and talked frankly about the ways their lives had intertwined, both with each other and with Gibran. She told him how Gibran had helped her develop her career, how great of a mentor he had been in her first years out of school. And how over time they had developed a more personal relationship, and ultimately a romantic one. She had cared deeply for him, despite their age difference, and she had thought that his feelings were also sincere. But she soon realized that Gibran was simply using their relationship to control her, the way he did with everyone around him. The way he had tried to do with Reza. And he had succeeded in doing so with Clara. Until, that is, he asked her to turn Reza in to the authorities. That is when she realized that she had to take back control of her life, and her destiny.

Without very much hesitation, Reza told Clara how much he still cared for her, and asked her to return to Washington with him. She could restart her law practice there, he suggested, and he would be able to help her find her way around the city, professionally. Plus, they would have a chance to get to know each other again, in a more genuine manner, away from the hurly burly that had come with Gibran and Ahmed. She was flattered, but, to his dismay, she declined the offer.

"I thought you'd know by now," she mumbled, "I'm not cut out for happy endings." She meant it to be funny, but they both knew that it was not so.

"Well, it's a long life," Reza said. "At least longer than it appeared to be this morning. We may have one more act left in us, a bit further down the road."

"We might, Reza. But first, I have to sort out my life out a bit. I'm going to go back to Chamonix for a while. I promise I'll find you when I've sorted things, when I know I can be good to you. That's the least you deserve. Until then, please remember the good things between us. And please know that I never stopped loving you." Those were the last words that she spoke to him before she left for France.

In late July, Reza and Maryam began their several week long journey to Washington. It began with a non-stop van ride to Kabul, courtesy of Rashid, followed by a short, chartered flight to Islamabad, Pakistan, aboard an old Tupolev TU-154. Reza tried, throughout the bumpy flight, to avoid thinking about the many corners that the Russian pilots had undoubtedly cut in their maintenance of the aging plane. From Islamabad, they flew a brand new Etihad Airlines Airbus to New York's John F. Kennedy International Airport, via Abu Dhabi. As they approached the airport, Maryam begun to panic. What if the Green Card that she had obtained from Rashid was fake or flawed in some way? Would she be separated from Reza again, after having come so close to realizing her dream, only to be sent back to Tehran all alone? Fortunately, she was admitted uneventfully into the country.

"Welcome to United States," the obese, mustachioed Customs and

Border Protection Agent said nonchalantly as he stamped Maryam's passport. "Please proceed through to baggage claim." She took back her passport and Green Card, with trembling hands, and walked as quickly as she could to the baggage claim area, where Reza was waiting anxiously for her. She jumped into his arms, and finally allowed herself to cry freely. "We're really here, Reza, safely in America. I can't believe it! I can live a normal life now. Thank you, Reza, thank you for everything." Reza held her tightly, and he too allowed himself to cry freely in his sister's embrace.

Maryam insisted that they spend some time in New York City before making their way to Washington. "I have to see Times Square, Central Park, the Empire State Building!" Reza wanted nothing more than to return to his home in Washington, to his own bed, but how could he deny Maryam such a simple request? He booked them two rooms at the legendary Carlyle Hotel, on the Upper East Side of Manhattan, where she had relatively easy access to all the popular sites that she wanted to see, and Reza could instead take long, quiet walks down Fifth Avenue, along the cobblestoned edge of Central Park. They met for dinner every night in the lobby restaurant, where Reza could enjoy the live jazz, and Maryam could excitedly describe for him her experiences in the city that day.

"You're not going to believe this, Reza," she said after her second day in the city. "There was this middle-aged guy walking his dog in the middle of Time Square today, wearing a top hat, a full length fur coat, and sandals!"

"I believe it," Reza chuckled as he took a sip of his peaty, single-malt scotch, "it's New York."

"No, wait, that's not my point. The strange thing is not that he was dressed that way, though that was obviously strange. What was strange was that I was the only person who even looked twice at him! No one else even seemed to notice him!" Having lived in Tehran, Maryam had been used to the sights and sounds of life in a big city. Even the skyscrapers had been relatively easy for her to absorb. But what she had not been used to — what she could not possibly have been ready for before arriving in New York — was the limitless personal freedoms that Americans enjoyed. Nowhere else in the world, Reza agreed, could you live as freely as you wanted to, dress as you wanted, love who you wanted, and be sure that no one else had any legitimate right to question you for it. "I love this place!" Maryam beamed.

By mid-August, Reza and Maryam came to live in his home on H Street, and they spoke with their mother each week by telephone. Maryam was quick to integrate into the Washington social scene, and she had found several Iranian-American friends. She also had secured a job working for Sonia Jimenez, at the First Metro bank branch that had declined Reza's request for a loan weeks earlier. Reza's career job prospects, on the other hand, were murkier.

It was clear the day Gibran was arrested that, one way or another, Reza's days at Henderson & Humphries were over. They had been professional enough – or perhaps self-interested enough — to pay his salary while he was on indefinite "medical leave," but that could not go on forever. Plus, Reza knew that the United States Attorney's Office was continuing to investigate Double H's role in the Gibran fraud, and it seemed impossible to Reza that his old colleagues could work with him again without holding him in some way responsible for that misfortune. It all became much easier for Reza to sort through, however, when he learned in early September that Travis' estate had finally settled, that he did have a will after all, and that he had left all of his possessions to Reza. That meant the six million dollars in the brokerage accounts would be released to him. So it was with great ease of mind that Reza met for one last time with John Burlington and resigned from Double H later that next month.

"I didn't think it all would end this way," Burlington said, over a cup of coffee at a Starbucks down the block from the office.

Reza, who hadn't seen his former mentor in several weeks, thought that he looked particularly old. "No one did."

"You were a damn good attorney."

Why the past tense? It rankled Reza. "Please give Jane my best."

Burlington, Reza knew, caught the inference. Reza then handed to his boss a check for four hundred and fifty thousand dollars, the full amount that he had borrowed. Reza did not hug him when they parted; instead, they simply shook hands, as men, as equals.

Reza went home, packed a small bag, left instructions for Maryam about how to access a new checking account in her name, and called for a car service to Dulles International Airport. He was finally going to take the trip that he had promised Travis he would take. Sure, he was taking the trip alone, but that was okay — he felt comfortable, even content with the idea.

Five hours later, he arrived at the modern Princess Juliana International Airport in St. Maarten, the Dutch side of the lush Caribbean island. And about one hour after that, having sat in much more traffic than he thought was possible in the Caribbean, he checked into the spartan but elegant Presidential Suite at Le Coloniale, on the French side of the island. He quickly changed into his swimsuit, walked down the rickety steps that led to the sandy beach in Orient Bay, and waded into the turquoise sea. Yes, he thought as the water crashed softly against his knees, Travis would have liked this very much.

Reza aimlessly wandered to a nearby boat launch. A gangly, dark-skinned boy with an easy smile waved to Reza from a nearby Century 1800 boat, a small, sprightly vessel with a powerful engine. "How about a ride," the boy shouted. "One hundred US dollars for two hours. Just what you need to get you on island time!" He spoke perfect English, with a slight French accent. Was it so obvious that Reza had just arrived?

"It's a deal," Reza smiled back. "But only if you have drinks on board." The boy pointed to a large, white styrofoam cooler that sat beside him, and Reza climbed on board. The boy introduced himself as Didier, shook

Reza's hand vigorously, and turned on a sound system that blared obscure, bad reggae music. Reza grabbed and sipped a cold Red Stripe beer as they puttered out of the dock, towards the nearby island of St. Barth's. He leaned over the side of the boat as they picked up speed, and dipped his hand in the ocean. Yes, he'd only been on the island for a couple of hours, but Reza was more relaxed than he had been in some time.

Soon after they hit open water, Didier cut the engine and dropped anchor. "You can go for a swim here, if you'd like," the boy said.

"No, thanks. I'm doing pretty well right here. But feel free to jump in if you want." Without any further prompting, Didier pulled off his fraying t-shirt, waved adieu, and dove in. He remained underwater for a surprisingly long period, before he emerging roughly thirty feet away. Reza leaned back in his chair, closed his eyes, and allowed the bright sun to warm his face for several minutes. Then he shook the ocean water from his hands, finished his beer, and made his way to the cooler for a second beer.

As he neared the cooler, a small but distinct design on the inside of the boat caught his eye. Drawn clearly in blue ink was the image of a small boy with big hair, racing goggles, and a mischievous smile, racing what looked like a classic Karmann Ghia sports car. Reza rubbed his fingers across the image, as though to confirm that it was not a mirage. It wasn't. He quickly shot up and looked around. No one was there but Didier, who was now floating on his back about 20 feet from the boat, singing a French song that Reza did not recognize. Reza felt a brief sense of vertigo and grabbed the side of the boat. He then called to Didier, who swam back and effortlessly climbed on board.

"Everything okay?"

"Everything is fine. But I have to ask you a very important question," Reza said, pointing Didier to the design. "Did you do this?"

"That, no. I'm not sure who did that. Why, do you like it?"

"No... I mean yes... I mean, that's not the point. I need to know who drew that!" Reza grew more and more animated.

"Probably one of the customers."

"When? I need to know when!"

Didier raised an eyebrow. "I'm not sure. Maybe in the last couple of days, because we had the boat serviced and washed a week ago. Couldn't have been there before that. If it's bothering you, I can try to wash it off."

"No, no. Don't do that. It's not bothering me. It's just that it looks a lot like something a friend of mine liked to draw. A friend who is dead — he died several months ago."

Didier pulled his shirt back on. "I see. A strange coincidence."

A coincidence? Yes, that must be what it was. What else could it be? It's not like it could've been Travis. Travis was dead. Wasn't he? Reza quickly downed another beer, wiped his mouth with the back of his hand, and asked Didier to drive them back to shore. He needed to get some sleep, maybe the journey was starting to take its toll. The Caribbean sun sank low on the horizon as they bounced across the waves. Reza gazed at the craggy outline of St. Barth's as it faded farther and farther away.

"We still have some time left," Didier yelled over the roar of the engine. "Want to swing by Oyster Pond?"

"What's that?"

"A gorgeous little cove over there, on the Dutch side."

He pointed, and the two of them stood to try to get a better look. They could barely make out a small resort, under two bent palm trees, on the bay called Coconut Grove. What they couldn't see was a man looking right back at them, with binoculars. He put the glasses down when he spied them pointing in his general direction and turned back to the bar for another umbrella drink. He had a bandage on his nose. In a few weeks, the doctors had told him, the scar left in place of where the ugly mole had been would hardly be noticeable.

Author Bio

NADER HOSSAIN SALEHI grew up in Teheran, Iran and studied
English and French Literature at the University of Virginia in Charlottes-
ville, Virginia. He also received a J.D. and an M.B.A. from the University
of Richmond in 1995. An avid fan of Arsenal Football Club, really well
constructed pencils, and Tin Tin comics, Salehi currently resides in New
York City with his wife and three children where he conducts a securities
enforcement defense practice at a leading, international law firm.

CPSIA information can be obtained
at www.ICGtesting.com
Printed in the USA
BVOW06s1943290617

488170BV00011B/235/P